eye
opener

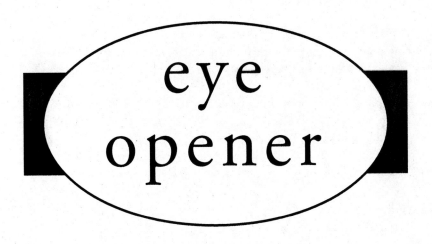

eye opener

Michael Z. —Lewin—

Five Star • Waterville, Maine

First Edition
First Printing: December 2004

Published in 2004 in conjunction with
Tekno Books and Ed Gorman.

Set in 11 pt. Plantin.

Printed in the United States on permanent paper.

Library of Congress Cataloging-in-Publication Data

Lewin, Michael Z.
     Eye Opener / by Michael Z. Lewin.
         p. cm.
     ISBN 1-59414-258-0 (hc : alk. paper)
     1. Samson, Albert (Fictitious character)—Fiction.
  2. Private investigators—Indiana—Indianapolis—Fiction.
  3. Indianapolis (Ind.)—Fiction.   4. Mystery fiction.
  I. Title.
  PS3562.E929E94 2004
     813'.54—dc22   2004056428

For my lovely sister, Julie.

0

The bartender was a chunky kid in his twenties. He set me up, and I bought a drink for him as well.

"Thank you, sir. I'll have a beer."

"I only came in here so I could be called 'sir,' you know."

"Oh yeah?" The kid smiled. He had no one else to serve so he stayed with me.

"Been working here long?"

"About . . . two years now," he said, "sir."

"Keep 'em coming." I downed my shot.

"The 'sirs' or the bourbons? Sir."

"Both." I sipped from my chaser.

He poured. "I haven't seen you in here before, have I, sir?"

"I stopped coming out to bars alone about the time you started here, but this is a special occasion."

The kid looked bartender-quizzical. "Birthday?"

I shook my head. I said, "Did you hear the one about the guy who's walking down the street and he meets a friend walking the other way with a dog?"

"No, sir."

"The guy says, 'Does your dog bite?' and the friend says, 'Nope,' and the guy bends over to pat the dog and the dog bites him."

The kid smiled.

" 'I thought you said your dog didn't bite.' And the friend says, 'This isn't my dog.' "

The kid chuckled and tapped on the bar like a pool player does to compliment an opponent's shot. "Be back in a sec." He walked to the other end of the bar where a guy who'd been sitting with a redhead at a dark table was standing with two empty glasses.

Maybe it was a good move for the kid. I'd been about to launch into an explanation of how this "joke" was a paradigm of my life. Not only that you mustn't jump to conclusions in my business—my former business—as a private investigator. But also that it's dangerous to trust people you think are your friends.

Even your best friend. I downed my shot.

No, I don't come to bars any more. I did for a while, but the last time I drank alone I got into trouble. Serious ex-girlfriend stuff. It ended in tears.

The kid returned. "Your glass is empty again, sir."

"Well you know what to do."

He did it.

I said, "What's your name, son?"

"Kyle, sir. Kyle Cooper."

"Well, I'm Albert Samson, Kyle. At least I used to be."

His eyes narrowed in thought but he surprised me with his question. "Would you be related to Posy Samson that runs the luncheonette up the road, Bud's Dugout? Sir."

"My mother drinks here? I didn't know she'd become a bar bunny along with everything else."

"No, sir, she doesn't drink here. But pretty much everybody round and about knows who Posy Samson is. It's because of how she's real active in community affairs and the neighborhood."

"She's been keeping busy since she decided to give up working behind the counter, that's for sure." In fact "busy" isn't an adequate word. When Mom's not out killing targets

8

at her gun club, she's hunched over her computer or off
partying with her legion of wrinkly friends. I don't know
where she gets her energy.

"Bud's isn't going to close, is it, sir?"

"My daughter's running the place while Mom decides
what to do with it."

"Well, I hope it all works out, sir."

"Thank you, Kyle. Let me buy you another drink."

"I'll have another beer when I finish this one, sir. Thanks."

"Meanwhile let's toast my mother." I lifted my shot
glass. "Mom."

"Your mom."

We clinked. We drank. I said, "Now set me up with
another shot and we'll toast the famous Jerry Miller."

"Jerry Miller . . . ?" Kyle said as he poured. "I'm not
sure . . . Who does he play for?"

I couldn't tell whether the kid was joking or whether all
the Colts, Pacers, Indians, and 500 stuff on the walls
insulated him from a world outside professional sports.
"Jerry Miller's the talk of the town, Kyle. You don't know
the name?"

"No, sir. To tell the truth, I don't."

"Have you ever lost a friend, Kyle?"

"Uh, you mean . . . who died?"

"I mean someone you thought was a friend who
suddenly wasn't."

"Oh, like he started fooling around with your wife?"

"I was thinking more a guy you'd count on to warn you
about a dangerous dog and he doesn't. A guy you'd think
would look out for you."

"No, sir. I'm glad to say that hasn't happened to me,
touch wood." He tapped his knuckles on the bar. "I guess it
has to you, though, huh?"

"It sure has. Do you have friends, Kyle? Good friends?"

"I do, I guess. Yeah, I do."

"Well, don't trust them too much. Don't rely on them for anything you can't afford to lose. Take the advice of someone who's learned the hard way. Even the best friends can be like dogs. They can turn on you when you least expect it."

As Kyle said, "Oh yeah?" a boisterous group of young men in matching track suits streamed into the bar. A team of some kind.

"Remember that, Kyle. Remember what I said."

"I will, sir."

"I've got something I want to show you," I said. I took the morning's *Star* out of my jacket pocket.

"You're going to have to excuse me for a sec, sir." He nodded in the direction of the thirsty team, and went to serve them.

"Sure. Of course." But I spread the newspaper out anyway.

The headline was: ***TRUNK KILLER ARREST—AT LAST!***

The supporting text filled more of the *Star*'s front page than anything had since September 11th. The hunt for the "bodies-in-the-trunks killer" was a big deal in Indianapolis. The headline caught my eye even before I realized its real significance for me.

The first body-in-a-trunk was discovered by the owner of a dog when his pet wouldn't leave the back of a parked car. More than three years had passed, during which four more women had been killed. All five were raped, strangled, and then stuffed into the trunks of their own cars. And four other women were now known to have been raped by the same guy in the two years before the first murder. All the victims were either in or near their cars when they were attacked. Every sober woman in Indy thought about the danger whenever she reached for her keys.

Public pressure to catch the killer rose after each new victim was discovered. A series of top-cops had headed the investigation, and then been replaced. It was an excruciatingly long time for a monster to be loose in our city.

Eventually local businessmen—all with car-driving wives and daughters and mothers and grandmothers and mistresses and friends—took their own initiative. They assembled a reward of a hundred and ten thousand dollars. It was far and away the biggest bounty ever offered in Indy and, according to the *Star* report, it was the reward that did the trick. Ronnie Willigar, aged thirty-two, white, unemployed, unmarried, was arrested after an anonymous caller gave his name to Crime Stoppers.

At the press conference announcing the arrest, Chief Cohl claimed that Willigar's name was already high on a new list of suspects, but he did concede that the Crime Stoppers tip-off had accelerated the arrest. Cohl also announced that "important evidence" specified by the anonymous caller was found in Willigar's house. I took the phrase as cop-code for "we've nailed the bastard" and Cohl showed no caution as he urged us to celebrate this long-awaited police success on behalf of the city's women who could now feel safe again as they went about their business.

But, for me, the significance of the *Star* story was not the fact that the cops had finally made an arrest. Though I did have a car-driving daughter and a car-driving mother, if no longer a car-driving girlfriend.

For me, the significance was the identity of the cop in charge. The cop who succeeded where the rest had failed. The cop who purged the terror from the streets of

Naptown, leaving them merely dangerous once again. That cop was Captain Gerald Miller.

Miller got a panel to himself on the front page. It said he was one of IPD's highest ranking African-American officers. It said he was Indy born and bred and joined the force in his early twenties. It said he was a family man with four children. It said he liked to fish in his spare time.

A photograph showed a handsome guy with a strong, mature face. It showed a full head of hair, a graying moustache, and a good smile.

But neither the words nor the picture showed the reality of this man, this Gerald Miller, this cop.

The reality was of a guy who was never completely comfortable with his contemporaries. Of a guy who as a teenager latched onto a white kid from the southside who felt just as much an outsider in his own neighborhood as the cop-to-be did in his. The reality was that these two isolated young men hung out together, learned about dangers and words together, and grew up together.

And the significance for me—the real significance—of this *Star* story was that Indy's new lap-of-honor hero was the very guy, the so-called best friend, who caused my private investigator's license to be revoked.

It was a horrible, destructive betrayal for Miller to do that. Being a private eye defined me every bit as much as being a cop defined him. And by losing me my license, this best bud cost me more than my livelihood. He cost me my identity. And even my woman—who couldn't endure what was left of me.

I fought to get the license back. Of course I fought. I was still fighting. I had a persistent lawyer who was certain he'd succeed. But he'd been persistent for years. He'd been certain for years. "Soon," he said, recently. He said "soon" a year ago too.

My lawyer guy is good. I'm not one of the people who thinks there's no such thing as a good lawyer. I like the way lawyers talk and think, generally, which is just as well since most of a private detective's work is for them. And I planned to work for lawyers again one day. My plans were mapped out. When I got *the call*, I'd be ready. Whenever "soon" turned out to be.

It was now that I was struggling with.

Now Jerry Miller was the toast of Indy. I was not ready for that when I picked up the **TRUNK KILLER ARREST** issue of the *Star.*

Not that I wasn't happy for the guy.

Of course I was.

Not that I didn't think he deserved some success.

Of course he did. He'd suffered a lot as he worked his way up the spine of command at IPD. Not only was the guy black, he was scrupulously honest. He only needed one more strike to be out.

So, Kyle, when you get back from serving the jocks jockeying for attention at the other end of your bar, we'll toast the toast of Indy. We'll fill our glasses and drink to success in one's chosen field of endeavor. Then we'll drink again, to enduring friendship.

Here's mud in your eye, Jerry.

Mud. Yeah, that would be a good start.

I kind of lost track of Kyle.

Then I heard pounding. But I couldn't see anything. It was too dark. Even when I opened my eyes.

"Steady big fella," a man said. I didn't recognize the voice. I wanted to see who it was. I tried to rub my eyes but I couldn't move my arms. What was wrong with my arms? Why was he pinning them to my sides and holding me close? What was going on?

"Someone's coming," the same voice said. "Just try to keep on your feet."

Who . . . ? Where . . . ? Why . . . ? But the questions wouldn't form sufficiently to make words in my mouth.

Then there was a light. I couldn't rub my eyes, but I could see the light.

A door opened. "Yes?" A woman's sleepy voice. I recognized it.

"Mrs. Samson?" the man said. "The bartender at the Pitstop asked me to bring—"

"Oh Albert," my mother said. I recognized the disappointment in the voice too.

"You know him?"

"Oh yes."

"It's not what you think, Mom," I tried to say.

The man said, "He had maybe one or two too many. The bartender called a cab—that's me—but before I got there it seems he fell off his stool."

"I'm so sorry you've been put to all this trouble," my mother said.

"Whereabouts would you like him?"

"Just inside the door, thanks. Lay him on the floor, would you?"

"It doesn't look like he hurt himself, ma'am, but you best keep an eye on him."

I felt myself being lifted. Was I going to heaven? "Heaven?" I tried to say. But nobody laughed.

My mother said, "I thought he'd got himself past this way of solving his problems, but it seems he lapsed."

"It was a special occasion," I tried to say.

"What did he say?" Mom asked. "Did you make it out?"

"No, ma'am," the cabdriver said. "Here by the wall?"

"Yes, thanks. I'll bring down a pillow and a blanket in a minute."

I felt myself being lowered to the floor. I'd been down before, but I'd bounce back. "It was a special occasion," I tried to say.

"Thank you so much. Just let me get my purse."

"No need for that, Mrs. Samson. Folks know what you do round these parts."

"Well, at least let me get you something to eat. Nice piece of pie? Or I could rustle up a sandwich."

"No, thanks, ma'am. I'll just run along now," the man said. "Oh, he had this. The bartender said something in it set him off."

"This morning's newspaper?"

"Looks like."

"Leave it on the floor beside him. He might like something to read when he wakes up."

"No," I tried to say. "No."

"It sounded like he said, 'No,' " the driver said. "Maybe he doesn't want the paper."

"Whatever he thinks he wants now, chances are he'll think better of it later, wouldn't you say?" Mom said.

1

The call came on a Thursday morning little more than two weeks later. I was asleep at the time, with the ringer off. Not from drinking. Other things can keep you up late. Like waiting for phone calls.

My lawyer left a message: "This is Don Cannon, Albert. Judge Darling nodded it through half an hour ago. You are restored, pal—it's official. Congratulations."

When I finally woke up, I played the message from the bed. Then I played it again with the volume up.

This was the call I'd waited forever for. It was no longer "soon." It was "now."

At last.

In the few short seconds' worth of message, I felt not only restored but renewed, redeemed, and maybe resurrected too, not that I could recall having been newed, deemed, or surrected in the first place. Stored, however, that I remembered all too well.

No matter. "Now" was now. All the plans I'd made for how I would start my life again were in play. And this time I'd get it right. I was ready. Boy oh boy was I ready. Or I would be as soon as I managed to hoist myself out of the bed.

Sam was at the cash register when I arrived downstairs. She beckoned me over. "Daddy, Mr. Cannon called down here a while ago because he didn't get through to you upstairs. You might want to check your messages."

Mom was there too, at a table having coffee with three

old men. "Sam, honey, I bet he took his message already."

"You think so, Grandma?"

"Look how he's walking without the slouch. I bet the news from Mr. Cannon was good."

Sam turned my way expectantly. "Daddy?"

It crossed my mind to drag it out, like easing the cork from a champagne bottle instead of popping it, but I was unable not to grin and giggle. "I cannot tell a lie," I said.

"That'll be a first." The sizzling comment was from Norman, Mom's one-armed griddle man. He doesn't like me.

"You hush, Norman Tubbs," Mom said. "We been awaiting this for a long, long time. This is a good day for the Samson family."

Sam hugged me tight. "Congratulations, Daddy! I am so happy for you."

"I'm so happy for me too," I said.

"How are you going to celebrate?"

"Get drunk?" Norman said.

I ignored him. "Before I do anything else, I'm going to turn on my sign."

"The sign, really?" Sam laughed and clapped. For an instant she was the young, carefree daughter I so often wondered about while her mother was bringing her up halfway around the world. Sam it was who gave me the sign in the first place.

"I need to tell the world that I'm open for business again, right?"

"Right."

"You and your grandmother go out on the street and watch. I'll go up to the office and flip the switch."

My office is next to my bedroom upstairs in the Bud's Dugout building. After years of shabbier and more temporary arrangements, I came back to where I'd grown up by

17

special arrangement with my mother. The game plan was to focus all my resources on making my business zing. The game plan did not include being called for a technical foul and being kicked off the court.

But now I was back. By God, was I back.

I turned the sign on and then stepped out onto the iron porch at the top of stairs that lead up from the street. Sam, Mom, Norman, and Mom's three old-guy pals made up the admiring throngs.

But they weren't cheering. "What?" I called.

Several spoke at once and some pointed. I couldn't make out the words, but the pointing was signward.

My neon lure was supposed to read, "Albert Samson, Private Investigator." However vandals must have broken some of the glass tubes. When that might have happened I couldn't tell you. I never noticed. What remained was, "Albert . . . gator."

Snappy.

"I'm sure it can be fixed, Daddy," Sam said when I joined them in the luncheonette.

"And fix it I shall," I declared, "for have I not already triumphed over a greater adversity?"

"That's the spirit, son," Mom said.

"I think I'll have some breakfast first, though."

Norman sniggered.

"If people eating breakfast is a problem for you, Burger Boy, then you're in the wrong business."

"Albert, please," Mom said. For reasons I've never understood, Mom likes Norman. Sufficiently to give him a small room on the top floor at the back as well as allowing him to work as her cook. Not that he was always one-armed. During my fallow, licenseless years Norman had a

18

horrific motorcycle accident. However he'd lost his personality long before he ever arrived at Bud's.

While Sam undertook to assemble me some breakfast, I had a quick test of my reflexes and anticipation at the pinball machine Mom has tucked in a corner. I heard the phone ring but had no reason to believe it had anything to do with me until Sam called me.

Another day I would have told her to take a message while I finished the game. But this day, *this day,* I left the last silver ball to trickle unimpeded to oblivion and took the call. Maybe, I thought as I walked over to the phone, Jerry Miller had heard my news and wanted to beg forgiveness and bury the hatchet. Well, I'd see how well he groveled. I'd rate him for content and for style. "Albert Samson, Private Investigator."

"Hello, Mr. Samson," a woman said. "My name is Flossy McCardle and I'm a reporter for *Nuvo.*"

"Hello." *Nuvo* I knew—Indy's most popular alternate newspaper. Flossy McCardle I didn't know. She was my first ever Flossy.

"Your lawyer, Mr. Cannon, e-mailed us a press release about your getting your license back and about how you're considering lawsuits against the city and the police for loss of livelihood. I'd like to come over and interview you about what it's like to be back in business and what's it's been like during the period when you weren't. Would two o'clock be convenient?"

I didn't know Cannon was issuing contentious press releases. Having just finished one interminable legal fight, the last thing I wanted to do was get into a new one, but since my relaunch planning didn't include TV commercials or skywriting, a relicensing article in *Nuvo* sounded fine. "Two o'clock it is. See you then."

I'd mused many times about how to relaunch myself in

the cutthroat world of Indy private eyeing if . . . when . . .
But I'd come up with nothing more sophisticated than
calling everybody I knew, beginning with lawyers and former
clients. The list of telephone numbers was on the desk in my
office. I dusted it regularly, along with my Client's Chair.

"So you've got something at two o'clock, Daddy?" Sam
asked when I hung up.

"Yeah. You're not going to be alone here, are you?" Among
the many odds and ends of work I'd filled my detection-free
years with was helping out at the luncheonette when it was
needed.

"Martha's already in the back changing her shoes."
Martha waits the tables during the lunch rush while my
baby, my only child, my heart's delight, minds the counter
and the cash register.

Sam grew up in Europe, but she fled the South of
France for Indianapolis—as so many do—when she realized what scum her sculptor husband was. Why she's
stayed on here is less clear. I don't ask. I fear breaking the
magic of her presence.

After coffee-bagel-juice-more-coffee, I brought the
dishes back to the counter and said to Sam, "I'm heading
out in a few minutes, but I'll be back before two."

"OK, Daddy."

"Client to see?" Norman asked. "Oh, I forgot. It's your
regular park basketball appointment."

To an outsider, shooting hoops in a park in the middle
of the day might seem like an escape from reality. The
truth is that it's been important to getting me through the
waiting and uncertainty. Physical fitness supports mental
fitness. Blood oxygen fuels the brain and fires the senses.
Samson fakes right. He puts the ball on the floor with his

left. There's that devastating crossover! He's in! He scores! He's back in business!

I'm in better shape than I've been in years. I'm lean. I'm mean. And, at long last, I'm back on the scene.

My warm-up moves from stretches to ball handling to underbasket shots with each hand. I was about to shift into my "jazz" phase when a guy about thirty appeared from somewhere and sat down on the bench near the basket. Knowing someone was watching me meant I fired my jumpshots from a centimeter or two higher than usual. It's an automatic response.

When a shot went in, I said to the guy, "You want to shoot?"

"Save your lunch money, Grandpa."

I'd only been thinking of sharing my ball, but his dismissive tone made me consider speculative possibilities in the free throw sector of the market. I sink a mean free throw when I'm on. But when I looked at the guy again, he seemed familiar. "Do I know you?"

"Yeah, right. We probably met at a boiled chicken potluck your friends threw to celebrate me and my family moving in next door."

"Have you been shooting in this park for a long time? Since you were a kid?"

After a pause he said, "As a matter of fact I have."

"I think maybe we played once."

"Yeah?"

"One on one, a long time ago. When you were about up to my kneecaps."

"Unless you were a whole lot better then than you are now, I bet I skinned your white ass."

If he was the kid I was thinking about, he did. "I was recovering from an injury at the time."

"So what's the excuse today?" He stood up and took off his jacket.

I got back to the luncheonette figuring I had just enough time for a quick shower before I faced my two o'clock interrogator. I got Sam's attention as I passed the counter. "If I'm a couple of minutes late coming down, tell Flossy I'm busy on a murder case, all right?"

"Tell her yourself, Daddy."

A girl sitting at the counter in front of Sam spun her stool and put out a hand. "Flossy McCardle, Mr. Samson. I'm pleased to meet you."

She looked about eight. "Are you sure you shouldn't be in school?"

"I'm twenty-three, Mr. Samson, so I'll take that as an unreconstructed attempt at flattery."

"Oh. Right."

"It's me who's early, not you who's late. When your daughter said we'd be meeting in a luncheonette, I thought, what the heck, have some lunch."

Yeah, go crazy. "There is a logic to that. Maybe you could take notes for a restaurant review while I take a shower."

Her face was impassive. "There is a logic to that."

I had a bad feeling about Flossy McCardle. You know how you go into a house and sometimes it just feels weird? Not that I was thinking about going into Flossy McCardle, but I had a fearful wave as I contemplated the interview.

Oh well.

Two things had already gone well—the license, and then hammering Joe Ellison on the basketball court. How many successes is it reasonable for a guy to expect in one day?

True, my park triumph did involve my opponent shooting his free throws with his back to the basket. "You sure you don't want to blindfold me too?" But that was just his little joke.

Joe liked that I'd remembered him. "I was some *hot* shit when I was coming up," he said when he made his first basket to trail 3–1. "I just never grew."

He was about six feet, tall enough for college and semi-pro, so maybe the true story was a different one. It often is. I missed my next shot.

At 5–3 Joe described himself as employed "at this and that." At 6–5 he was "taking stock of my life." At 9–5 he thought maybe he "ought to settle down."

Those things all said as much by what was omitted.

Once I had won 11–8 and returned from my lap of honor, he said, "So what job lets you shoot hoops in the middle of the day, Super Al?"

"I'm a private investigator."

"And I'm Michael Jordan."

I shrugged.

"Show me your license."

Ah. "Well, funny thing, but at the moment . . ."

"Let's start with the basics," Flossy said as she settled into my Client's Chair. Her shoes didn't touch the floor. Seeing her there made me flash back to past clients who had applied backsides to that very seat. Young clients. Old clients. Clients in trouble. Clients in masks. Even a few clients who told me the truth.

Maybe Flossy herself had a problem that could be solved by a professional asking questions on her behalf. A lost relative, maybe, or a cheating boyfriend, or— "The most basic thing is that I am genuinely delighted to be able to work again for people who want me to help them."

"Uh huh." Flossy flipped the notebook open. With that

simple action the child-reporter suddenly looked for all the world as if she knew what she was doing. "First off," she said, "is Samson your real name?"

"Excuse me?"

"Or is it a name you chose for its value in advertising? Maybe to present prospective clients with an image of strength tempered with vulnerability?"

What? "Is that a serious question?"

Her humorless expression told me it was.

"It's my real name."

I watched her write.

"The chef downstairs was very helpful while I was waiting for you to finish your shower. He explained how your mother supported you during your difficulties—not just giving you encouragement, but providing a place to live, and feeding you, and sometimes pocket money."

"I worked for her sometimes, but—"

"And I thought to myself, hey, what a great hook for my piece! Can't you see it? No matter how old you are, you're always Mama's little boy. So, how old are you, Mr. Samson?"

Flossy left a little past two-thirty. I began making phone calls immediately.

Nuvo is published on the north side of town, in Broad Ripple. I live on the southside. Being Flossied probably wouldn't do me much harm. And the whole experience underlined that the real way for me to get back into business was by personal phone pitching to all and sundry.

The city's law firms were the key—lawyers provide any investigator's bread and butter. "Hi. This is Albert Samson, the Private Investigator . . ." As long as I could say it better than my neon sign read it, I'd do myself some good.

2

I completed calling all the city's listed law firms on Friday morning. I'm not a natural self-promoter so I promised myself a treat for when the lawyers were done: a call to the law. Telling Captain Hero Jerry Miller that I was back in business would be something to savor. During the Licenseless Years there were so many other things that I'd wanted to say to him. But this . . . This would be good.

And he was at his desk—as Indianapolis Police Department captains so often are in my limited experience. "Miller."

"I'm glad to see my direct line number still works," I said. "Will you take it to the new office when you're promoted?"

There was silence at his end of the line. Could he possibly not have placed my voice? "This is Albert, Jerry."

Still no response. Had the guy blotted recognition out? This was someone I'd stolen cars with. Someone whose wife I knew before they got married. Someone whose complaints about work and home provided condiments for more lunches than I could count.

"Is this the famous silent treatment Janie complains about? Well, I've got an idea. Why don't you suggest she gets a divorce? Tell her you can recommend a good PI— very reasonable. Tell her the PI you can recommend *has his license back at last!*"

"I know," Miller said. "I heard."

"Of course you know. I just called to check whether the

25

congratulatory bunch of flowers yesterday was from you, or whether it was the fruit basket this morning. Or both— yeah, that must be it. They're both from you. Thanks, pal."

"I . . . I can't help you, Al."

"Did I ask you for help?"

"Don't call me here again." He hung up the phone.

I had anticipated several possible responses from Miller to this call I'd waited so long to make. Being blown out as if I didn't exist was not one of them.

I shook my head, as if that might free up a fact to help me understand. Did Miller feel his contribution to the loss of my license so strongly that he needed to turn me into a non-person to cope? Guilt does wreak terrible ravages on its sufferers.

The only problem with that analysis was that my—considerable—knowledge of Miller did not include evidence that he had the slightest aptitude for guilt.

"Don't call me here again." Here being his direct line at IPD. Was the number set aside for a different purpose than talking to him now? Maybe reserved for a new Dial-A-Hero-And-Save-The-City plan that was about to be launched?

I didn't get it.

And despite myself . . . despite the abiding sense of grievance I had, I wondered if he had some kind of problem, whether something was wrong with him.

What could be wrong for a Captain Hero?

How would I know? I hadn't spoken to the guy in years.

I made more calls. This time from the list of former clients who weren't lawyers and who I classified as Very Satisfied, Satisfied, or Moderately Satisfied.

Then, as lunchtime loomed, I got an idea about Miller's

26

stony silence. I dialed a social work agency and asked the receptionist for Mrs. Proffitt. When I got through I said, "This here is detective Samson, ma'am. I sure do want to speak to you about some police business."

"Albert?"

"In the electronic flesh."

"It's been a long time."

She wasn't wrong about that. I said, "I have my license back, at last."

"I can imagine how much that must mean to you."

"But I called about something else."

"What?"

"I talked with Jerry Miller this morning, and I came away with the distinct feeling that something is wrong with him."

"I'm sorry. What is it?"

"That's what I was hoping you might help me with."

"Me?"

"Since he's suddenly got this hero profile he's bound to be the subject of conversation around the water coolers. So what I wondered was whether you'd be willing to speak to Lieutenant Proffitt and ask if he knows anything."

She was silent for an extended moment. "You want me to ask Homer about Jerry Miller?"

"Yes." During another silence, it occurred to me that there might have been more to her question than a wish to confirm her understanding of what I was asking. By way of explanation I added, "The circumstances of my license thing mean I don't have much inside contact in the police these days."

"Tell me, something, Albert."

"If it's within my power, ma'am."

"Why did you call me instead of talking to Homer yourself?"

"I didn't think Homer was likely to do me a favor."

"There was a better chance I might?"

"Well, yeah." It sounded kind of crass the way she put it.

"This strikes me as unacceptable behavior, Albert."

"Then don't do it, ma'am."

"I mean for you to call me after all this time for a trumpery reason like that. It will take me quite a while to work out what's really going on here."

"It'll take you zero. Miller's manner on the phone this morning made me worry. I can't call his wife because she hates me. I can't call a girlfriend because I don't know who's current. There's no hidden agenda."

"So it wasn't a convoluted way to make sure I knew about the restoration of your license?"

"I called you for the reason aforementioned. If I done wrong by your behavior book, I'm sorry. Have a nice day. Ma'am." I put the phone down.

However I didn't get up immediately to go down to rustle up some lunch—life is so full of ups and downs. Mrs. Proffitt's tone on the phone left me pissed off. Not least because Homer Proffitt's woman used to be my woman. Not least because of course I had wanted her to know I had my license again and I didn't like proof that I was so transparent these days.

At the bottom of the stairs I pushed through the curtain that separates the luncheonette from the rest of the building and I came face to face with the Abominable Norman. He was holding a plastic bag of garbage.

"Let me hold the bag for you," I said. "It'll be easier for you to get in."

"Your mother's with some friends in there," he said, "so don't embarrass her by taking money from the register."

28

We traded places in the passage and crowded each other just a little bit. He nearly dropped his garbage bag. I nearly laughed. Some of my feelings I don't mind being transparent.

In the luncheonette all the tables and most of the counter seats were taken. Sam and Martha were rushing around trying to cope with the midday rush, so I helped clear plates and refill coffee cups until the peak passed.

My work in the family business has had more formal periods, times when I was between the many odds and numerous ends that I made a living from during the dark days. At one point Mom even suggested that I consider taking Bud's Dugout over. "I'm getting too old for the daily grind, son," she said, which was a general comment and not one limited to the daily grind of chunks of beef for the makings of hamburgers and meatloaf.

"I'm not much of a cook," I told her.

"I thought you'd be more interested in other parts of the business. Maybe give the whole thing a fresh spin, with new names for the menu items."

"Budburgers?"

"Or maybe you'd want to organize pinball competitions. Whatever. Use your flair. Norman would take care of the food side."

"If I took it on, the first thing I'd do is fire Norman."

"Oh, I couldn't have that, son."

Which kind of finished the conversation.

Even so, I recognized a lot of people in the place as I helped out. "Hi." "How you doing?" "Looking great."

And things finally calmed down enough for Martha to take a plate of fries and fill a counter stool. Fill it she did. Martha had back.

Then, as I stood with Sam, a woman came into the

luncheonette. She stopped in the doorway as if she was looking for someone. I knew her face, and her name—Yvonne—and I was surprised to see her in the middle of the day. Usually when she appeared at Bud's it was on her way home after work. She'd have a piece of pie, a cup of coffee, and a quarter of an hour's complaining about her problems.

Her problems were not unique ones, especially since the gentrifiers began to turn their acquisitive gaze on Fountain Square. Yvonne lived in a rented house with three children she'd brought up on her own. Only now her landlord was taking his profit and selling up. Whatever rights she might otherwise have had were compromised because she hadn't always managed to pay her rent on time. The ex-husband was no help. Neither was her oldest kid, a wild boy in his early teens. "Look on the bright side," I thought about saying more than once. "Rory will be in jail soon, so you won't need to find as big a place." Ha ha. But, of course, I didn't say it—what kind of insensitive boor would even think of such a thing?

Today, however, Yvonne didn't order food. Instead she went to the window table where Mom was sitting with a couple of her wrinkly pals. Mom turned in her chair to face the newcomer. But instead of saying hi, how you doing, or looking great, Yvonne dropped to one knee, took Mom's hand, and kissed it.

It was over in an instant. Yvonne rose and moved to a spare chair and then she and Mom and her pals started talking like they were already in the middle of a conversation.

Sam was making change. I said, "Did you see that?"

"What?" She waved goodbye to a homeless guy who comes in sometimes with a camouflage sleeping bag.

"That woman just kissed Mom's hand."

"Who?" Sam looked over toward the window. "Oh, Yvonne?"

"Yeah. What's that about?"

"It's . . . I think it's like a game they have."

I looked at the table again. There was nothing odd about anybody's body language. Maybe it was me. Nevertheless . . . "Funny game."

"You play pinball machines." Sam's attention left me for no better reason than that a woman wanted to settle her check.

When the money thing was done and Sam came back to me I said, "So how long has it been going on?"

"What?"

"Your grandmother's 'game.' "

"I don't know."

"Why haven't I seen it being played before?"

"Daddy," Sam said, "if you haven't seen it, either you've been out at the time or you didn't notice. It's no big deal."

"So I'm noticing now. Tell me the rules of this game. Is it always kissing her hand like she's the Pope or do they kiss her feet sometimes too?"

"I think whatever it is maybe it began during the rehearsals for her play."

"What play?"

"Daddy!"

Which served to remind me that my mother did take part in an event last Halloween. Something about vampires, put on in a gutted movie house in the neighborhood that's used for community events while the new owners decide how to extract top dollars from it. But, hey, that was six months ago and I was away the whole week of the performances. I was playing my own role as Inter-State Delivery Man—one of many short-term superhero roles I played during what could—at last!—be called my interim period.

But was there hand-kissing in vampire stories? I looked

31

back to Mom's table. Mom, Yvonne, and a gray couple were chatting.

"Daddy?"

"What?"

"Is it all right if I come to your office after work?"

"Sure. What for?"

"I want to hire you."

"You what?"

But Sam waved me away. "I'll explain later." She turned to a couple who wanted to pay their check.

Back upstairs I made more calls. Then, I heard an unfamiliar sound. Footfalls on the metal steps. Someone coming up them. A . . . client? My heart raced. I admit it.

What did I used to do in this situation? Sit all casual, with my feet on the desk? Hunch over papers making notes? The doorbell rang. I grabbed the phone. I called, "Come in!"

The maybe-client turned the handle.

Unfortunately, the door was locked. Oops.

I left the phone and strolled to the door. Outside I discovered a short, paunchy middle-aged guy. He wore a dark rumpled suit but no tie. He said, "I saw your sign."

"Come in. Sit down. I was just on the phone."

"Oh. Right." He put an index finger to his lips and came in. He sat in my Client's Chair.

I retrieved the phone receiver as I took my position behind the desk. "Sorry for the interruption, Mr. Lilly. Where were we?" The dial tone did its level best to explain its problems. I said, "Uh huh," a couple of times and Maybe-Client maybe looked impressed.

Suddenly the dial tone was replaced by the penetrating sound that comes on when a phone's been left off the hook accidentally. The sound cut to my very soul. I hung up without even saying, "I'm not cheap, Mr. Lilly, but I'll get it done for you."

If Maybe-Client had ears in his head and enough brains between them to tie his own shoelaces he must have understood the charade I was trying to perpetrate. But I continued to play my part. I made a few notes on my pad before I looked up. "Right then. You saw my sign."

"Your sign, yeah. You got some letters out on it. Did you know?"

My silent stillness would have made a bunny caught by bright lights look like a fidget.

The guy just figured I was stupid. "What I mean is, some of the letters in your electric sign, they don't light up."

Leaving Albert . . . gator. That I had not turned off since yesterday. "I know."

"It's a bitch when that happens, ain't it?"

"Let me guess. You can fix it."

"Me? What? I look like a sign guy to you? That's what I look? I got to start working out."

"So what did you come up to talk about? Hiring me?"

"For what?"

"I'm a private investigator."

"Oh is that what it's supposed to say? 'Albert Investigator'?"

"Albert Samson. Yes."

"So you are a Samson. I wondered that too, being how you're in the same building as Posy Samson."

"You know my mother?"

"Yeah. Well, no. Not exactly. But I'd like to. She's a neat lady, is what I hear."

"Look, Mr. . . . ?"

"Jimmy Wilson."

"Mr. Wilson . . ."

"Call me Jimmy."

"Jimmy . . . You came up because you wanted to meet my mother or because of my sign?"

"Hey, I didn't even know you had a mother, Albert Gator. Course it was the sign. It's got letters out. I drive up and down Virginia Avenue every day, a lot—don't ask. It's what I do. So all of a sudden your wall, where there's been nothing, it's lit up with neon, and I think, 'Wow, I ain't seen that before, but it don't make no sense.' "

"And your journey has not been a wasted one, Jimmy. I'm going to find myself a repairman right now. See, I'm getting out the Yellow Pages. I'm picking up the phone. Thanks a lot for coming in."

"That's all right. No problem."

Also no movement from where he was seated. I said, "How would you like a cup of coffee?"

"Coffee would be good. Thanks."

"You know where the luncheonette is. Just go in and tell the pretty girl behind the counter that I said to give you all the coffee you can drink, on my tab. And ask her to introduce you to Mrs. Samson, if she's there. How about that?"

Jimmy Wilson looked embarrassedly pleased. "You ain't coming?"

"No. I've got a sign repair to arrange."

And as soon as Jimmy was out the door, I did. A guy in the phone book said he'd come out to look at the sign first thing Monday morning.

3

After about four o'clock the people on my phone list started being in meetings. Rather than call the bars where the meetings were probably taking place—it *was* a Friday afternoon—I called it a day. No doubt the top agenda item for most of the meetings was already the hot news that I was back. Don't get in a tizz, Mr. and Ms., let Albert Gator do your biz.

I headed downstairs with the idea that maybe I could still get in a few muscle-toning hoops. Or some timing-and-reflex-honing pinball games. Or both. Toned and honed and fit to be cloned, that was me.

But at the bottom of the stairs as I turned into the luncheonette I saw a cop. He was standing with Sam. "Daddy," she said, "this man is a—"

"I know exactly what the man is," I said.

"It sure has been a heap of time since I last laid eyes on you, Albert Samson."

"Still playing the country boy, Homer?" Homer Proffitt spoke with a Southern Indiana drawl. After all his years in cosmopolitan Indianapolis, it had to be an affectation by now.

I turned to Sam. "Honey, give the Lieutenant some grits, on my tab."

"Sir?" Sam said.

"He's not serious, Miss," Proffitt told my daughter. "Don't pay him no heed."

"So what are you here for, Homer?"

"Oh, I was in the area. We've had reports of a lot of nasty incidents and malicious damage in this neighborhood and—"

"*That's* what detective lieutenants spend their time investigating these days?"

"Seeing as I was already nearby, I thought I'd stop for a word about another matter."

"What matter might that be?"

"I do believe you asked my wife to pass a request on to me."

For info on Miller. So she'd done it. Well, well. "That's true."

"I think maybe it'd be better for us to speak in private, Albert. So long as you can spare the time."

I prefer to have witnesses when I speak to cops, but because this concerned Miller, I led Proffitt upstairs. If whatever it was needed privacy, it did not sound good.

"So, what's up with my hero pal?" I asked when we got to the office. I dropped onto my desk and gestured to the Client's Chair for him.

But Proffitt did not sit. He took a position facing me squarely.

"What?" I said.

"I am not staying, Albert. And I don't have anything to say to you about Captain Miller."

"But the message I gave Adele was—"

"Listen up. Hear me good. I am not a source of police information for you, and I never will be."

"I just thought—"

"So don't you be calling Adele."

"Is that what this is about? You don't want me to call my ex?"

"She's my wife, and she'd never come back to you."

"I have absolutely no—"

"Give it up," Proffitt said, waving a finger in my direction. "And mind you pay attention here. It would be imprudent of you to ignore my wishes in this matter."

"Oh, I won't ignore it, Homer. I definitely won't ignore it. Or the fact that you win the prize for being the first cop to threaten me since I got my license back."

"If you take it as a threat, that's up to you." He glared and pivoted and was out the office door before I could think of a killer retort. Or turn my tape recorder on and get a repeat performance. The truth was I was struck dumb. What was with the guy?

When Adele was doing the "this is the hardest thing I've ever had to do" speech, I annoyed her by asking what on earth she saw in Proffitt. "He's a cop, for Christ's sake," I said. "Granted, he's younger, better looking, and more ambitious than I am. But apart from that and his pension, what do you see in the cornweed hillbilly goofus?"

I went downstairs again and found Sam alone in the luncheonette. She was up-turning chairs onto tables. "What did the police officer want?"

"Not much. He just had a window in his bullying schedule."

"Am I right about who he is? Isn't he Adele's husband?"

"Yes."

"And?"

"And what?"

"Daddy, you're not being very informative."

"What's to inform? I have a feeling that something's up with Jerry Miller and I took a chance that Proffitt might get his mind out of the trailer park long enough to help me find out what. Unfortunately help is not what he's good at. He preferred to use his time to instruct me not to call his wife."

"Do you call Adele?"

"I called today to ask her to pass a message on to her husband. Wives still do that, don't they? I know it's been a long time since I was married but . . ."

"Is the problem that Lieutenant Proffitt thinks you want Adele back?"

"I don't know what he thinks. I only do joined-up thinking."

"Do you want Adele back?"

"No."

"Are you sure?"

"Of course I'm sure. What kind of question is that?"

She shrugged, seeming diffident. Then she decided to speak. "The truth is, Daddy, you're not the same since you two broke up."

"I'm not? How not the same?"

"You act angry a lot."

"Don't I have things to be angry about? First I lose my livelihood. Then my girlfriend dumps me. I was even in jail, for crying out loud."

"That was only for a few days, and it was a long time ago now, Daddy."

"Seems like yesterday."

"It's other things too. You've been a lot more self-absorbed. And you say nasty things about people lots more than you used to. Your tolerance of people's idiosyncrasies used to be one of the nicest things about you."

I was not aware of being intolerant about people, except those who gave me special cause. Like Proffitt. And his wife. I was on the verge of promising to give the matter some serious thought when Sam said, "Take Norman for example."

"Honey, my failure to see a good side in Norman is nothing new." I looked around. "Speaking of idiosyncrasy, where is he? Why isn't he helping with the chairs?"

"He's with Grandma. I think they're playing Scrabble."

"Has she finally managed to teach him which way up the letters go on the rack?"

Her face indicated disapproval.

"Sorry. Sorry. I'll think about it all. I'll try to become a better person."

"Daddy, if you dislike Lieutenant Proffitt so much, why did you pick him to find out about Uncle Jerry from?"

"He was the only cop I could think of to ask."

"But you know other police officers, don't you?"

"Who?" But as soon as I asked, I knew who she meant. There was another law enforcement officer I had history with. Granted, he made Homer Proffitt at his most threatening seem like a cream puff. "Ah. Leroy Powder."

"He might know about Uncle Jerry, mightn't he?"

Powder was less a gossip-over-the-water-cooler kind of guy than Proffitt, but it was certainly possible he would know about Miller, if there was anything to know. But I felt a gut reluctance to expose myself to the vicissitudes that were Leroy Powder.

"Daddy?"

So did my reluctance mean that my call to Adele had really been just an excuse to tell her about my license after all? Down deep, did I really want her back again?

"Daddy?"

No, not that. Surely. Too much betrayal to go there again. To have a girlfriend would be nice, but not that one. "No way," I said.

"Daddy, are you all right?"

"One hundred percent right." I had my license back!

"Does that mean when I finish here it would be an OK time for me to come up to your office to talk business?"

I helped with the chairs and left Sam to finish a couple of other things downstairs. I went up to change clothes. I still had it in mind to shoot some hoops, assuming whatever her "business" was didn't take too long. The park courts were not empty in the late afternoons but I still might find space enough to work up a sweat somewhere away from the good players.

I changed quickly, then settled to wait in the office. There I discovered a message on my answering machine. A message . . . Could it be . . . a client . . . ?

It turned out to be Joe Ellison, my free-throw buddy. In answer to my outgoing message he said, "Hey, I guess maybe you really are a private eye."

What he wanted to tell me about was a man he knew. "There's this guy in the neighborhood—well, not a guy exactly, he's a reverend. He's been having trouble at his church, vandals, they've been coming in and defacing the place and doing damage. A few days ago it was sledgehammers at the brickwork. The cops claim they can't do anything for him, surprise surprise, so I thought if, well, if maybe you were looking for something to investigate, like to get your eye in with, like on the court, well, you might have a talk with my man, the rev. Or maybe you don't give a fuck about a church being vandalized if there's no money in it for you, which I can see if you're trying to get your life back together. Been there, done that myself. But you don't ask, you don't get." And he left an address for the church and a name for his man, the rev.

I played the message a second time, and wrote down the name and address. I didn't quite know how to react. Is a client a client when it's not a paying client? And is a cop a cop when it's Leroy Powder?

Philosophical issues for a late afternoon.

I didn't notice Sam till she was nearly in front of me. "Daddy? The door was open."

"So what's up, kid? You looking for a divorce? Oh, I forgot. Been there, done that."

"Thank you, Daddy. That's ancient history now."

"Well, take a seat, Ms., Ma'am." When she was settled in the Client's Chair, I opened my notebook. "First a few details. What's your name and address?"

"It's about my mother."

"Mom? What about her?"

"No. *My* mother."

"*Your* mother?" Talk about ancient history. Sam was the only valuable artifact to have survived that civilization.

"I don't know where she is. I want to hire you to find out."

Whoa, whoa, whoa. "Whoa."

"It's exactly the sort of work you do, Daddy. I have the money, and you can't possibly be too busy to take the case."

"You're moving too fast," I said.

"What's too fast?"

"First, it's not exactly the sort of work I do. Missing people, sure. But missing people last seen in Europe? I don't think so."

"Why not?"

"There's no good reason to believe that I could find someone in Europe."

"Have you ever tried?"

"No."

"I want you to try."

"Which brings us to second. Do you have any idea what it would cost?"

"You don't have to go to Europe. There must be lots of ways you could look for her by computer now."

We both glanced at the winkin', blinkin', and nod machine that, with its paraphernalia, was the only substantive addition to my office in the recently completed interim period of my career. What I might yet come to call The Calm. I saved up. I researched. I bought wisely.

"And you did take some classes . . ." she said.

That too. But isn't there an IT rule against using technology to find an ex-wife? One who was so ex that I probably wouldn't even recognize her anymore. "Well . . ."

"But let's say you do have to go somewhere in Europe—to confirm a sighting or something. I have money to pay for that."

"What money would that be?"

"I own some stocks."

"What stocks?"

"Various. A portfolio."

"My child has a portfolio?"

"They were part of the settlement. I ignore them."

"Meanwhile spending your time as a cashier and waitress in a luncheonette in Indianapolis."

"I won't be doing that forever. I like working in Bud's, though. It's not like a job. It's a family thing."

"Only now you want to go and spoil it by finding your mother?"

"Daddy, I just want to know where she is. For years, I got letters from her every month. Now I haven't had one since Christmas."

Making it five months. "Where was she at Christmas?"

"Basle. It's in Switzerland."

"And you're afraid she was caught in an avalanche or a

cuckoo bit her writing fingers off, or what?"

"I'm afraid," my daughter said, "that something's wrong and she's not telling me about it."

"Which would mean that she didn't want you to know. Doesn't she have that right?"

"Sure. As long as she writes me a letter every month."

Was this really something I might consider getting involved in? I took one of the deepest breaths of my life. "If . . . If I were to try this, I would need to know a lot of things about your mother that I've never had the slightest inclination to know."

Sam pulled out a plastic folder that had been spooled up in her handbag. "I tried to think out what might be useful for you."

I put the folder next to my notebook. Less than two days back in business and I already had two potential non-paying clients. Because not even I—a down-and-out-of-work private eye—would take divorce settlement money off my own kid. "I'll read it. No promises."

She nodded. And I saw in the grimness of her expression that she was seriously worried about her mother. Had the concern been there since Christmas and I hadn't noticed? How much else was there in my life, among the people in my life, that I hadn't noticed?

I said, "Honey, I'm sure she's OK. She's too tough to crack."

"You're not making it better, Daddy."

"Sorry." I patted the folder. I smiled my most fatherly smile.

"Thank you. And there's something else I want to talk to you about," she said.

Whatever it was couldn't be worse than this. "Fire away."

"Grandma and I think you need to get laid."

4

I didn't know if Leroy Powder still lived at the address I had for him. Or even if he still lived at all, the cantankerous old coot. But wasting a journey was better than sitting with my hands folded while my well-intentioned daughter outlined the benefits of my return to the dating scene. "I know it must seem hard now," she said. "Sorry. Got to go to an appointment," I said.

The used-to-be Powder house was in a downtown "Historical District" called Lockerbie Square—a few blocks of carefully restored houses from the late nineteenth century. Powder's, if it was, showed no signs of internal life from the street. Nevertheless, I walked up the path and rang the bell.

Nothing happened, and I wondered whether trying to find Powder another way would be worth the effort. Then, the door flew open. Leroy Powder, heavier, grayer, said, "What?" He had chopsticks in one hand.

"I don't know if you remember me," I began.

The chopsticks twitched at my face. "You're the private dickhead. We've had you in jail, haven't we? More than once."

"Old news."

"The last time's not so long ago. You were done for drunk and disorderly, criminal damage, disturbing the peace, right? Outside Adele Buffington's, wasn't it? Boohooing to the moon, and everybody else ten blocks in each direction."

I'd forgotten that Powder knew Adele. "It was a mistake."

"You're not going to break any of *my* windows, are you?

Because I tell you now, I won't drop charges in favor of a goddamn restraining order."

"I'm regretting that I came here now."

"So leave."

I probably would have if he'd shut the door. But he didn't. I said, "I need some help. A couple of questions, a few minutes. I wouldn't be here if I could think of some-place else to go for it."

He scratched his forehead with the chopsticks. "Did I hear you got your license back?"

"Good news travels fast."

He rubbed his face with the stick-free hand. "I'm eating dinner." He turned and took a few steps into the darkness of his hall. "You coming in or what?"

Powder's kitchen table and chairs were plastic resin, the kind normal people put on their lawns or patios. "Take a pew," he said.

As I sat opposite he began to poke at the food on his plate: broccoli florets, mashed potato, and cut-up pieces of a pork chop.

I said, "Captain Gerald Miller."

He captured an elusive piece of pork. "What about him?"

"The guy's my oldest friend. We've been out of touch but I called him today."

"To rub it in that you got your license back after he lifted it off you?" A chopstick clattered onto the table as Powder tried to pick up a piece of broccoli. Disgusted, he speared it with the other stick.

"I called to say no hard feelings and to invite him out to lunch. It's something we used to do every few weeks."

"And?"

"He blew me off."

"Yeah?" Powder lifted his eyes and smiled as he recovered his missing chopstick.

"Unless something serious is up, Miller just wouldn't do that to me."

"It's that kind of friendship, huh?"

"Yeah."

"Buddies from birth. Peas in a pod."

"At least we both know how to eat pork chops."

Powder looked at the utensils in his hand. "So why do they call them *chop*sticks?"

"To baffle the literal."

"Your old pal," Powder said, "your childhood sweetheart, has just wrapped up the biggest case in his life."

"Bodies in the trunks. He's a hero."

"You'd think so, wouldn't you?"

Before I could encourage Powder to expand on the doubt he implied, he got up from the table and went to his freezer. He took out a tub of ice cream, flicked the lid off, and scooped out a few mouthfuls with the chopsticks.

"What the hell is with the chopsticking?"

"I got a date tomorrow night with an Italian girl."

"I hate to break bad news, but they use forks in Italy. They invented the damn things."

"Yeah?" He smiled. "Now suppose, just suppose, suppose I already knew about Italy and forks."

"I guess I could stretch to that."

"In light of the date with the Italian girl, what do you conclude?"

"What?"

"Think it through. Become a better cop."

I thought it through. "You're taking her to a Chinese restaurant?"

He applauded me by clicking the sticks together, then

put the ice cream away. "So, private eye, what you doing for a girlfriend now that Homer Proffitt's got Adele? Or are you still getting rat-ass drunk every night about it?"

"It was once. One mistake. Done and gone."

"Society and I are relieved to hear it." He ditched the chopsticks in the sink. "Hate to love you and leave you, but I've got a job to go to."

"Where are you assigned these days?"

"Northside, night shift, doing what I can to turn the baby blues into competent cops. You're not planning to come by for advice on your love life, I hope."

"Not from you, if it means eating pork chops with chopsticks."

"Pisser is that I don't even like Chinese food much these days."

"No?"

"But she does, and she's only thirty-three and you hate to disappoint a kid."

"Aren't you kind of old for a thirty-three-year-old?"

"I'm not too old for her. The question is whether she's too young for me."

"Powder, does Miller have trouble at work?"

"It's not for me to tell you stuff about your own damn pal."

"So why imply he's not IPD's bright-eyed hero-boy when it would seem he ought to be?"

"What exactly did the guy say to you?"

"He said, 'Don't call me here again.' And his tone of voice totally blanked me."

"Think it through. Become a better cop. What might 'Don't call me here again' mean?"

"Call him when he's somewhere else?"

Which anyone with half a brain would have thought of

47

for himself. I drove away and felt stupid while I cruised the streets for a phone booth. I found one at a gas station and I called Miller's home number.

But it was Janie, not Jerry, who answered. I bit the bullet and said, "Hi. This is Al Samson. Is Jerry there?"

"The last thing we need now is the likes of you."

I said, "Uh," by way of preparing to ask her to tell him I'd called, but she hung up.

She'd confirmed that *something* was up. Miller not wanting to talk at IPD implied it was work-related. But something that spilled over into their home life. It wasn't obvious what that might be.

I thought about calling again.

Janie answered once, probably she'd answer again.

I thought about driving to the Millers' house.

Maybe not.

I thought about going to 42nd and College, where IPD's North Quadrant HQ was, to try to get more information out of Powder.

But finally I thought it might be better to think about it all some more first.

5

I did not go home. Whatever Sam got up to on a Friday night, I wanted her to have plenty of time to go out and get up to it. I was not eager to renew the conversation with her that I hadn't wanted to have in the first place.

It wasn't that I was opposed, in principle, to going out on dates—however alien the word felt. Feminine company is desirable, in principle. But after Adele ditched me I never felt I had anything to offer a feminine. I probably had nothing to offer long before that, which was why it happened. Not that I saw it coming. Such were my powers of observation.

Well, Adele was history, if not yet ancient. And I was whole again, with a license to prove it. So why not start thinking about a social life?

Because it just didn't feel right, that's why. There wasn't much inside me that I wanted to talk about.

I could hear Sam saying, "All you have to do is listen."

Well, I didn't feel much like listening either.

So instead of going home, I drove to the address Joe Ellison had given for the vandalized church of his pal, the rev.

The church turned out to be closer to Fountain Square than I'd thought—maybe half a mile. It was also only a block from Virginia Avenue and a slip road leading to the multi-lane state highway and occasional interstate that circles Indy. Very convenient for sinners on a schedule.

49

The location might have felt part of a formula for modern, efficient worship if the church building had looked more hip. In fact it looked rural rather than urban, its color and shape being barnlike. Up close the barn red turned out to be brick red but even so, a roof ad for Bull Durham wouldn't have struck me as out of place from a design point of view. There was also a rural amount of land on two sides of the building, far more than had been paved for parking. Maybe what I was seeing was a church for urban folks with rural values, a niche market. When I pulled up and parked, it was clear that business was good. The paved lot was nearly full.

As I got out of my car I heard a soaring angelic sound pouring out through open windows. A choir was rocking with the Lord and as I approached the harmony and harmonies of it all lifted even my weary heathen spirit. I remembered to be thankful. I had my license back. Alleluia.

The two things I knew about the church were the name of the minister, Timothy Battle, and the fact that vandals had been at work there. With a service apparently in progress, I decided to begin my investigation with a walk around the building to see what I could see.

I went from the parking lot to the front of the church, where all that was evident from the nearby sidewalk was a well-maintained building that sported signs about forthcoming activities. The church was on a corner and the side opposite the parking lot was also unremarkable. Then I turned a corner where the church faced a neighboring house, if distantly, across a stretch of unpaved and unattended land.

A rough gravel path ran close by the church building. I was only a few yards along it when I saw where yellow paint had been sprayed on the brick wall. Efforts to remove it had been made, but how you do you get yellow paint out of red brick? The message was not hard to read: "Blackies Not Welcome."

Although it was an oddly old-fashioned wording, I found myself really offended. The Fountain Square area has been a mixed neighborhood for a long time. There's plenty of racial hostility of all kinds in Indianapolis, but that's elsewhere somehow. Not here.

I moved along the wall. More racial messages were supplemented by the remains of two erect penises alongside what was probably a legless vagina. There was also a telephone number, and a flower of indecipherable species.

Near the end of the wall I had to duck under some shrubbery to turn the final corner of the building. When I got there I might just as well have asked, "What corner?" Where the path made the turn, bricks were missing from the church wall. Not just a few. A panel of brickwork had been removed that was about four feet high and perhaps six feet in length.

This was not the work of your average disaffected racist middle-schooler, even if these days some of them are big enough to wield a sledgehammer. This destruction had been done with care, and not with the purpose of getting inside. The internal wall had been exposed but not hacked through. The removed bricks where piled on the other side of the path.

Vandalism is often described as mindless. That a mind was at work here was evident, if not the purpose it was working toward. Was it some kind of threat of a future intent to bring the whole building down?

I disliked what I saw here. This church might be at the edge of the neighborhood, but it was still Fountain Square side of the highway around the city, so it counted. The damage was shocking.

Also shocking was a guy walking toward me along the back of the church. It wasn't just his football size—something like three hundred pounds—or his scowl. It was his shotgun, which was raised to his shoulder and pointed at my midsection.

He said, "You got ten seconds to convince me not to pull my trigger."

It took me nine-point-eight to get the words "Joe" and "Ellison" out. There are guys who can run a hundred meters in that amount of time.

Mr. Juice Jackson, sir, and I sat in the foyer inside the front door of the church and waited for the service to finish. Folding tables near us were loaded with food. I saw platters of little sandwiches, fried chicken, and deviled eggs. There was potato salad. There were cookies, cakes, and pies. There was a big bowl of red punch. The smell of it all, the sight of it all, along with the first twenty-five minutes of not conversing with Mr. Jackson, sir, combined to remind me that I had not eaten for hours.

At twenty-seven minutes past doing nothing, I asked sir if I might lighten a plate or two. There looked to be enough to snack-feed an army.

He said, "No."

Eighteen more minutes later the service was suddenly over and well-dressed people streamed through double doors. They went straight to the food and drink. In moments the room was packed. Only the final few seemed disinclined to eat. One of these was a stocky guy in his late forties who wore black robes and a kente cloth stole. It didn't take a Gold Medal Noticer to work out that this was the Reverend Battle.

I was working out a way to suggest to Mr. Jackson and

his shotgun that we might call the rev over when the rev came over on his own initiative. "What have you got here, Brother Jackson?" he said, but he was looking at me. Battle's stare was penetrating.

"Found him outside by the hole."

"The back of God's house seems a strange place to be found, brother," Battle said. "If you're lost, you'd have a much better chance to find relief inside."

"I was marking time until the service was over," I said. "Joe Ellison asked me to stop by."

"You know Brother Ellison?"

"Told me that too," Juice said. "It's why I didn't shoot him."

"Joe told me you've been having some trouble here," I said. "He suggested I talk to you."

"With a mind to serve what purpose?" Battle asked.

"Maybe none, but I am a private investigator, and if you're interested, I can listen to what's been going on and decide then if there's anything I can do."

"I'm Reverend Timothy Battle. You are?" I told him. "We are not a wealthy congregation, Mr. Samson."

"Joe made it clear that it would not be a paying gig."

I was on the end of the piercing stare again as he said, "How is it that you know Brother Ellison?"

"We shoot baskets together now and then."

"And is that sufficient connection for you to be offering us your professional services for free?"

"It's a complicated story, but what's sufficient is that my family has been in this neighborhood for a long time. I don't like bad things to happen around here and the damage I saw out there is bad. I don't like it. Anyway, all I'm offering at the moment is a consultation."

He looked at his watch. "Would you be able to hang

on for about fifteen minutes?"

"Sure."

"Meanwhile, please feel free to partake in the collation."

Fifteen minutes turned out to be closer to thirty but I didn't mind a bit. I was quite content to let some of the women in the congregation make sure I sampled each of the delicacies and introduce me to their creators. Sister Vernette's pound cake was my favorite but Mother Moore's triple-layer coconut with banana filling ran it a close second.

I had just refilled a cup with punch when Juice Jackson appeared by my shoulder. "Reverend's ready for you."

I followed Jackson up a flight of stairs. He left me in an office room that sported enough full mahogany bookshelves to convince me Reverend Battle was a reader and enough autographed pictures on the wall to convince me that he was a player. But in what league?

Battle was waiting in a leather swivel chair, his back to a window that overlooked the street. I had a sudden impulse to move Battle to one side so that he would not be so easy a target for a sniper. Why was I thinking like that? Jackson's shotgun? Or just the serious aggression that the damage to the fabric of the church's wall represented?

Battle said, "I trust you've been made to feel welcome, Mr. Samson."

"Very, thank you." As I sat, I shook my head to clear it.

"I see you've taken to the punch."

"It does have a certain *je ne sais quoi*." I sipped.

"I believe it's widely referred to as 'red church juice,' although none of my flock would do so in front of me."

"Just so long as it's not the blood of my host," I said. "So, tell me about the hole."

"You've seen it."

"I'm puzzled about the effort it took to remove that many bricks without breaking through to the interior of the building."

"It certainly appears to be damage for damage's sake. It was done on Wednesday night. And, before I forget, let me apologize for Brother Jackson's zeal. This incident was one of several we've suffered recently, although by far the worst. Because of the escalation, the Board of Trustees organized a rota of volunteers to stand guard. However guns are not part of the strategy. I'll have a word with Brother Jackson about it."

I nodded to acknowledge the gesture and said, "I managed to make out the ugly graffiti on your wall. Is what's been done to your wall all that's happened?"

"We had bricks through windows on two occasions and some excrement in the mailbox once."

"What time period?"

"All in the last couple of months."

"I take it these are unusual events."

"The congregation has been in this building for twenty-eight years. I've only been here for a year and a half, but I'm unaware of any serious problems before now."

"And what do you think all this vandalism is about?"

"Frankly, Mr. Samson, I don't know what to think."

"I take it you reported the incidents to the police."

"The recent one, yes."

"And?"

"I told them about the hole that had been created. They said they'd look into it."

Battle's face was expressionless. I said, "Was that an intentional joke?"

"Sure."

"I think it might prove expensive to play poker against you, rev."

"A few guys in Vietnam were of the same opinion. Fortunately, they only learned by experience and I thus accrued sufficient financial reserves to provide a few creature comforts during my years at Divinity School on the GI Bill."

6

It was nine when I arrived back home. I parked on the street across from the stairs that led up to my professional world. To my hopes. To my dreams.

The neon sign was on, advertising a version of my existence to the world. It crossed my mind that a few judiciously flung stones might save me a substantial repair bill. "Albert . . . gator" could easily become "Albert." Singers go without last names. Why not me?

Ah well. Perhaps talk to the prospective repairman before loosening up the old pitching arm.

In the office my answering machine was blinking. I played the messages immediately, hoping that one would be from Jerry Miller. Maybe he wanted to meet tonight, sneak out of the house after Janie went to bed. So what that I hated the guy. He was still my oldest friend.

Message one was not from Miller. Instead it was from that most prized of species—a possible client. William Allen was considering the purchase of a condo, but before he committed himself he wanted to know what his prospective neighbors were like. Did I do such work?

Did he have a checkbook?

Message two was from Jimmy Wilson, "the guy that came in about your broken sign." Wilson wanted to thank me for laying on free coffee for him in the luncheonette. "Your girl, the daughter, she was very civil to me which is a credit to you. She also introduced me to your ma, when I asked. She's a pistol, your ma. I'd like to help her. I really would." Gee, as much as you've helped me, Jimmy? He said I could call him back if I wanted to know how he'd gotten my phone number.

From the phone book?

The last message, however, was from the pistol herself.

I found Mom at the computer she'd installed in her living room. "You're leaving messages on my machine now?"

"Well, if you'd check your e-mails . . ." She didn't look up.

"Maybe I should call you back and suggest that we do lunch."

After a moment to suspend whatever she was doing, Mom swung around to face me. "I don't mean to be formal, son. But these days they can forward calls to your cell phone."

"I don't have a cell phone, Mom."

"No? I thought you might have got that set up now you're back in business."

I was about to observe that my poor powers of observation might be a genetic inheritance when I realized that this was a Mom-like way of telling me that I ought to have a cell phone now.

She said, "I really am so glad you got the reinstatement you wanted, son."

"Thanks."

"Your plan is to return to being a detective full time, isn't it? You're not going to carry on jumping from doing this to doing that any more, are you?"

"Mom, I took whatever I could find that would earn some money."

"And I guess none of those jobs appealed to you enough to give up the investigating."

"I was never looking for a new career."

"And now you've got your old one back. Well, isn't that nice."

She leaned back in her chair and folded her hands. For that moment she looked like a grandmother who knitted. Active, elderly, sweet. Can you knit on a computer?

"So, Albert, are you all right for money?"

"Rolling in the stuff."

"Please try to control your flippant side, son. I'm really busy here." A wave to the silent screen.

"Contrary to what your pal, Norman, seems to think, Mom, I've never taken money from you and I don't plan to begin now."

"I do wish you could see Norman's good qualities."

Why does everyone keep saying that?

"And no matter what the history is, if you do need a bit of cash to tide you over—"

"No, Mom. Thanks. I may need a little grace period before I begin to pay rent, but that's all."

"You know I don't need rent from you, son."

"Then when it starts to come in you can use it for champagne and cruises."

"And were you with a client when I called?"

When I left the Reverend Timothy Battle, I told him that I would look into what I could do to help take his security to something a little less basic than Juice Jackson. Therefore . . . "Yes."

"Albert . . . ?"

"A *pro bono* client is still a client."

"Oh, Albert."

"You wouldn't want me to charge a church, would you? Not one more or less in the neighborhood."

"What church?"

I gave her the address. "They've had some serious vandalism."

"What happened?"

I described what I'd seen and what I'd been told. "It upset me, to tell the truth. So I'm quite happy to see if there's anything I can do. I'm unlikely to find the culprits, but maybe I can come up with some economical ways they can scare the bad guys off. Maybe some floodlights, or some ersatz alarm boxes that have little flashing lights so intruders would think they've been caught on a surveillance video. Of course, if something paying comes along, that will have to take precedence."

Mom didn't respond. I didn't know if she was thinking about what I said or whether her attention was wandering back to whatever she'd been doing on the computer.

"In fact, another message just now was from a prospective client, so I'm heading back upstairs to deal with that."

"Mmmm."

"Are you all right?"

"Me? Good heavens, yes. And Albert, even if it doesn't all work out the way you hope, I'm truly happy for you because you're focusing on what you want to do."

"Thanks."

"And now that you're settling down to work here at your agency, maybe you'll have a little more time for Sam."

"For Sam?"

"Your daughter."

"I know who . . ." Ah, a joke.

"Because I've been wanting to talk with you about Sam for quite a while, son. It's just you've been so . . . so involved in your own problems."

"Mom, what are you talking about?"

"I do hope that now you'll be able to spend more time

with her. Your daughter needs you to be around, son. She needs that fatherly input. Sam is drifting, son."

"She is?"

"Of course she is," Mom said sharply. "It's all right for you. You're where you want to be. But Sam . . . A grown-up girl her age . . . To be here . . ."

"You don't want her here?"

"I want what's best for her, son. For her. Sam is so bright . . . My, she even speaks French. And she could—can—be something, do something. Do you want her arriving at your age and still be living under my roof? Is that what you want?"

"What does she want?"

"That's a very good question. And, as her father, don't you think that you should be asking it of her?"

7

Problem is, it's hard to ask a kid a question if the kid's out somewhere.

So instead I called William Allen back and agreed to check up on his prospective neighbors in return for a check from him. Then I spent the best part of two hours at the computer. Doing some gen-u-wine de-tec-tive work. And for my pains I turned up information about four nearby condo neighbors. One was an ex-bankrupt, one had an expired pot conviction in Hawaii, and two had unpaid parking tickets. No felons or politicians. It would be up to the estimable Mr. Allen to decide if that was the kind of neighborhood he wanted to live in.

When I turned the computer off, I turned me off too.

Or so I thought.

I found it hard to get to sleep.

Was it neglectful of me to let my only child find her own path without active intervention, or at least attempts there at?

Ah, but Mom wasn't suggesting intervention. She was urging *communication*—the chant word honed in the old century to be ready-sharp in the new.

And, like many a mother, chances were she wasn't far wrong. I talked to Sam every day, but we rarely said anything.

Once upon a time I communicated with my kid. I wrote her letters, especially when she was young. Often they had stories in them—fancies, fantasies, whatever came to mind when I sat down to commune with paper and pen. As I remember it the stories were more interesting than anything I could have reported about my actual life, with few exceptions.

And now my kid and I lived under the same roof for the first time since she could speak sentences and I might as well be the parent who'd stopped writing letters. It was nighttime, and she was out, and I didn't have the faintest idea where she was or who she was with.

Was that so wrong? Was that so bad? The "kid" in question was a grown-up, so in that sense it wasn't wrong. It wasn't bad. But it wasn't right and it wasn't good.

And I certainly did not know what my child's objectives in life were.

Except that she wanted me to solve the problem of her mother's missing letters.

Probably j, c, and r.

Ha ha.

No, no, better: whatever the missing letters were, they wouldn't be any that helped spell "money."

Ha ha ha ha ha.

I got out of bed. I went to the office and dug out a piece of plain paper. I sat down to write whatever came into my mind. I wrote "duck." Then I drew something that looked to me impressively like a creature that would quack. And then I wadded it up and flew it away.

But as I sat, uninspired, I felt comfortable. My life was whole again. I could *feel* it, in my shoulders, in my limbs. The bits of my body were individually and collectively more me than they had been for a long, long time.

Can a job really be like a body part?

I guess it can, if the job really resonates in you.

But why was being a private investigator, a *licensed* private investigator, such a big deal for *me?* Why was I not whole without it? It's not like I spent my sandbox years telling kiddy colleagues, "Only twenty-four more years and I'll have my PI license."

It was a strange process. A step in this direction, followed by two steps in another, and then, whoops, how about one backwards? And I'd ended up in the problem-solving business.

At least I hadn't ended down.

Or ended altogether. Not yet.

8

When I woke, it was morning and a Saturday. Weekend though it might be, I rose and shaved and renewed my vows to work hard.

There were a few Former Clients yet to entice, along with a long list of Other Things To Do On Reinstatement. For instance, I could use my work for William Allen to construct template documents for future reports to clients, expenses records, and final bills. I'd been given a second chance, so no messin'.

But even hard workers need to eat, right?

Saturday mornings are busy at Bud's. Sam was working up a storm when I came downstairs, and it hadn't slackened off much when I went back up. In the meantime I said three things to her: "Have a good night last night?" "Do something fun last night?" and "Could we have a little chat later today?"

She said, "Sure," each time.

Ah well.

Once back in the office I had the computer up and thrumming in a trice. In a trice and a half the doorbell rang.

Could it, possibly, be Miller?

What I actually found on the landing was a gal in overalls. She was maybe just shy of forty, bleached blond, and she had a cigarette dangling from her lips. Ash was dangling from the cigarette. She seemed not to realize it because she was looking at something off to the right.

I put my hand out. The ash dropped into it.

That she noticed. "Thanks," she said. "I'm Mary."

I said, "I try to keep pretty cheerful myself."

Smoking Mary was the neon. "You got a lot of options out there," she said from the comfort of my Client's Chair. "Your wiring and transformers are good and there are plenty of mountings we can tie into." My office ashtray is brass and looks like a shoe. Mary tapped her habit into it. "The question is, do you want to duplicate what was there before or do you want something new. And you'll have to decide how much you want to spend."

"How much I *want* to spend? I'm eager to spend a buck, maybe a buck and a half. Do you think it should be all on the sign or should I save some of it for a new car?"

"A clown . . ." She rubbed her eyes, then looked up, the better to address God. "Saturday morning at the big top . . . Thanks, Big Guy."

"I wasn't expecting you till Monday morning."

"Tell the truth, Mr. Clown. You weren't expecting *me* at all."

"You, as in the last smoker in Indianapolis?"

"Me, a feminine female woman neon person."

"I don't think I had expectations one gender-way or the other though, true, I did speak to a man on the phone."

"Dick."

"Excuse me?"

"You spoke to Dick. My assistant, Richard Kless."

"So it's your own business?"

"Yeah. And please don't ask how a nice girl like me got herself into neon signs, because I'm not a nice girl."

"I'm beginning to sense that about you, Mary."

"My dad got sick. I came back to help. He got sicker. I

stayed longer. He died. I inherited. And now fate has delivered me up to your scruffy office. Life's a bitch, huh?"

My part in the conversation was interrupted when I suddenly realized that Sam, by returning to Indy when I had troubles, had duplicated a path I took long ago. Did that mean Sam *was* doomed to end up like me?

And then Mary said, "Something connected with you about what I said?"

"Am I so transparent?"

"Beneath the white paint and red nose? Yeah, maybe you are. What, you gave up something when there was family trouble?"

"College, as a matter of fact." The story wasn't that simple, but hey. "Though I wasn't thinking about me."

"Who?"

"My kid—my daughter. Tell me, Mary, what would you have gone on to do if your father's illness hadn't brought you back at that particular time?"

"Me? It would have been a tough call between singing opera and being an astronaut."

Which I took as a way to say it was none of my business. Fair enough. "So, what's my sign repair going to set me back?"

"To make it say what it used to?"

"Yeah."

"Well, to make it look perfect I'll have to replace the whole thing. If I just fill in the missing letters, you won't get an exact color match."

"Oh."

"Ballpark, and without measuring . . ." She gave me numbers for the two options that made me appreciate Sam's generosity in giving me the sign in the first place all the more.

"Or," she said, "you could do something different."

"Such as?"

"Change your message. Or goose up what you've already got a little. I was thinking when I was outside your door . . . Suppose *none* of the letters and colors matched. We could give the whole thing the impression of being a ransom note." She stubbed out her cigarette and tapped another out of a box.

"Kind of subtle for Virginia Avenue, don't you think?"

"Am I doomed to work forever for people with no imagination?" She sighed. She lit the cigarette. "Mind if I smoke?"

"I don't mind if you burst into flame."

She looked at me, her head still. It was as if she was seeing me for the first time. A smile flickered across her face. I was pleased by it—a feeling that took me by surprise. It felt like a gift.

And then Sam walked in. "Oh, sorry," she said. "I didn't realize you were with someone."

"I found a neon doctor who makes house calls," I said. "Mary, this is Sam, my daughter. Sam this is Mary Contrary."

"Hi," Sam said.

"Want a cig?" Mary said.

"Great, thanks."

My jaw dropped as for the first time in my life I watched my only child put a white stick in her mouth and set fire to it.

"What?" she said.

"I didn't . . ."

"There's a lot you don't know about me."

"Is he one of those fathers you feel you have to hide it from?" Mary asked.

"Exactly," Sam said.

Mary wrinkled her nose.

"I don't think he's ever smoked a cigarette or a joint in his life," Sam said.

"There is something pious around the eyes," Mary said. She and Sam studied my eyes.

I struggled to find something snappy and amusing to say about my daughter taking poisonous fumes into her lungs, but I failed. They found my discomfort humorous.

"Smokers are much better company," Sam said.

"Better than what?" I asked.

Their laughs mutated into giggles.

And then the telephone rang. I was grateful.

A reassuringly male voice said, "This is Christopher P. Holloway from Perkins, Baker, Pinkus and Lestervic. You called here yesterday, I believe. Left a message about your availability for investigative work?"

My God! A lawyer! "Yes, I did."

"One of our partners is defending a client in a criminal case, Mr. Samson. Our partner asked me to find out if you'd be available to do some work for it."

"Well, 'available' is a relative term, but I can probably make some space."

Christopher P. Holloway hesitated. "What's that noise in the background?"

"I'm playing a surveillance video. Just a sec." I put my hand over the receiver and said, "You two: shut up or get out."

The Giggle Girls rose and went out to my porch. "Sorry about that, Mr. Holloway."

"I think I need to make something clear before we go any further, if I may, Mr. Samson," Holloway said. "My instructions are to engage your services, by which I mean you yourself. Nothing against your employees—I'm sure they're great—but it's your expertise and knowledge that we're after. Is that going to be possible? Of course, we do understand that hiring the engineer and not the oily rag implies paying a premium."

Premium. He said premium. "I should be able to give it my personal attention, assuming we can agree to terms."

"Good. Excellent. In that case, let's meet."

"Are you thinking today?"

"If it's possible. I am at our offices now."

"Let me check my book." Check and book? What's on my mind here? "Mmm, yes. I can make a window in . . . about fifty minutes?" Or, if you'd rather have a door . . .

Christopher P. Holloway gave me directions to Perkins, Baker, Pinkus and Lestervic.

Yes!

When my employed heart stopped racing, I went out to the porch. Sam said, "I like Mary's ransom note idea."

"She'll have to kidnap you first. It's a protocol thing."

Mary said to Sam, "I told you he didn't like it."

"I had an imaginectomy when I was a child. Sorry."

"So we'll imagine for you," Mary said. "How about this? Sam's told me she helped you out on some cases years ago."

"True."

"Well, why don't have your sign say 'Samson' instead of 'Albert Samson.' That way it could include her as part of the business too."

I looked to Sam. She seemed as taken by surprise as I was.

Mary said, "The sign would just leave the option open, unless you're saying that you would never want to work with your daughter."

"What I might or might not want isn't the issue. The truth is that Sam is much too smart to end up like me." I gestured to Albert . . . gator.

"Or maybe," Mary said, "the truth is that the old man is scared that the young woman might do the job better than he can."

"I've got to go out now," I said to Sam. "We can talk about this later, when we're alone. But you do know, don't you, that this company has a strict no-smoking policy?"

9

I left Sam with Mary Contrary so I could ready myself for Christopher P. Holloway. The Christopher P. Holloway who had asked for me, not my oily rags, on behalf of a partner in the esteemed downtown law firm of Perkins, Baker, Pinkus and Lestervic, Attorneys at Law and Lords of the Universe. I didn't know what to wear.

Even sixty seconds in front of my open closet didn't resolve me. I was rescued from my indecision when the telephone rang again.

Only as I walked to answer it did it cross my mind that "Christopher P. Holloway" might be somebody's joke. A fiction. A prank. Who would do something so grotesque? Norman? Homer Proffitt?

The caller, however, was Joe Ellison. "I heard you met Reverend Battle."

"I went there last night."

"And?"

"And what, Joe?"

"What do you think?"

Think? It wasn't even noon yet. "I talked to the guy. I looked at the damage, which really appalls me, by the way. And I think . . ."—winging it—"I think it would be a good idea to talk to the police."

"Oh." The way he said it made it sound like it was an oath.

"Battle couldn't give me any leads about why it should have happened other than random vandalism."

"Somebody's trashing the church. Vandals might write on the walls but they don't hack out holes."

"So we need to put it in some other context. I already happen to know that there's been a lot of malicious damage in the area recently." If Homer Proffitt was to be trusted. "The police can tell me whether that damage differs from what the church has suffered. If it's the same, it means one thing. If it isn't, that means something else."

"So you're going to talk to the police," Ellison said with a sigh. "What else?"

"I'm going to put my pants on one leg at a time and do some breathing. I don't know yet what else I'm going to do."

"Sounds a lot like 'nothing' to me."

"So you going to ask for your money back?"

"Ah, money. Of course."

"Look, you've got a building that's been defaced and damaged. The perpetrator failed to leave a business card at the scene of the crime. What do you expect me to do?"

"Something more than put it in a 'context.' What about when it happens again?"

"Are you so sure it will?"

"Of course it will. Damage like that is to scare folks. Make 'em uncomfortable being there."

"So who might want to scare Reverend Battle or his congregation?"

"If I could answer that do you think I'd be talking to a so-called detective who can't shoot free throws for shit?" On that note of radiant confidence Joe Ellison decided he had better things to do than continue to talk with me.

Bummer.

Christopher P. Holloway was real. His law firm was real.

His desire to see me was real. He met me at the front door and thanked me for being on time. "The office is closed over the weekend," he said, to explain why he was handling the meeting and greeting himself. "It's only hard cases working on hard cases on the premises today."

All in all, it was a pleasant introduction to a new client. Holloway, in his thirties, was one of those guys who's been bald since he voted for the first time. He retained a black rim of hair around the edges of his head. A good-luck horseshoe?

The office he led me to wasn't impress-'em large, but it did overlook Canseco Field House and that was plenty to impress me. Canseco is where the Pacers shoot free throws even better than Joe Ellison.

Holloway sat across from me at a low table beside his desk. He offered me whiskey.

I declined. "We're both busy, I'm sure," I swanked. "What's the case? Who're you defending? Anyone I've heard of?"

"Our client is Ronnie Willigar."

I should have taken the whiskey when it was offered. Ronnie Willigar was the bodies-in-the-trunks killer. The alleged bodies-in-the-trunks killer. Miller's bodies-in-the-trunks killer. This had to be the biggest, most public case in town.

"I can see from your face that you've read newspaper accounts of the crimes our client is charged with," Holloway said.

"Refresh my memory. Was it more rapes than murders or more murders than rapes?"

"Mr. Samson, I hope we're not about to debate the wisdom of the Constitution's guarantee of a vigorous defense even for people charged with serious crimes."

74

"The Constitution's cool," I said. "It's just that my impression from what I've read is that there's a lot evidence against Mr. Williger."

"Our client will be pleading not guilty."

"Oh."

"There is a lot of evidence in the prosecution's quiver," Holloway said. "However . . ."

"Call me psychic, but I knew a 'however' was coming."

"That evidence is flawed, Mr. Samson. Deeply flawed."

"Wasn't a box containing items taken from the victims found in Willigar's bedroom?"

"Yes."

"What would the flaw about that be? Are you saying the police planted it?"

"Not the police, necessarily, but our case is that someone put the box there. The most likely candidate is the informant who called Crime Stoppers."

"OK." I nodded, absorbing that.

Holloway said, "There are many facets to the case we're building, Mr. Samson. For instance we also believe that the police search itself was flawed. So, basically, our defense will be that the whole thing is a crock of shit. To use the technical term."

"The crock-of-shit defense, got it." A flawed police search? A framed client? Conducted and orchestrated by Jerry Miller?

"But before we proceed, Mr. Samson, we should talk about money."

"Before we proceed to talk about money I think maybe I ought to tell you I may have a conflict of interest on this case."

"How can that be?" He frowned. "You're an investigator, not a judge, a juror, or a lawyer."

"The police officer in charge of the case and the arrest of Mr. Willigar . . ."

Holloway moved a couple of papers. "You're referring to Captain Gerald Miller?"

"He's my oldest friend."

"So?"

"Well . . ."

"He does his job and you do yours. I don't see the conflict unless you're saying that you would betray the confidence of this office to assist the prosecution."

"I would never do that. I've been to jail rather than do something like that."

"Well, even if you have talked with Captain Miller about the case from time to time . . ."

"Which I haven't."

"Then I don't get it. Are you saying that you refuse to work for the defense on any case that Captain Miller is involved in?"

"It's never come up before."

Holloway took a deep breath and raised his eyebrows. "It's come up now, Mr. Samson. Time to piss or get off of the pot. Are you in or out?"

Was I really going to turn down paid employment in order to keep from hurting Jerry Miller's feelings? I could still worry about the guy having problems, if he did. Couldn't I? "I'm in."

"In that case let's deal with the financial side so we can get on to what we want you to do first."

On my way into the city I'd thought about money, what I would ask for from Perkins, Baker, Pinkus and Lestervic. It had to take account of how much I'd be paid up-front as a retainer, what would constitute a reclaimable expense, and how often they would settle my account if the case dragged on. Considering that Holloway had introduced the concept of a "premium," I decided to push him up from whatever his offer was. Begin my new business life as I meant to go on. Engineers do not come cheap. If you pay peanuts, you get oily rags.

However, I had not planned my response if the numbers and terms Holloway started with were already better than what I'd decided to shoot for. My "That sounds fine," may have been a meek precedent but on my drive back to Virginia Avenue I was a happy engineer. An ecstatic engineer. An employed and highly paid engineer.

They wanted me to start work right away. My first assignment was to see if I could find any alibi witnesses who would confirm Willigar's presence in the bars he said he'd been in when the prosecution said he was committing unspeakable crimes. One day I was an unlicensed private depressive. Two days later I was being paid more money than I'd seen in years to go to a bunch of bars. Life is fucking amazing sometimes.

When I got back home I went whistling into the luncheonette. All the tables were full, so I sat at the counter. I whistled as I watched Sam help the Saturday girl, Paulette, dish dishes.

I was floating. I was flying. I was death-defying. The only problem in the World of Samson was that my bank wasn't open on Saturdays. Thus I'd have to wait till Monday to deposit the largest retainer check in Samsonian History.

Suddenly I was so hot I was glowing. I would prove Ronnie Willigar to be such an innocent babe he'd be cast as the star in a nativity play.

Once I finished with that, I'd set Sam up as the world's

first French-speaking opera-singing astronaut.

Then I would find a severed arm that would, somehow, send Norman to the slam for six consecutive life-means-lifes. However, on the witness stand I would argue against giving him six death sentences. I don't believe in death sentences, even for Normans.

I tried to catch my kid's eye and call her over. I was eager to let her know that her old man was back on the high road. I passed some of the time by watching Norman cope with the grill and the griddle. He wasn't bad at it, although that acknowledgment did not mean I was softening about him. Enjoy it while you can, sucker.

Then Sam was in front of me. "I like Mary," she said.

Mary? Oh right, Mary. "Good. I've got something—"

"Are you eating, Daddy?"

"Is God Hoosier?"

"How about a BLT club plate?"

"Sounds good."

She dropped a club plate in front of me. "It was a mistake on an order. It's only been sitting here for a couple of minutes."

"Cool." I tucked into a chip.

"So what about Mary?"

"What *what* about Mary?"

"Did you like her?"

"I'll tell you that when I get her quotes."

"I don't mean repairing the sign," Sam said with a touch of irritation. "Did you *like* her? Because we sat out on your stairs for nearly an hour, talking, and I like her a lot. And, she's single and not involved with anyone right now."

Finally I got it. Did I *like* her. Ah. "Ah," I said, but by that time Sam was gone, an angel of mercy ministering to the hungry. I applied myself to the BLT club plate, for which Mom's specs include mustard in the mayo, a pickle that puckers, and Cape Cod chips. Runs a classy joint, does my Mom.

And it tasted *good*. Even better than when I couldn't afford to pay for it.

Mary Contrary, huh? Between relationships, huh? How surprising was that?

Sam reappeared with coffee. "So what *did* you think of Mary?"

"Got a quick tongue on her, that gal."

"But you liked her, right?"

"Ah, but did she like me?"

"Daddy, that is such an immature way to approach a situation like this."

"It is?"

"You like her. Why not just tell her, without making a big dithery deal out of it? You didn't know her before today. What would it matter in the fullness of your life if she turns you down? You're only asking for a date. What's to be scared of?" Sam slapped her cell phone down on the counter and returned to the masses.

What I'd taken as a hypothetical conversation suddenly morphed into the piss and pot thing. Again. Call Mary? For a date? Me?

I returned to my food. I savored the bacon. I puckered the pickle. I crunched a chip. I also absorbed some fragments of conversation from nearby. ". . . a slut. She'd tell you so herself . . ." ". . . thirty percent off the original twenty-five percent off. Does that make it less than half price? Ralph said it does, but Linda-Lou's not so sure."

Sam passed by again, pausing only long enough to give me a slip of paper. "I've written out her number."

"There's a problem."

The problem held fire while two customers paid their bills.

"What problem?" Sam pushed a cup of coffee toward me.

"I've just taken on a major job. A really big one, honey. Maybe a bigger one than I've ever had."

I waited for her to cheer. She said, "So what's the problem?"

"Well, it means I'll be working evenings for the foreseeable future."

"Doing what?"

"The first thing I have to do is to go to some bars and show a guy's picture around. My client is trying to build an alibi for his client."

"Ask her along," Sam said. Then she was gone.

Ask her along? But what if . . .

And then I thought, fuck it, why not? I was hot, was I not? If she didn't want to come along, let her tell me herself. I picked up the phone. I dialed.

A woman answered, "Yeah?"

I wasn't sure. "Mary?"

"I'm not here."

"Sorry to hear that."

"Who is this?"

"Mr. Saturday morning neon."

"Oh. Funny, I was just thinking about you."

"Yeah?"

"Because if you do go ahead with the sign that says, 'Samson Private Investigations' that would mean you could use the acronym, S. P. I. Put it on your business cards, your website, make it a brand."

"S. P. I.?"

"It's pronounced, 'spy.' Get it? 'Cause that's what you do, isn't it? Basically. You spy on people."

"Ah."

"I'm so wasted in this town. What were you calling me about? You've decided to ditch the neon and go with a guy who'll walk up and down the street wearing a sandwich board instead?"

"No, though it's tempting."

"What, then?"

"Uh, I called to, uh . . . to ask you out."

There was a silence long enough for me to wonder if we'd been cut off. But then she said, "I was waiting for the punchline."

"No joke. I liked talking to you this morning. I'd like to get to know you better."

"Where are you calling from?" she said.

"The luncheonette below my office. Why?"

"With the noise in the background, I thought you might be in a bar. Maybe had a few."

"Got me." I held my coffee cup close to the phone and slurped from it. "But I would have to have had a lot more before I could have come up with something like S.P.I."

"So where was it you want me to come out to?"

"Other bars. Lots of bars."

10

And just like that I had a date.

Life surely is a wild ride. Now I was an ex-private depressive being paid to go to bars with a date.

Sam materialized in front of me. "Well?"

"Neon Mary and I will meet at the Slippery Noodle at six-thirty."

Sam's reaction was the slightest of nods and the slightest of smiles. They added up to colossal smugness. For an instant I was reminded of her mother. Can facial expressions be inherited?

Sam said, "I hope the two of you have a good time, Daddy."

"Thank you."

"But please keep in mind that you're only just out of a serious relationship. That means you should take things slowly and not expect too much."

"Thanks, Mother."

"I'm only trying to help."

"Speaking of help . . . About tracking down your mother."

"Yeah?"

"I haven't read the notes you gave me and, with this new job, it'll be a long time before I get to them. But if you want to use my computer yourself, then I could give you some ideas of where and how to look for her."

"Oh that's a good idea, Daddy. Thank you." And she was away again.

How to look for my ex-wife on the Net? Try sites devoted to men whose brains were tied in knots before they died.

I met Sam's mother far away from Indy. Having dropped out of college when my father died, I went back to the books when Mom was on her feet again. But then, out of nowhere, there was this beautiful woman . . .

People—some of them even called themselves my friends—said she was out of my league. They were wrong. She was out of my planet. The woman was glamorous, sophisticated, and rich. Why shouldn't she make a beeline for me? Why she did was because she had just been dumped.

I may have been what they called later a "mature" student, but I was way too green to know better than to get hitched and make a baby, though not in that order. And by the time we split I was too cowed, too ignorant, and too angry to work out that I could have fought for a share of my child. Besides, what could I have offered the kid? The opportunity to live on scraps in a provincial city as her father tried to invent a life that would suit him?

So Sam was raised—and "finished"—in Europe. Most of the time she was based in Switzerland, but she—and her mother—got around. No doubt fueled by the fast and furious lifestyle, my daughter married young and lived in France. However that was already over when she heard about the troubles that cost me my license and came to Indy to pitch in. And, amazingly, stayed. It was hard to believe that Sam could find life in Indianapolis sufficiently . . . sufficient. Yet here she still was, passing back and forth in front of me. Taking time out from waiting tables and counting cash to arrange my social life and worry about a mother who had managed to lose herself.

Sam would never locate her mother anywhere that was

cheap. Of course her father was no longer cheap himself. I patted the pocket that held my check from Perkins, Baker, Pinkus and Lestervic. Roll on Monday morning.

Upstairs I opened up the summary case notes Christopher P. Holloway had given me with my retainer. My homework.

Certain things were easy to work out. Like, whoever did commit the crimes I was going to clear Ronnie Willigar of was a Grade A All-American psycho. The details of the case were essentially as they had been reported in the **TRUNK KILLER ARREST—AT LAST!** edition of the *Star*.

A key part of the case Perkins, Baker, Pinkus and Lestervic intended to build focused on the informant who had called Crime Stoppers to name Ronnie Willigar as the killer. The partner in charge of the case was a Karl Benton and Benton was already pressuring the courts to require identification of the informant. "That's because he's almost certainly the bodies-in-the-trunks murderer himself or knows who is," Holloway told me. "How else could he have known about stuff that was planted in Ronnie's house?"

The "stuff" was a box. It was mentioned by the informant and found in Willigar's bedroom. It contained things like a kitchen knife "compatible" with the wounds that had caused all five deaths. There were also "souvenirs." Forensics had connected at least one item from the box to each of the nine known victims. Two of these *aides-mémoire* were pieces of clothing soaked in blood.

No matter what other evidence against Willigar came when it was time for "discovery," the forensic confirmations alone underlined the logic of an I-was-framed defense. What else could there be?

I would have no reluctance about investigating the honesty of Captain Jerry Miller. No one knew the essence of the guy better than I did. His work would come up clean. The other officers in the raid might be a different proposition though, obviously, the informant was the hottest bet. A reward of a hundred and ten thousand dollars can buy a lot of evidence-planting.

But Holloway did not want me to wait for the informant's identity to begin my work. I'd begin by trying to establish an alibi for Willigar. Oddly, for that purpose it was good that he was charged with so many crimes. To cast serious doubt on all the accusations I would only need to find an indisputable alibi for one.

Unfortunately Ronnie Willigar was indisputably vague about where he was or might have been on the key dates. Mind you, the murders alone were spread over nearly three years, with the rapes covering four years before that. How many of us could account for our whereabouts on nine particular nights out of the last two odd thousand?

Nor did Willigar offer names of any friends he associated with regularly. His only family was a sister who lived in Oregon. Their mother died before the period of the accusations, while Willigar was in jail—for an indecent assault carried out while he was a teenager. It was from his mother that he inherited the little house he lived in, along with a small income. He did not have a job.

Before the search that had led to his arrest, Willigar was questioned three times in connection with the bodies-in-the-trunks investigations, but officers hadn't thought him a likely candidate. There was no evidence that he had committed crimes of any kind since he was released from jail, except for his car having twice been found to have faults with its bulbs.

Willigar told the police—and his lawyers—that he spent

most evenings at home watching videos. The raid turned up a sizeable collection. The tapes ran from *Debby Does Dallas* to *The Sound of Music*, but no one had suggested that he was involved in making or distributing either porn or unlicensed copies of Julie Andrews.

Willigar's only contribution to establishing an alibi was to say that he sometimes went to bars where he'd sit in a corner and watch people or listen to music. However he was unable to say he was more likely to have done that one night of the week than another. Nor was there a particular bar that he patronized regularly. The case notes gave me the names of a dozen bars he said he'd been to more than once. That was the list I was using to show his picture around. My chances of finding a useful witness that way were about the same as winning on the Lotto, but Holloway said, "Do it." The check in my pocket answered, "My pleasure, boss."

11

The Slippery Noodle on South Meridian purports to be the oldest continuously serving bar in town. Also to have been a stop on the Underground Railroad before the Civil War. What can be confirmed without library work is that its stage at the back is Indy's leading venue for blues music. Slippery Noodle is also a record label.

I arrived early. I wouldn't want a gal to get blue from having to spend time in a bar alone, which is not to say that Ms. Contrary struck me as a gal who couldn't cope. But hey, first date . . . I'd even put on clean clothes.

While I waited I got the attention of a child woman behind the bar and pulled out my picture of Ronnie Willigar. It was not one that had appeared in the newspapers. "Could you tell me if you've ever seen this guy before?" I asked.

She took the picture and held it close enough to suggest mild myopia. "What it about? He somebody baby-daddy?"

"He's in trouble but not that kind. I've been hired to try to help him."

She pushed hair out of her eyes. It fell right back to where it started. "He do look kind of familiar."

"Have you seen him in here maybe?"

"Could be."

"Any chance of your working out when that might have been?"

"It would have to been a Saturday. I only work here on Saturday."

"It could have been a Saturday." The third Saturday in

January was the seventh rape and fourth murder. "He maybe nursed a couple of beers for the evening. About five-nine, thin guy."

She frowned. "I wouldn't been out here then. Seven o'clock I move from out here to the tables in the music room."

"He might have listened to the music. Maybe if you think about it, you'll put his face together with a particular band."

"Mmmm." Which meant, I doubt it. But then she said, "I'm sure I seen him."

Be still my beating heart. How hot was I? Private eyeing doesn't go like this, but what a coup it would be if my first stop produced an alibi witness.

Mary Contrary appeared at my shoulder. "Already trying to pick up other women, Albert? This does not bode well for our future."

I knew Mary was just funning me. On the phone I'd explained about the work I needed to do. "The young woman is trying to work out which Saturday she might have seen my client."

"That's right, miss," the child behind the bar said. "He didn't hit on me or buy me a drink or nothing, I swear."

"Like I'm going to believe that," Mary said. She snatched the picture. Then raised her already rather fetchingly arched eyebrows. "Is *this* the client you're trying to build an alibi for, Albert? The bodies-in-the-trunks killer?"

"The alleged bodies-in-the-trunks killer, emphasis on 'alleged.' It's an important judicial—even Constitutional—point."

The bar child grabbed the picture back. "That's it. That's where I seen him. It was on the TV. I knew I seen that face." She turned. "Gordie, come look. This guy showing round a picture of that raping bastard stuffed the used bodies into car trunks."

"The alleged raping bastard," Mary said. "Please remember he hasn't been convicted yet."

"What?"

"He must be deemed innocent till he's proved guilty."

"Oh yeah," the bar child said. "I heard about that."

Two beefy bar boys materialized behind her, seemingly pleased to have an excuse to push up close. "Let's see," the more tattooed one said, but the less tattooed one got his hands on the picture first. "Fu-uck. This is that killer guy."

Mary said, "My friend Albert is trying to free him."

Les Tattooed curled a lip and looked up at me. Morey Tattooed said, "You want to let him loose so he can kill more old women?"

"He raped them too," the bar child said.

"Not so much of the 'old,' if you please," Mary said. "Five of those rape victims were younger than I am."

"Alleged rape victims," I said. I regretted it as soon as the words were out of my mouth because all the bartenders and three nearby patrons looked at me as if I was the bodies-in-the-trunks killer myself. Anyone who knew me would know how desperately unfair of them that was. I have back trouble—I would never be able to put a victim's body into the trunk of a car.

"Thanks so much," I said, once Mary and I were safely on the sidewalk.

"Showing around pictures of a rapist on a first date. Honestly, how tacky is that?"

I couldn't deny that it was pretty seriously tacky. "I did explain about this evening being partly work."

"Along with going to lots of bars, and eating great food, and dancing the night away, and having a real good time."

"I said all that?"

"You would have if you hadn't been so nervous when you called."

"Nervous? I thought I was pretty smooth."

She laughed.

"Wasn't I clear? Wasn't I direct? I called, I asked you out. I didn't say, 'Um,' more than twice."

"Yes, Samsdad, you were very efficient."

"And that's supposed to mean I was nervous?"

"Sam did tell me I shouldn't be put off if you seemed strange at first. She said you've been locking yourself away for months and that you're scared of women because you got badly dumped."

"Did she also say that she was only around to talk to you because there's a day-release program at the asylum?"

"Where are we headed for now, by the way, Mr. Cool? Or has fear driven out the memory that our cars are back at the Noodle?"

In fact, I wasn't headed anywhere, except away from the tattoos. There was another downtown bar on Ronnie Willigar's list but it was Tailgators—on the same block as the Noodle. I said, "You were surprised I called?"

"Yes." She stopped for a moment to shield a match and light a cigarette. She inhaled deeply once she was successful. "So what's behind it? There's an insect infestation in your office and you think tobacco smoke might cure it cheaply?"

"Cynicism is going out of fashion, you know."

"Oh yeah?"

"The truth of the matter is that I called you for no more reason than that I'm unbelievably smitten."

"You're right."

"What?"

"That is unbelievable."

"Why?"

90

"Because Sam said she'd make you call me."

"She would *make* me?"

"I told her not to do me any favors but she said that any favor would be to her, because you've been so strange for so long."

"Oh great," I said. "So, you're here as a favor to Sam?"

"We're not getting paranoid, are we?"

"It's important for me to know if you're the kind of gal who does favors for near-strangers because I may need to ask a favor too."

"And what might that be?" The eyebrows again.

"I may need some help putting a young woman's body into a trunk."

We walked the long way round to Tailgators. Once there, I bought us a couple of drinks and didn't flash the Willigar picture until we decided the menu was not up to tempting a high-class broad like Mary Contrary. The only bartender who would even take a look was a kid and he shook his head even before we established that he hadn't been working behind the Tailgators bar long enough to cover any of the relevant dates.

Mary and I amscrayed and went to the Noodle parking lot. "One car or two?" I asked.

"Two. Where now?"

Next on my list was Turk's. We drove. We parked. We bought drinks. I said, "You want to get something to nibble on?"

"You nibble all you like, pal," she said. "I'm chowing down."

It wasn't until sixteen out of a possible twenty ounces of rare peppered rump steak had disappeared between her thin but not unattractive lips that Mary said, "So why do you think this lawyer hired you to work on the Willigar case?"

"To explore every possibility of an alibi for his client, I guess."

"No, I mean why hire you, as in you, Albert of S.P.I., as opposed to anybody else?"

I hesitated over a drumstick while I realized that the question was one I hadn't asked for myself. I had taken Christopher P. Holloway at face value. He said he'd been instructed to engage my services, my expertise, and my knowledge. Mine and not that of an oily rag.

Mary said, "I don't mean to suggest that S.P.I. is anything less than the best spi option in town. On the other hand, a guy working on his own doesn't seem the obvious choice for a defense strategy that wants to beat all the bushes."

"No . . . But maybe I was fresh in their minds. I had just called the law firm the day before to tell them I was back in business."

"You pitched to the guy who hired you?"

"Well, not him himself." Nor to the partner who had given Holloway the instruction to hire me. I put my drumstick down. Not so hungry anymore.

"I'm not meaning anything bad by asking." Mary's appetite was undiminished.

"I know."

"You still don't like it, though, huh?"

"I was so pleased to be hired for a major job right after getting my license back that I let my skepticism down."

"You having dessert?" Mary said. "It's probably they think that if you're hungry for work they'll get good value out of you."

"Maybe." But then why give me a really big retainer and

a payment schedule that could only be called bargain hunting in a gold mine? Fuck.

"Will it wipe that nasty frownikin off your face if I tell you I've been having a really nice time?"

"*Are* you telling me you've been having a really nice time?"

"I have never ever had more fun on a hunt for a rapist."

I smiled for her.

"And," she said, "this is not the first rapist hunt I've been on."

"No?"

She cut the remains of her steak in two and sent one piece on the trip no good steak ever comes back from. She wiped her lips. "A friend of mine was raped. This was before I came back home. My friend knew who it was. So she, I, and two others went out to hunt him."

" 'Hunt' rather than 'find'?"

"Hunt."

"And?"

"And we found him."

"And?"

"And we bagged him."

"Was that rifles or shotguns?"

"Two-by-fours in three-foot lengths."

"He must have looked pretty good on the roof of your car as you drove back."

"We left him in the road, hoping a speeding semi would be next around the corner. And I'll tell you, I can't speak for stones, but sticks will definitely break your bones."

"How did you feel about it later?"

"Satisfied." Mary sighed, then reached for a cigarette. "And that's why I brought it up, Samsdad. I'm having even more fun tonight."

★ ★ ★ ★ ★

When Mary savored her final bite of cherry pie, she mused aloud about a liqueur.

"I don't know of they have a liqueur license," I said, "but I'll ask."

At the same time I showed the woman behind the bar my Ronnie Willigar picture. When she shook her head slowly, I realized I didn't really care.

It wasn't that I had lost the will to work. It was the realization that what I was doing wasn't much of a job in the first place. What were the odds I'd stumble across someone who'd say, I remember the guy and it was at such and such a time on such and such a date? Even if I did, it couldn't be useful without confirmation.

I sorely wanted to be able to deposit the big retainer check on Monday without qualms, but the "job" I'd been asked to do stunk. What it stunk of needed working out. But even the mere possibility that I might not deposit the check made me sad.

I delivered an orange liqueur.

"Not having one yourself?" She sipped.

"Mary, I've had a good time too."

"The way you say that makes it sound like we won't be hitting any more bars tonight."

"I'm not sure there's much point."

"You're worrying about why they hired you?"

I nodded.

"I'm sorry I asked it then."

"It's a good question. One I should have asked myself. But, you're right. No more bars tonight."

"What about the dancing?"

"I don't feel much like dancing either."

"Albert, you're about to ruin a very nice evening. OK,

the work part suddenly sucks. Can't you compartmentalize enough to set work aside, and concentrate on play? I thought boys were supposed to be good at stuff like that, or are you one of these sad-sack guys who can't ever leave his work behind?"

Was I? "Mary, may I borrow one of your hands for a moment?"

"To do what with, you saddo?"

"To hold, briefly."

She finished her liqueur. Then she extended a hand. "Or would you prefer the less tobacco-stained one?"

"This will do fine." I held her hand in both of mine. "I need to say that no matter how this evening came about I've enjoyed it a lot. I've enjoyed you a lot. I'm really glad to know you better."

"It's nice to hear that."

"It's what I feel. And, yes, you can have your hand back now." I let it go.

"You're not one of these guys who does the hand-squeeze and soulful look and then jumps away and says 'G'night' without making a pass or even trying to kiss me, are you?"

Later, she said, "Thank you."

"I should be thanking you."

"You did."

"Ah."

"Is that a quote?"

"Not exactly, no."

"I need a cigarette." She leaned to her bedside table and tapped one out of a pack. "Have you never smoked?"

"Not that I've noticed."

She lit and inhaled. "Aaah."

"Enjoy."

"You're a nice man, Albert Samson. Of course, I might be wrong, but it's what I feel at the moment."

"Nice?"

"Mmm."

"May I ask you a question?"

"Mmm."

"Why did you come out with me tonight?"

"Sam said she'd pay me to have dinner with you."

"She what?"

"I think she was joking."

"Ha."

"Don't not-laugh at me, Mr. Private Eye. Not-laugh at her. I'm just the messenger."

"OK. I will definitely not-laugh at her, later."

"Why did I come out with you?"

"Yeah."

"Because I have about me an air of quiet desperation."

"Yeah? And I just thought it was smoke."

12

At about noon Sam failed to knock on the office door. "*There* you are."

Yup. At my desk, hard at it. I riffled the stack of paper I had out in front of me. "Where else would I be?"

She dropped onto my Client's Chair and drew it close. "So?"

"I won't play games and pretend I think you care how my work went last night."

"Daddy, you were out past midnight."

"I was out past three."

"So, you had a good time?" She nodded several times with her eyes opened wide.

"After a sticky start." It was all too easy to visualize the Brothers Tattoo. "We got along just fine. It turns out we have something in common. We both hate people who try to manipulate our lives."

"What manipulate? I just found myself in the middle, guessing you might get along." She looked very pleased with herself.

"And Mary and I would like to thank you appropriately for your contribution to our destinies. The best we came up with is a blind date for you with Mary's Kentucky cousin, Luther, if his appeal's successful."

"Daddy, what are you complaining about? You must have had a good time, if you stayed out that late."

"Sam, honey, you do know, don't you, that, despite my recent neglect, I really am concerned about your future?"

She squinted, not understanding where this apparent change of subject was leading.

"And I know you've thought about getting into the detection game. We've talked about cases, when there were cases. You've even helped me."

"Yeah . . ."

"So, Sam, honey, you do know, don't you, what is at the absolute heart of any investigation?"

"Do tell me."

"It's being able to tell what the information you have means."

A shrug.

"And what it doesn't mean."

"What are you getting at, Daddy? Because I'm meeting someone soon."

"A moment ago you said I must have had a good time if I stayed out so late. Well, it just struck me as an apposite moment to point out that my staying out late doesn't necessarily mean that Mary stayed out late. Do you see?"

"So did she?"

"As a matter of fact, she didn't."

"Oh."

"We each had a car. Mary drove home after only our third bar. That was at a little after ten."

"Oh." A frown. "Well . . . Sorry."

Far be it from me to put a pushy kid out of its misery. "The fact that I was working during the 'date' didn't entirely enhance the experience."

"But will you ask her out again?"

"Not if you get involved."

"Honestly, Daddy, I just saw that you were miserable, and then the sign repairman happened to be Mary, and she's outgoing and funny and . . ."

I held up a hand. "I do not have immediate plans to ask Mary out again."

"Why not? Sometime when you aren't working. I'm not asking as a failed matchmaker. I'm asking as your daughter."

"Well, I'm not saying that this is a definitive factor . . ."

"What?"

"But Sam, honey, you know, don't you, that there is something . . ." I wrinkled my nose. ". . . about women who smoke."

Before Sam left to meet whoever she was meeting, we talked about her using my computer to attempt to locate her mother. My find-people-with-the-computer skills were primarily for people in the U.S. but I had a few ideas I could get her going with. "Start tonight, if you want," I said.

"Great." Then, "If you're sure you won't be using it."

"I won't be using it."

"Thanks, Daddy." She departed.

I liked the idea of having some idea what my daughter was up to of an evening, at least the once. And I had no intention whatever of using the computer. My intention was to spend the evening with Mary.

"I'll call you," I had said as I was leaving.

"Don't do that. Let's meet at—what's the next bar on your list?"

"My plan was to punt the list."

"Let's go to the bars. You can collect matchbooks to prove to you were there, and take the money with a clear conscience."

We left it that we would meet at Harry's Hideaway. If one or other of us thought better of it, there'd be no embarrassing wait for a phone call. Whoever got stood up could go inside and drink him, or theoretically her, self into a stupor.

Not that I did things like that any more in the face of disappointment. No no, not me. But I'd be sad if Mary stood me up.

I didn't know quite what had hit me so hard about Ms. Neon. Could life really be so quirky as to put a genuinely *simpática* woman in my path at the very time I was getting the rest of my life back?

Or maybe that wasn't the right question. Maybe my kind of women traipsed and lollopped around me all the time and it was only the relicensing euphoria that opened my eyes enough to see this one.

Either way, I was smitten. I'd even have gone and bought some cigarettes for her, if she said please.

13

With Sam gone I applied myself to shuffling through the papers I'd spread across my desk. They were the Ronnie Willigar case notes and I was trying to find some explanation for why Holloway, and Perkins, Baker, Pinkus and Lestervic had hired me at high rates to do an extremely unlikely job. I leaned back, put my feet up on the desk, and tried to unhook the leash of likelihood.

Could it be . . . What could it be? Did someone out there want to *make* some work for me? But who? My mother? No. Not her style.

The one person who made any sense in that scenario was the client on whose case and behalf I'd lost my license in the first place. But that bit of guilt had already provided the get-the-license-back legal services of Don Cannon. Our agreement was that she'd do no more.

So, who else?

No one else, that's who else. And even if there was such a person, the way to send a CARE package wouldn't be to put me to work on the Willigar case. Easier, less suspicious, would be to commission a long-term surveillance. Of almost anybody.

There had to be some other reason I'd been hired. I just couldn't think what it might be.

Of course, Holloway only assigned me to doing the bars until the identity of the reward claimant was known. Maybe that's when things would become clearer. Meanwhile, I would continue to think about it all. Then I found I could think about it all more clearly with my head on the desk.

The phone woke me. I was out cold. "What?"

"Samson?"

I knew the voice, but couldn't place it. "Jerry?" but as I said it I knew it wasn't Miller.

"Joe. Joe Ellison."

"Hi, Joe. How you doing?" I told him I'd talk to the police, didn't I. Ah well.

"I'm doing good. I want to thank you."

"Thank me?"

"I didn't believe you'd come through. I had you figured for another all-talk crap-out-when-the-chips-are-down whitey, but I heard what you did. You delivered. You done made a believer out of me, and I owe you."

Was this one of those dreams where the more you hear the less you understand? "You're going to have to spell it out for me, Joe."

"I don't mean I owe you money, if that's what you're asking, but if you ever need the kind of help me and my friends can give, you got it."

"I'm still not with you."

"What's so hard? Another fifteen minutes and the whole place would have gone up."

Place? "Sorry to be so dumb, but I was asleep when you called. I had a late night."

"Well, I *know* that. Reverend Battle says the cops told him the call came through at five minutes past four. The first patrol car got there at four-twelve, just before the first fire truck. And he says the cops told him the pictures were so good they'll be making arrests today. He says they think the motherfuckers didn't even bother to steal a car so they'll have them through the plate too. Those two assholes are tied up tighter than a rabbit's ass. And I just want you to remember, I'm not the kind of guy who forgets it when people do something for me. That's what I called to say."

After he hung up I pinched myself until it hurt. But I still didn't wake up. I couldn't even go back to sleep.

Did I miss something?

I got to Timothy Battle's church a little after two. I parked in the church's lot along with about a dozen other cars.

There's a smell that lingers when serious burning is put out with water. I smelled it as soon as I got out of my car. All around the church building's corner that had been attacked before the vegetation was trampled and hacked down. I could see from a distance that where there'd just been a hacked hole, now there was a burned and blackened area the size of a trailer. If this was the result with the fire department on the scene quickly, then surely the whole church would have gone up without the mysterious intervention.

Lucky for Battle and his congregation, but puzzling— even without all the stuff I was getting credit for. Like, if the idea now was to burn the place down, why not do that the first time? It was all so puzzling that I actually scratched my head.

I went back to what I knew from Joe. That two assholes started the fire just past four in the morning. That a non-asshole had called the fire department. And called the police. And taken pictures of the perps. And recorded the plate of the car they drove away in. And provided pictures and plate to the cops.

I also knew I was not the non-asshole. Given Joe's presumption that I was, it seemed that the real non-asshole had not identified him, or theoretically her, self.

So, who are you, Mr. or Ms. Non-Asshole? Well, you are a person who is up and about at four in the morning. You carry a camera, and a phone. You're quick-witted enough to use both, and record a license plate. Yet you choose not to be identified.

Or was I jumping to a conclusion? Was it simply that the police hadn't passed your name on to Reverend Battle? Would a cool customer like Battle be too upset to ask? Well, asking the police a few questions might resolve that. I'd already told Joe Ellison I'd be talking to the cops.

Nevertheless, Mr. or Ms. Non-Asshole, who are you going to turn out to be, up and about at four a.m.? Owner of a restless dog? That you walk while carrying camera, phone, and notepad . . . ?

Or are you a neighbor, maybe already awake, or awakened by the noise? With a camera, phone, and notepad by the bedside . . . ? Well, plenty of people are poor sleepers.

I looked around. Only one house was placed to overlook the part of the church that had been set ablaze. It was a one-story frame house clad in dark green boards and bounded by a link fence. Quite a way away, though, and from what I could see it looked poorly maintained. However it did have some windows facing the fire and the hole.

So I headed for next door.

The closer I got, the worse the place looked. A pane in one of the front windows was broken, although it had been boarded from the inside. A couple of timbers on the porch were broken and partially caved in.

I knocked. Nobody rushed to invite me in. I knocked again. And again.

The front door was locked when I tried it, but around the back I found a door that wasn't. "Would you care to come in, Mr. Samson?" "Don't mind if I do, Mr. Samson."

I entered a small utility room that might have begun life as a porch. There was enough light for me to see marks on the linoleum that showed where absent machines had stood. From the utility room I moved into a kitchen. Here there were more gaps, but it wasn't in bad condition. The floorboards sagged a little in the middle but felt solid enough. There was dust but no apparent decay.

Straight ahead was a small living room. Off to the left—the church side—I found a bathroom. Its window was blocked by a tub but although the glass was opaque, if the window was opened there would be a view of the church. However instead of trying to open the bathroom window, I decided to check out the final room.

It was a good decision. The last room, also on the church side of the house, was a bedroom. Here I found signs of recent occupation. A folding chair stood open by the window. On the floor there was a milk carton. A dozen cigarette butts were lined up on the sill like spent cartridges.

The final confirmation that I'd found a surveillance site came when I picked up the milk carton. It was partly full, but not with milk.

The history of surveillance is littered with the sob stories of surveillors who missed the biz because they left their posts to take a leak. Whoever had watched from this room knew enough to come prepared . . . And from the shape of the container, I felt safe concluding that the watcher was male.

So, scratch the dog walker or the sleepless neighbor. The guy whose work I'd been given credit for was here on purpose. Maybe Homer Proffitt's claim to be working on the neighborhood was genuine. Might Proffitt have expected the attack? But would cops take pictures and make calls without arresting the assholes who were so literally *in flagrante?*

Maybe it had nothing to do with the cops at all. Maybe a church member—Juice Jackson, say, deprived of his shotgun—had decided to wait for the assholes' next visit. There was a logic to that. But no logic as to how that could lead to me being given the credit.

Pleased as I was to have found the observation site, I needed to establish whether the cops knew who'd done the observing. Little as I liked the idea, I'd have to contact the police myself.

So I decided to go downtown rather than try to get anywhere on the phone. There was always the chance that I would run into Miller. He might say, "Hi, Al, let's catch some coffee."

Not much of a chance, maybe, but I was on a roll, right?

14

Inside the front door at IPD there's a little booth from which access to the public's servants is controlled. I presented myself and asked to speak to any officer who was working on last night's fire in the church near Fountain Square.

Without ceremony or a superabundance of civility a call upstairs was made and I was told someone would come down. As soon as the words were spoken I knew in my heart who that someone would be. And it was.

"Well, well, well. Lookee who's come to visit." Homer Proffitt flicked a nod to the guardians of the gate and I was permitted to enter. "Let's us find some privacy," he said. We rode the elevator without speaking. I passed the time by wondering if maybe he wove a little straw into his hair every morning, supplied by Hillbillies "R" Us. Adele would know, by now. Would she tell me if I called?

Proffitt led to an interview room where he settled himself and took out a notebook. "Fellas downstairs said you want to talk about last night's church arson, Albert. What's the story? You come in to confess, boy? It sure will go a whole lot easier on you if you do."

"They'd sure throw the case right out, Mr. Homer, yes they would, 'cause I don't match up with them fellas in the pictures that was taken at the scene."

Proffitt absorbed that I knew about the pictures.

"And, Mr. Homer, you fellas must already know that license plate you got sure ain't registered to no vehicle of mine, no sir, no how."

The eyebrows went up and created a row of wrinkles on his forehead. Quietly, and less accentedly, Proffitt said, "What happened last night was a serious crime. I'd like us to treat it that way."

I just waited.

"Did you come in to say it was you who e-mailed in those pictures and that license plate number?"

Just by asking the question he'd told me what I'd made the trip for. Plus that the pictures had been e-mailed. I was already ahead of schedule. I said, "I didn't come in to tell you anything. Do you have the two arsonist assholes in custody?"

"We're working on it."

"You've got their pictures. You've got the car they drove away in. What's so hard?"

"It's an ongoing investigation. Albert, let me get this straight. Did you take the pictures?"

"Is it just the pictures you're asking about, or do you also want to know if I called the police and the fire department?"

"All of it, damn it. Yes or no."

"Let's do it this way," I said. "I promise I'll make a full, frank, complete, and truthful statement about the pictures and the rest of it, if—but only if—you do something for me first."

I could almost hear the cogs whirring in his head as he went through his options. After a moment he worked out that he lost nothing by asking, "What something?"

"I want everything you know about what's up with Jerry Miller. Otherwise I'm out of here."

"Miller?" He took a few more seconds to decide between the hard path and the easy path. He chose easy. Miller was nothing to him. "In exchange for everything you know about last night, a formal statement, and agreement to testify if we need you?"

"The whole banana," I said.

"I take it what you want to know is that Captain Miller is under departmental investigation for corruption."

"Corruption? You gotta be kidding."

"It's no joke. Serious issues have been raised. They concern allegations that Miller participated in a fraudulent claim of the hundred and ten grand reward for the bodies-in-the-trunks killer."

"I don't get this. Cops can't claim rewards."

"The allegation is that Miller gave information to a co-conspirator who used it to claim the reward, the agreement being that they share it."

"And they actually think Jerry did that?"

"I don't know what they think. But that's the hypothesis that's being investigated."

"Who made the allegations?"

"I don't know. But they also say Miller has financial problems."

"What financial problems?"

He shook his head and shrugged.

"To do what you're saying, wouldn't Jerry have to hold back decisive information about the killer's identity so the co-conspirator could call it in?"

"That's what's being alleged, yes."

"That is not something Jerry Miller would ever—*ever*—do."

Proffitt shrugged.

"What conceivable evidence could they think they have?"

"I don't know the ins and outs. All I know is that the alleged co-conspirator called the Crime Stoppers number and gave Willigar's name three days after Miller got it from somewhere else."

"Who's the alleged co-conspirator?"

"I can't tell you that. But I do happen to know that his identity will be made public at a press conference to-morrow."

"So there's no harm telling me now. You know for a fact that I don't rat people out." He knew that because I lost my license in the first place when I refused to give the police names they wanted.

Proffitt sighed. "The guy is called Carlo Saddler, nick-name 'Chip.' He works part-time at the Milwaukee Tavern. It's on North Illinois Street."

"I know it," I said. And I was not happy that I knew it. For years—before he became a Captain and Janie pressured him into moving—Miller lived on North Illinois. We met sometimes in the Milwaukee. Janie never liked me coming to the house. "Has Jerry been suspended?"

"He's restricted to desk duty. And that, Albert, is every-thing I know about the situation. So tell me about last night."

I nodded. It was good to know that Proffitt could be civil, if he worked at it. He'd earned my end of the bargain. "Homer, I had nothing whatsoever to do with the photo-graphs, the plate number, the telephone calls, or anything else connected to the church arson at or around four a.m. yesterday morning. That is the full, frank, and complete truth."

Tempted as I was to up sticks and leave it at that, I made a gesture of good faith and outlined the events that led me to know about the church fire. I also shared my discovery of the next-door observation post. He had no more idea than I did who the observer had been.

I even shook the guy's hand as I left. Such are the

sacrifices that an ambitious practitioner of the detective arts must sometimes make.

It was about four-thirty when I emerged into the civilian world. I wanted to sit and think for a while, but where? With nearby places like the City Market closed for the Sabbath, I opted for fresh air and headed for the steps on Monument Circle.

Indianapolis was an invented city. Its location as state capital was picked by a committee of early nineteenth century politicians. Once their collective genius settled on a swamp by the White River, they commissioned a couple of surveyors, one of whom was from the team that invented Washington, D.C. Thus early Indy's streets, like D.C.'s, radiated like spokes from a hub. But in one particular the plan was brilliant. It called for the state governor's house to be inside the hub—the Circle. Where better to put your head honcho—or, theoretically, honcha—than where all his or her dirty linen would always be on public display? Would JFK have smuggled in his broads, or Reagan his Aricept with half so much abandon if the White House was in a traffic circle in the middle of town?

Ah well.

In modern Indy an obelisk stands where the governor's mansion should be. Surrounded by fountains and statues, it makes a monument to Indiana's war dead. There are also lots of steps for a meditative private eye to choose from. I chose one where the head of a lion guarded my back. I don't know what the lion represented but it made me feel safe. I wondered when Jerry Miller last felt the same. If there was ever a situation where the crock-of-shit defense was called for, Miller conspiring to obtain money by fraudulent means was it.

How could I be so sure? I just could. Half of a hundred and ten grand was serious money, but not enough to alter a guy's very nature. Therefore I had an advantage over IPD's internal investigators. I knew Miller didn't do it, whatever "it" turned out to be.

In fact, I was in much the same position that Christopher P. Holloway claimed as Ronnie Willigar's representative. My guy didn't do it, therefore no matter what the evidence is, the truth is different. Would the parallel continue? Would the line of Miller's defense be the crock of shit? That someone was setting him up? If so, who? And why?

My musings were interrupted by the approach of a dog. He—definitely a he—was of no breed I recognized and black. He was a big guy. His shoulder would have stood at about my knee height, if I was standing and next to his shoulder. And there was something about him, a confidence maybe. I'm not a major doggy person, but this guy made an impression on me. It was as if he was comfortable with who and what he was. Was it too anthropomorphic to call it charisma?

He stood looking at me with what seemed mild curiosity. Maybe he thought it was unusual for a man to be leaning against a lion and doing nothing much. Then his interest passed and he got on with his own business, which was to take a drink from one of the monument's pools.

I said, "Do you mind helping me out here, Fido? A pal of mine's in trouble and I don't know what the best way I can help him is."

Fido lifted his head and glanced my way. Something about his eyes said, "What help can you offer?"

"Well, as a non-cop I might be able to follow investigative tracks that he, as a cop, couldn't follow, legally or professionally."

Fido sat down. It was like, "Go on."

"Miller may have cut a corner or two to further his career. In fact, more than once he's helped me out on my cases because he figured they'd give him a leg or two up the career ladder."

Fido had a scratch.

"Which they did. So it's not like he's a total straight arrow. I mean, he's had a lady friend or two on the side over the years, but they were never the kind who would break up his marriage. And who could knock him for taking a little comfort when what he came home to every night was a whatever-you've-done-it's-never-enough specialist like Janie?"

Fido rose to return to the water. I wasn't certain whether it was renewed thirst or the comment of a committed monogamist.

"I'm not knocking Janie's strengths, Fido. She's been with the guy from the start. She did the housewife and mom thing and worked hard at it. All four of those kids went to college, and how many cop-wives can say that of their progeny?"

In fact, I didn't have certain knowledge that the youngest, Helene, *had* gone to college. She was in her teens when Jerry and I stopped communicating, but she was doing well in high school—better than any of the others—so I figured the assumption was reasonable. No point in complicating the story for a dog unlikely to know the ins and outs of the educational system.

In what was possibly a gesture of gratitude, Fido left the water and lay down, watching me.

"My problem is picking which investigative track would be best for me to work on. Is someone in the department so jealous of the big arrest he made in the bodies-in-the-trunks case that he—or maybe she—is trying to pour cold water on Jerry's accomplishment?"

Fido declined to opine.

I said, "Should I try to find out who in the department might benefit from Jerry being taken down a peg or two? What do you think?"

Silence can be assent, but Fido's expression gave me the impression he was thinking, "Rather than shoot ducks in a barrel, why don't you ask your friend what would help him most?" He looked like he might have a little hunting dog in him.

"I'd like nothing better than to talk to Jerry about it, but when I called, he as good as hung up on me."

"Why would he do that?" Fido's expression suggested.

"Well . . ." And then it struck me. Jerry was restricted to desk work. Maybe his phone at work was being monitored while they investigated him. What he said to me was, "Don't call me here again."

When I was with Leroy Powder I took, "Don't call me here again," to mean I should call him at home. Janie blew me off when I called there, but maybe there was more of a reason for that than just her chronic dislike of me. Maybe the home phone was tapped too.

In any case, my next move was clear now. I should go to Miller's house. If I showed my face, then maybe he would lead me to a place where he felt comfortable to talk.

I checked my watch. It was not quite five and I wasn't due at Harry's Hideaway until six-thirty. There was time for me to drive to Miller's house and either have a quick talk or make plans for when to talk.

"Fido, it's been clarifying to talk with you." I stood up.

Slowly he stood too.

"I wish I had something on me to give you. A hunk of meat or . . . I don't know, a doughnut. But I can offer my undying friendship and admiration." I stuck out a hand. He wore no collar, but maybe in his colorful past he'd been trained in the civilities.

He studied the hand for a moment. Then he gave me a look that would have been disdain in a human being and trotted away. He might not wear a collar, but I do.

15

The Millers now live in a suburb called Wynnedale. It's not as far from the Circle as the most fashionable parts of greater Indy but neither is it the 'hood. Overlooked by the city art museum and the other side of the White River, any swamps in Wynnedale are landscaped swamps.

The Millers' property itself is modest for the area—a ranch house set in less than an acre and with only a couple of trees that might be older than the game of basketball. Nevertheless there's sufficient space at the ranch to allow the Miller buckeroos and buckerettes to come back and bunk for a spell. Just not all at the same time.

Or so I'd been told. Never been inside myself. Janie . . . You know . . . Meet in town . . . No point ruffling feathers . . .

Today, feathers were not a consideration. I drove up the driveway. I parked close to the front door, where I figured an invited guest would park. I strode up the path. No messin' with Samson on a roll.

I guess I half-thought Jerry would answer the bell, and I was prepared for Janie. I certainly didn't expect the tall, languid young woman who looked at me through tired eyes and said, "What do you want?"

Could this possibly be . . . "Helene?"

"I know you?"

But before I could say, I dandled you on my knee when you were no bigger than a big bag of potato chips, she said, "Are you the private eye guy?"

"In person."

"Oh, right." She nodded slowly. "What was your name again?"

I told her. "The last time I saw you, you were about to start high school."

A brief laugh. "Those were the days."

"I heard you did well, that you were headed for college."

"Yeah?" She yawned sleepily.

Was Helene old enough to be out of college already? She didn't look it, but since it wasn't a social call I said, "Is your father home?"

"No. They went to Gramma's. In Terre Haute. Mom's mom. She's supposed to be sick." She sucked air through her teeth. "She's supposed to have heart trouble."

"It sounds like you're not convinced."

"A narcissistic personality like hers is never going to let somebody else have a crisis without trying to have a bigger one."

"Ah." Of course, a narcissistic personality . . . Silly me. "Do you know when your father will be back?"

"They didn't say," Helene said. "But hey, I didn't mean to be rude, Mr. Samson. It's just not everybody who comes to see Pop is a friend. Please, come in."

I felt I couldn't refuse, but as I crossed the threshold I glanced at my watch. I had a six-thirty appointment I didn't want to be late for.

We sat in the living room. "The reason I came out was to offer my help to your father."

"What kind of help?"

"There might be things your dad wants to know but can't investigate for himself. I can't be more specific, because I don't know that much about the situation."

"The situation is shit," Helene said.

"Oh. Right."

"Of course a lot of it he brought upon himself."

"He did?"

"You'd think—wouldn't you?—that if he's *got* to have a girlfriend, the least he could do is not get caught."

"I didn't realize there were troubles like that going on. I've . . . Well, your father and I have been out of touch lately."

"Some guy came out and gave Mom chapter and verse. Poor Pop didn't stand a chance. It's not like it's my business, but if you're living in the same house you can't avoid it. And Mom doesn't exactly make the best of things. Pop's no saint, but as far as Mom's concerned, she's the only injured party. Poor Pop tries to cope, but he's out of his depth."

We shared a momentary silence.

Helene said, "Of course, the guy telling Mom about the affair isn't the only creep we've had out here. Yesterday it was the Chief of Police."

"Cohl? What did he want?"

"That creepy snake-face was all smiles and hugs, and then he said if Pop resigns now they'll stop the investigation and he can have a full pension."

"There's nothing quite like support from your superiors in times of trouble."

"Why should Pop resign? He didn't do anything wrong, so how can anybody prove he did?" Helene made a face. "Mom says that's naïve."

"He's not going to resign, is he?"

"Mom thinks he should, but he won't. You know, they're even following him around, the dummies."

"Following him? The police?"

"Hey, maybe they'll bug Gramma's house and have to listen to all her moaning."

"Why would they follow your dad?"

"He says they think he might contact the guy who's claiming the reward. But he doesn't even know who the guy is."

I hoped that when Carlo "Chip" Saddler's name was made public, Miller still wouldn't know who he was. I left Wynnedale with just enough time to make it to Harry's Hideaway by six-thirty. I was glad I'd gone to Miller's house, and that he'd be given a clear message that I wanted to help him, despite everything.

I didn't know if I could help his case, but I was pretty sure I could help him. Does it really matter how much money you can make by calling yourself guilty if the fact is you're innocent? Sometimes money can be way too expensive.

I was musing about all that when one of my tires blew.

16

Never has a tire been changed so quickly without benefit of power tools and a 500 pit crew. I'd barely caught my breath when I finally rolled into the parking lot at Harry's Hideaway.

Mary's car was still there. Good.

Mary was in her car and backing up. Bad.

I jumped out. "Stop, stop, I'm here, I'm here."

Her car stopped. She rolled the glass down. I said, "I had a flat."

She thought about it, then pulled back into her space and got out. "Show me."

The dead tire was on the back seat. She pulled it out and rotated it till she found a nail. "Yeah, right."

"What?"

"You're probably one of those guys who always carries a flat so he's got a handy excuse."

"I thought if I didn't show up, you were supposed to go inside and drink yourself into oblivion."

"I wasn't feeling oblivious."

"No?"

"I've always wanted to have a one-night stand. I thought maybe I was going to get my wish at last."

"That doesn't sound like an unattainable ambition, if you put your mind to it."

"They keep coming back for more," she said. "What can a girl do? So are we going in?"

"Would you mind if we don't?"

"I thought we were doing your list."

"Well, what I was hoping we might do this evening . . ."

"Yeah, Eye Spy, tell me. What were you hoping we might do this evening?"

In our two cars, we went to the Milwaukee Tavern on Illinois Street. Not a venue of sufficient salubriousness that I'd have chosen it for a second date. Or even a hundred-and-second date. It was a dark place. It was ugly. It was smoky. It smelled of men.

Mary got excited as soon as we walked through the door. "Look, look."

"What?"

"See the Pabst sign, next to the wooden arrow with 'restroom' on it?"

"The neon, you mean?"

"I haven't seen one of those puppies for years. Do you have *any* idea how long it's been since they made signs like that?"

I didn't. She told me. "So, what's to eat, Samsdad? Oh, the blackboard, right. I think I'll start with the chili. Do you think it's hot? I love it hot."

Even Miller and I never ate here. "Are you sure you want to eat anything that doesn't come to the table in a sealed package?"

"Sure as men are faithless bastards. After the chili I think . . . the meatloaf special. And then maybe . . . chocolate cake. Do you think they'd put vanilla ice cream on that for me?"

"If they've had a delivery from their organic ice cream suppliers."

Mary chose a table, astonishing me, in the circumstances, by picking it because it was the only one with a clean ashtray. As she sat, a man in fringed leather shuffled his chair to make space. "Thanks, pardner," she said.

When it came the chili was not particularly hot. Mary studied it closely after the first bite. "Look. Don't you love the way it goes all rainbowy when it reflects the light?"

Like oil in a puddle in the street. "I regret not having ordered some for myself."

"Well, don't think you'll be sinking your spoon into mine."

"Or my straw?"

"You bring me to the best places, Albert. Are you sure the guy we're looking for here isn't a rapist?"

"He might even be the bodies-in-the-trunks."

"I thought that was Ronnie Willigar."

"The guy here is an alternate hypothesis."

She turned to the bar. "Which one is he? They all look like they're capable of it."

"I wouldn't recognize him. I don't even know if he's in tonight." Behind the bar there was a choice of three.

"I'll find out for you."

"You will?"

"What's his name?"

"Carlo Saddler. They call him Chip."

She rose. "No sneaking from my bowl while I'm not looking. If there's anything I hate, it's a guy who says he doesn't want chili and then eats yours."

I watched as she spoke to the closest bartender. She was probably saying, "Is Chip here tonight?"

The bartender looked toward a light, thin guy about five-ten whose hair was wound onto the top of his head into a knob. Then he probably said, "I'll get him for you." I could tell by his hand gestures.

The knob head—presumably Carlo "Chip" Saddler— looked Mary up and down as he went over to her. They exchanged a few words and then something she said made him frown and stiffen. She pointed my way. Chip wiped his hands on his apron, came out from behind the bar. Mary led him to our table.

"He's the one that saw it," Mary said of me as they approached.

Chip was not happy about what I had seen. "Where? Where did you see shit like that written about me?"

"Well," I said, "of course it might not have been *you*."

"Don't wuss-out, Albert," Mary said. "You told me you saw a graffito that said, 'If you want your dick jerked off like a rocket, find the Milwaukee and get Chip in your pocket.' "

"It's just there might be more than one Chip. There might even be more than one Milwaukee."

"Where did you see that, man? Where?" Chip pounded on the table. Mary's chili shimmered a rainbow.

"At IPD," I said.

Carlo "Chip" Saddler froze, staring at me. He knew what the letters IPD meant.

"They have a men's room on the ground floor, next to the elevators. It was written on the wall in the second stall—in chartreuse ink."

Carlo "Chip" didn't like it. He looked from me to Mary and back again. "What is this? What the fuck is this about?"

Mary slipped onto her chair. "It came up because my friend Albert here was saying that he wanted his dick jerked like a rocket, and I wouldn't do it for him, so . . ."

"You're not safe to be let out," I said after we made an abrupt departure.

"You wanted to meet him. You met him." Mary was extremely pleased with herself. "Nice touch, by the way, making the graffito chartreuse."

"I'd have preferred meeting him in a way more condu-
cive to assessing his personality and character."

"You should have said. Shall we go back?"

"Possibly not in this lifetime."

"The guy's kind of cute though. You say he's claiming
the hundred and ten grand reward?"

"The suggestion is that he's claiming it fraudulently."

Mary considered this for just a moment. "No one is
saying that he thought up the scam for himself, right?"

17

In the morning I got up before eight-thirty. I thought that was pretty early and befitted a relicensed detective with a sense of responsibility. Also it was a Monday. Banks open on Mondays. Open banks accept checks.

Early for me or not, when I descended to the luncheonette Sam was already on a break. "Uncle Jerry called last night. He said you'd been out to his house."

Miller, at last. But, "Honey, are you saying you answered my phone?"

"I was in your office working at the computer. I picked it up without thinking. I left you a note, right on the desk. I thought you'd see it. Whenever it was you came in."

I hadn't turned on the office light—just looked to see if the answering machine was blinking. "Oh."

"I worked till after eleven." Sam made it clear that she'd welcome an exchange of information, but didn't ask.

I didn't volunteer. "Did you find your mother?"

"Not exactly."

"You found an arm and half a leg?"

"I found several things about her."

"Like what?"

"Well, she endorsed a line of jewelry in *Vogue France* last fall. There was a picture of her smiling and showing a bracelet on her wrist."

"She didn't snort the line of jewelry after the photo shoot, by any chance?"

"And," Sam said, "I found out that she got divorced three months ago."

Her face showed this was not junk mail to her.

"It was in Barcelona. Well, two months and twenty-five days ago."

"From anybody in particular?"

"I only met him once. Quite nice, quite good for his age. He was an admiral."

Swiss Navy, perhaps? "Well, I'm sorry to hear it, love."

"It just means that she's unsettled. She gets unpredictable when she's like that."

"Is it enough to explain why she hasn't been in contact with you?"

"Maybe. Have you ever been to Barcelona, Daddy?"

"No."

"Never wanted to go?"

Barcelona? Not on my owna. "There are plenty of other places I'd like to see that are a whole lot closer than Spain."

"Not Spain. Catalonia."

"Do you miss Europe?"

"More some of the people I know there than the place—the places."

I was going to ask about the people, but she was called away, by that old siren—someone wanting to pay a bill.

"She's really upset about her mother, Albert."

Norman was at my shoulder. I hadn't noticed he was within earshot. "What?"

"The poor kid is going half-crazy about not knowing whether her mother is all right."

"Shouldn't you be griddling something to a cinder?"

"Just trying to help," Norman said. "I know parenting doesn't come natural for you."

★ ★ ★ ★ ★

I was back in the office before nine-thirty. Not only did I find the note Sam left about Miller's call last night, my answering machine light was flashing. Miller again? It would be good to talk with him at last.

However the message was from Christopher P. Holloway. He wanted to know where I was.

"We had no meeting scheduled," I said when I called back.

"Wasn't it understood you'd keep me informed about what you're doing? I looked for an e-mail report about the weekend. And then I find I don't seem to have a cell phone number for you."

"There's not a whole lot to report," I told the firm's Number One client. "Although my researches have raised a question or two."

"Well, they can wait. I want you downtown by ten."

"Your office?"

"The Police Department. They're holding a conference about the reward claim. Do you know where it is?"

"IPD is like my second home."

"I mean the Press Room."

"Sure." By which I meant I was sure that I could find it.

He said he'd leave my name with the guy checking IDs at the door.

I said I'd leave immediately and come straight there.

That was a lie. I had a different stop to make before I went anywhere for anybody. I had a check to deposit.

My bank was only up the street. I had it all worked out. When I got there I would say I'd forgotten my glasses and needed help with the deposit slip. I'd ask a cute young banky girl to read me the amount off the check. I'd stand close by her shoulder as she read the number and turned to me with her baby blues open wide and her pupils dilating.

Hey, how many chances does a fella get? Even if it was all but certain to be a one-check stand.

I got to the Press Room at a quarter past ten. As I slid in at the back I was able to pick Holloway out—no closer to the front than me but on the other side of the room.

Chief Lew Cohl was at the microphone. I'd missed his statement but it seemed that I was just in time for questions from the assembled media.

A guy in the middle started it. "Chief, would you please explain the nature of the 'irregularities' in the reward claim?"

"Charlie," Cohl said, "if you had an attention span that was longer than a goldfish, you'd remember that only a couple of minutes ago I said that the irregularities we found are under investigation, and that's why I can't say any more in that information vicinity now. We've got to have the time we need to go through all the facts. You can understand that, can't you, I'm sure. Hey, you know I was just kidding about the goldfish, right, pal?" Chief Cohl was known for his sense of humor.

Maybe Miller laughed when Cohl offered to trade a pension for a resignation.

"I heard you loud and clear, Chief," Charlie said.

There were a couple of chuckles from around the room. Chief Cohl looked over his shoulder to where two young men stood. These guys looked borderline for being out of high school but they were both clearly there to support and assist the Chief. I wondered what their official status was. Do Chiefs of Police have spin doctors now? Or spin interns?

Charlie said, "Chief, you ought to be able to tell us at least whether the irregularities arise from Mr. Saddler's end, or from someone in the department, or because the reward money isn't really there, or something else."

"You're not going to get any more terrain in that vicinity out of me today. But nice try, Charlie." Chief Cohl looked for another question. He pointed to a television reporter known locally for her prominent teeth and for once having been married to a gubernatorial candidate. Possibly because of her intimate experience of politics she often made snide comments about the statements made by local government officials. "Veronica?"

"Snappy suit, Chief."

"You like?" Cohl showed off his sleeves. "See me after."

The two teen aiders smiled behind Cohl as Veronica said, "Chief, why are you the only member of the department talking to us today?"

"Everyone else is angry with you," the Chief said. "Hey, just kidding."

"Wouldn't it be more normal for the officer in charge of the case to be here? What is the significance of Captain Miller's absence today?"

"Before I answer that, as it happens Captain Miller's mother-in-law is unfortunately seriously ill, so I want to take this opportunity to wish the Miller family every hope of a speedy recovery on behalf of the department. I mean that sincerely."

"Are you saying Captain Miller is with his mother-in-law?"

"No, I'm just condoling. But even if the unfortunate illness weren't the case, probably Captain Miller wouldn't be down here today anyway, which on behalf of the populace you should be glad of, Veronica. The more time Captain Miller spends trying to solve our city's crime rate, the better for us all, including you and your viewers."

"Don't *you* try to solve crimes, Chief?" a woman in black called from near where Christopher P. Holloway stood.

"My point, Stella, is that having more than one senior officer at a press conference means one less at his desk doing other vital crime-solving." He held up a finger. "But let me clarify that to the extent that it's now, this particular time, that having more than one senior officer down here would be wrong, because we're real busy upstairs. I want to make that clear as *claro* so's you folks don't come back another day and ask me why we've turned out half a dozen guys to talk to you and give you more than one point of view."

There was mild, good-humored chatter in response to Cohl's butt-covering. Veronica, however, was not deflected. "Chief, I've heard a rumor that Captain Miller has been suspended." The reaction to this around the room clearly indicated that Veronica's rumor was news to the rest of the newshounds and houndettes. "Would you care to comment?"

Cohl sighed and looked disappointed. "Veronica, you know better, I'm sure, than to pay attention to rumors. My mom, bless her cotton socks, used to say a rumor and a tumor have a lot in common, and I think you'll agree if you care to look at it that way."

"You can kill the rumor once and for all, Chief. Tell us, is Captain Miller suspended or not?"

"Captain Miller is upstairs at his desk at this very minute. Does that answer your question, because that doesn't sound like suspended to me."

"If Captain Miller is under investigation, don't you think you ought to tell us about it?"

Cohl finally looked exasperated. "Veronica, I told everybody, and I told Charlie, the investigation we've got going is ongoing. Captain Miller was in charge of the case so of course we can't investigate without taking some testimony from him. But the guy is at his desk, right now, straining every brain he possesses to make Indianapolis a safer place. What more can I say?" The Chief turned away from Veronica. "Yes."

"Reinhold Massey, Channel 13, Chief."

"What can I do you for, Reinhold?"

"You've finally given us the name of the reward claimant."

"Because of the unusual circumstances, yes."

"And we all understand that the police have no official role in a reward offered by a group of civilians."

"We're only overseeing the reward thing through our Crime Stoppers program."

"Nevertheless I'm sure I speak for everybody here when I say I wish we could talk with Mr. Saddler ourselves. Can't you at least tell us more about him? How old he is, what he does for a living, what information he provided . . ."

One of the aides passed Cohl a sheet of paper. The Chief looked it over, nodded, and shook it out with a flick of his wrist. He read, "Carlo Saddler is twenty-four. He's a native of Orlando, Florida, but he moved to Indianapolis with his mother when he was seven. He went to Beech Grove High School and then worked in the library at the Purdue technical library and IUPUI for more than a year. He is currently in the refreshment industry where he has held a number of posts over the last several years. He hopes to use the reward money to further a professional career in music." Cohl put the paper down. "I've just read you part of the statement Mr. Saddler's attorney will release when he and his client leave the City-County Building from the courthouse entrance in a few minutes from now. Happy?"

This news was greeted by a roar. Almost as a single organism the people in the room rose and headed for the door. Moments later the room was all but empty.

Christopher P. Holloway was not part of the rush. He seemed almost to be making a point by taking his time to gather his briefcase and smooth out his suit. I waited for him near the Press Room door. From there I saw the Chief wink at his young assistants. The Chief wouldn't have timed the announcement of Saddler's availability to truncate his own interrogation, would he?

IPD and the courthouse share the City-County Building. I walked with Holloway around the block and although our arrival at the entrance to the courts was comparatively dilatory, we did not miss the end of Saddler's attorney's statement on the courthouse steps.

"My client is confident that his claim for the reward will be accepted as valid, complete, and justified once the police have concluded their investigation of the case. His willingness to forego his right to anonymity underlines the integrity of his position. However until the police have finished their work, my client will be making no comment whatsoever. Copies of this statement are available from my associate." A young woman in a suit waved a handful of papers.

Carlo Chip stood before the city's press in a suit and tie and an Indianapolis Indians baseball cap. He appeared to be uncomfortable, although he wasn't expected to speak. Maybe the knob on his head was finding it hard to breathe under the hat.

However Indy's assembled media had dealt with "no comment" before. While the photographers called, "Look this way, Carlo," and "How about a fist in the air, Carlo," and "Say cheese, Carlo," the reporters kept writing and the

TV cameras kept running. A few of the reporters called out, "Are you and Ronnie Willigar friends?" and "Are you going to quit your job when you get the money?" and "What does your girlfriend think of all this?"

The lawyer intervened with plenty of no-comments and he and his silent client probably figured they were in control. Then the reporters got down to work. One shouted, "Why don't you talk to us, Carlo?" Another called, "Are you as stupid as you look?" That drew the knob-head's attention and a scowling frown. So he was already on the serving platter when someone else shouted, "Can't you speak English, Carlo, is that the problem? *¿No habla Ingles?*"

"Of course I speak fucking English," Carlo "Chip" Saddler snarled. "What do you think I am, a fucking retard?" And the assembled media had their quote.

18

"Some witness *that's* going to make," Christopher P. Holloway said as we set out for the offices of Perkins, Baker, Pinkus and Lestervic. But his tone and his stride did not encourage conversation. At other times in my life I might have worried what the silence signified. Not today. I had money in the bank. It was a nice day. What's the worst that could happen?

A secretary stared myopically at a monitor outside Holloway's office. When he got to her he said, "Delilah, tell Karl that I'm back and that Mr. Samson's with me, would you please."

Delilah squinted up at me. She said, "Yes, sir."

I followed Holloway into his office and sat down. I said, "Now we're here, do you want me to summarize what I've done about the list of bars, or shall I cut straight to the questions that have come up?"

"Neither, thanks." He swiveled to look out the window. He fiddled with the blinds.

"So, do we play tic-tac-toe, or what?"

"We wait for the leader of the defense team. He'll lead the meeting."

"That's the aforementioned Karl?"

Holloway turned back to me. "Do you know anything about him? Karl Benton?"

"Nope." Then I remembered something. "When you first called me, didn't you say a partner had asked for me specifically?"

"That was Karl."

"Why me?"

"Maybe you should ask him yourself."

As if it was cued, the door of Holloway's office flew open. A man with floppy hair that was pineapple yellow entered the office at speed. The guy was thin and his head under the pineapple mop was big. He addressed Holloway with a tone of authority. "Have you laid it out for him?"

"I thought you'd want to do that. To make sure the slant's right."

Pineapple top faced me. "Karl Benton. I'm leading Ronnie Willigar's defense." I stuck out a hand and began to introduce myself but he cut me off. "I *know* who you are."

Holloway said, "We were at the press conference, Karl. They caved about the identity of the informant."

"I said they would."

"And then they produced this Carlo Saddler on the courthouse steps."

"What's he like?" Holloway began to respond but Benton cut him off and pointed at me. "You tell me."

"He's twenty-four, about five-ten, and he works part-time behind the bar at the Milwaukee Tavern. If you're thinking how he'll do as a witness, I think he'll appear presentable at first, but he's not smart, and he has a quick temper that could be made to get him into trouble in court."

Benton turned to Holloway. "You agree?"

But Holloway was studying me. "Nothing was said about the Milwaukee Tavern."

It showed he'd been paying attention. They might want to test me, but that didn't mean I couldn't test them back.

Benton smiled. A lot of lawyers like the adversarial. It doesn't necessarily make them bad people. "Samson?"

"You mean you guys didn't know who the reward claimant was until just now?"

"And you did?"

"I found out from a contact in the police department."

"Gerald Miller?"

"Someone else. So last night I went to the Milwaukee Tavern to take a look at Saddler. Without letting on that I'm part of the Willigar defense team, of course."

"We must make sure not to underestimate you, Samson."

"I don't mind. Underestimate away."

Benton turned back to Holloway. "At the press conference, what did they say about the reward?"

"Chief Cohl says they're investigating irregularities about the claim."

"The irregularities wouldn't be anything so helpful as admitting they arrested the wrong man, I suppose?"

"He refused to talk about what the irregularities might be, but you know that TV reporter with the teeth, Veronica Maitland?"

Benton's eyes narrowed.

"She got up and said she'd heard a rumor that Miller has been suspended. Cohl dicked around it, but neither confirmed nor denied."

Benton returned to me. "Samson?"

"What?"

"Is Miller suspended?"

"Chief Cohl said he was at his desk."

"I didn't ask what Chief Cohl said. I asked you whether Miller is suspended."

Proffitt had told me that Miller was restricted to desk duty. Was that "suspended" or not? Did Clinton have sexual relations with that woman, or not? I opted for, "I don't know any more about that than you or Mr. Holloway do."

"You used a police contact to find out Saddler's name, but you didn't ask the same contact what was happening to your oldest friend?" Benton said.

"I had no reason to think anything was happening to Miller."

"I don't believe you."

I felt like a witness who'd lied under oath. "That's your prerogative, of course."

"I do hope you're not going to make the mistake of underestimating me, Samson."

"I'll try not to." Especially since he'd caught me once already.

"Miller is your oldest friend, isn't he?"

I was not comfortable with this pineapple interrogator pushing me about Miller. "Unless you count Suzie. She and I used to play naked in a sandbox together."

"And you've had quite a hard time in the last few years, haven't you? While your license was suspended. That must have been tough."

"I got by."

"But you got no help from your good friend, the Captain, though. In fact it was Miller's decision that got your license taken away." After a moment, "Nothing to say about that?"

"Was it a question?"

"Want a question? OK, here's a question. Why do you think we hired you?"

"Because I'm honest, discreet, trustworthy, and good at what I do."

"Your friendship with Gerald Miller is why we hired you."

"I don't understand."

"Our defense of Ronnie Willigar will be based around the contention that someone framed him. Who would be in a better position to do that than the guy in charge of the investigation and his arrest?"

"You hired me to prove that Jerry Miller framed Willigar for the bodies-in-the-trunks murders?"

"That would do nicely," Benton said.

"There's no way Miller would do a thing like that."

"Then we'll have to settle for less. But make no mistake, Samson, your job, your full-time highly-paid job, is to investigate Gerald Miller. I want chapter and verse of every weakness. Does he take paper clips home? Does he cheat on his wife? Does he play the race card to get his kids better jobs or into better schools? I want anything and everything that we might be able to use to impugn his character in court. It's show time, Samson. Time to earn that corn in your suddenly-replenished larder."

19

When I left Karl Benson, my feet worked fine. Right, left, then right again. I just didn't know where I was going.

Or what I was doing. The big job to restore my self-esteem . . . Put my oldest friend in the shit. Just because I hated the guy didn't mean I wanted to do *that.* Jeez.

I discovered myself on Virginia Avenue. I was halfway over the barren bridge that crosses the interstate. The bridge that was built to reconnect Fountain Square to the city.

If there were no bridge . . . Would that protect Fountain Square from the gentrifiers who have transformed so many other near-downtown areas? Or without it would the neighborhood decay and decline because it was detached from the rest of urban Indy?

Can a neighborhood be cut off and still live?

Can a friendship?

Then I was beyond the bridge. I was across the street from my mother's luncheonette.

When I was a kid I walked to and from the city countless times, like the streetcar mules for whom Fountain Square's fountain was constructed. It was where the mules got to stop and sip before they turned around to lumber back downtown. Maybe they took the moment to reflect on their lives. On the endless cycles of work they exchanged for food and shelter.

The fountain, a bronze pioneer family spouting water, sits at the end of Virginia Avenue. If you didn't know better you'd think it had been there always. In fact for a while it was removed to Garfield Park, to help the movement of traffic. Protests, including from my mother, restored the fountain to its rightful place in 1969.

Can interrupted friendships be restored?

I walked to the fountain. It was in my mind to sit on the little island it occupies in the sea of traffic to reflect on my life. My work.

I never sat. As I crossed to the fountain I remembered sitting under the lion at the circle. Which reminded me that my car was downtown, parked in a lot.

Having gotten to the fountain, I should turn around and go downtown again. However I didn't set out immediately. I decided to stop and sip.

Roxanne's, among the neighborhood's new cafés, is the one I like best. It's long and thin, light at the front and dark at the back. A counter with stools runs along on one side, and other forms of seating—many of them upholstered—are scattered down the other. I like a place that can cater to many moods.

My mood involved a large sweet coffee and a saggy armchair by a bookshelf in a dark corner.

"Are you afraid to investigate your pal? Is that it?" Benton asked me.

What would I be afraid of?

"Maybe you think Miller might have committed the murders himself."

Of course not.

"Or maybe you're afraid that he did try to get himself part of the reward." Addressing Holloway, Benton said,

"Our boy Samson knows this Miller dude better than any-body, and he's scared of what he'll find out. Maybe we need to rethink our strategy here. Maybe we should train all our guns on the good Captain."

Of course I'm not afraid of what I'd find. Miller just isn't like that.

"So what is your problem?" Benton's eyes bore into me from beneath the pineapple topping.

It's just . . . immoral to dig dirt on a friend.

"I thought there wasn't any dirt. You can't have it both ways." Benton turned to Holloway again. "You know, I'm wondering if Samson's really the right man for this job."

"He knew that Saddler works at the Milwaukee," Holloway said. "Maybe it was Miller who told him."

I got that information from someone else.

"Suppose we do let him go ahead on Miller," Benton said. "Can we trust that he'll get everything that's there?"

"Or that he'll tell us everything he gets," Holloway said.

I will. I promise. I swear.

And so I left the offices of Perkins, Baker, Pinkus and Lestervic having not only agreed to investigate my best friend but having all but begged to be allowed to do it.

Why?

Was it so I could help Miller by being in a position to control the investigation? To keep someone else from doing it?

Or was it payback because he'd cost me my license? Did I want to be in at the kill if he did do something wrong?

Or was it because I didn't want to have to give back that lovely big retainer that was already in my bank account?

Or all of the above?

"Are you all right?" Roxanne was offering a refill.

"Great. No, awful. No, all right, fine. Sorry, I'm not really."

140

"I know exactly how you feel," she said. "And it's never as bad as you think. I promise."

"But doesn't it have to be as bad as you think sometimes? Otherwise nobody would never worry as much as they do."

She thought about that for a moment. Or gave up on me. I couldn't tell which.

Then she said, "There are scones in the oven. When they're done, I'll bring you one. They're really good when they're warm."

You *do* know how I feel. I almost cried as she retreated with the coffee jug.

20

Sam was tending the Bud's Dugout cash register. "There you are, Daddy."

"Here I definitely are. Can I have some change for the pinball machine?"

While she made change she said, "Daddy, are you all right?"

"Great."

"You don't look all right."

"I don't?"

"Your face . . . It looks droopy."

"I've got a lot weighing on my mind, honey."

Simultaneously two customers from different tables arrived to pay their debts. As Sam took one of the proffered checks she said, "Uncle Jerry called again."

"Oh yeah?"

"He said he tried the office number but was calling down here in case you were playing pinballs. It was about an hour ago."

Now, now he calls . . . "Great."

"I thought you were worried about him."

"I am."

"You don't look worried."

"Today my face is disconnected from my inner being. It's because I had a late night. With Mary, since you didn't ask."

"I know."

"How?"

"I called her."

★ ★ ★ ★ ★

I immersed myself in the transient fates of silvery balls. I did not play well, but as my flippers flopped, the balls' rolly dazzle did its job and took my mind off the real world.

But is a world real in which your daughter monitors your love life, in which your job is to discredit your best friend, in which you get credit for staking out a church when you haven't?

Then I won a last-number replay at the end of what was going to be my last game. Unreal!

Before I could begin to collect my winnings, Mom came into the luncheonette. She had a couple of friends with her and I wouldn't have noticed them but they were laughing to beat the ban. There was an old guy and an old gal, neither of whom I recognized. The gal carried a black plastic bag. They walked past me, headed for Mom's living quarters.

As Mom passed I asked, "What's so funny?"

"A ship full of red paint collided with a ship full of blue paint. The sailors were marooned."

The gal pal nearly split the sides of her plastic bag as she shook with renewed cackles. And then they were gone.

I returned to the machine. Suddenly I was a wizard. I earned a replay. Then another. I played thirty-five minutes without the aid of additional money and only tapped out when I began to play with my eyes shut because I knew I ought to go upstairs.

I had a stack of mail and I had an answering machine blinking like an angry stutterer. The top envelope was brown, so I opted for the messages.

The first was from Miller. He'd called not long after I left for the press conference at IPD. "Sorry not to get back sooner, Al, but you talked to Helene so you know how crazy things are."

I knew, but did he?

He left me a cell phone number.

The next message was from Jimmy Wilson. "I see your neon sign still ain't fixed. It's false economy leaving it that way. If you don't believe me, then ask your Ma. She'll convince you. Say hello to her from me. Tell her I'm trying to help you out."

There was a message that wasn't a message, someone who hadn't hung up quickly enough . . . maybe.

Then Mary, who said, "We need to talk neon. Or shall I ask Sam what your sign should say?"

Mary's call I returned. "Let Sam decide? I don't think so."

"So what is this sign supposed to say? 'Inert Samson'?"

We were already meeting at seven. I promised I'd think about the sign before then.

"But if you're thinking of trying the flat tire ploy again, forget it."

Ah. Have the flat repaired. I wrote myself a note. Then I turned to my mail.

I put the brown envelope on the bottom and found an invitation to change my life forever. I could combine all my debts *and* become the owner of a free nylon bag.

This once in a week-time offer came with a prepaid envelope. I stuffed it with its own paperwork, then added more from my wastepaper basket. They send me their junk, so I send them mine. And a prepaid envelope only costs a junk-mailer money if you use it.

The telephone rang. Obviously Mary calling back. "Hey, sweetie."

"Is that the latest thing from How To Be A Private Investigator?"

It was Miller. I didn't know what to say to him.

"Al?"

"I don't know what to say to you, Jerry."

"Then I'll say something. I *am* glad you're back in business. Really. It was never a personal thing. You must know that."

"I guess." Of course I knew that. "Yeah, of course."

"And I was sorry to hear about Adele. I'd have thought she'd stick by you. What happened?"

"You know the one about the social worker? She finds a guy bleeding on the sidewalk because he's been beaten up, and she says, 'The person who did this to you must really need help.' "

He laughed, too much.

I said, "To tell you the truth, I don't remember everything that happened around then. Maybe I should try to get a copy of the arrest report."

There was a pause.

He thought I was asking him for the arrest report. "It was a joke, Jerry."

"Oh, right." Then, "Did I hear something about Adele and Homer Proffitt?"

"Only that they got married. Defies gravity, don't it?"

He cleared his throat. "Look, Al, Helene said you offered some time and effort on my behalf. Is that right? Because I think maybe there are things you could do to help me."

Oh God.

"I'd pay you. I mean I'd hire you, naturally."

"Your money's no good. It's just I've got this client."

"Since yesterday?"

I heard sudden desperation in his voice. "Look, Jerry, I think we should talk. Are . . . are you at work?"

"Cohl sent me home. He has me taking my own vacation days. I'm paying for my own unofficial suspension. Can you believe that?"

My watch said three thirty-seven. "Let's meet somewhere. At a bar, say. You name it."

He paused to think. I almost said, "Please, not the Milwaukee," but he said, "Do you know the Working Man's Friend?"

"Yeah. Make it five o'clock." Which gave me more than an hour to reclaim my car from downtown and to work out what I could say to him.

21

The Working Man's Friend is on Holt between West Michigan and West Washington, in Haughville. There may not be much left of Benjamin Haugh's iron casting but the area named after him remains a mix of industry and European ethnicity. Wynnedale it's not. Nor black Indy.

If Miller chose the Friend to avoid people he knew he might also have chosen it because it stands on land by itself. From the parking lot it's easy to tell if you're being followed. Cars behind you either stop or drive by. There's no third option.

Inside, the bar faces an open room filled with square Formica tables and kitchen chairs. It's large and light for a saloon, and it's easy to have a private conversation and still see who's coming in and going out. I arrived early, got a beer, and waited on a stool at the bar.

There were only three other customers. They were near the TV and ignoring ESPN to talk about the Indianapolis Indians—arguably the most successful minor league baseball franchise in the country. The new Victory Field is one of Indy's many fresh landmarks.

But I didn't listen to the talk. I concentrated on the message in my bottle. And then the message in its twin. Miller arrived at five-fifteen, about the time I was beginning to feel more relaxed.

From inside the door, he surveyed the room, then caught my eye. I nodded toward a distant corner, bought two more beers, and carried them over.

147

Jerry had added some gray hairs, but he was still big and strong and comfortable-looking. "Long time no see," he said and stuck out a hand.

Our handshake was solemn, a symbolic reconnection. So was the clink of bottles after we sat and before we drank.

"So, how you doing?" I asked, but I could see areas under and around his eyes that were so dark he looked like a panda. "Getting any sleep at all?"

"Not much. But you're looking pretty good for an old guy."

"Slim and trim and full of vim."

"And you already have a client?"

A sore point, but my resolve was to forget my client long enough to hear Miller's story. "Money up front as a retainer and everything."

"Well, I hope it goes well for you, Al. Like I said on the phone, for me it was never a personal thing."

"Yeah, you said it on the phone."

"And I really do appreciate that you're willing to help me out."

"If I can."

We sat looking at each other for a moment. I broke the eye contact and drank.

He said, "Did you get what they're accusing me of from Helene?"

"Jerry, why don't you lay it out for me?"

"Yeah, all right." He took a long draw on the bottle. "IPD, my beloved employers, they think—they claim to think—that I've compromised my whole career—my whole goddamned life—for a few bucks from this fucking bodies-in-the-trunks reward."

"Did you?"

He gave a laugh. "Yeah. There was this horse. But it lost."

"Bummer."

"So, I was working the bodies-in-the-trunks, right?"

"Right."

"And one Monday Crime Stoppers gets a call. It's a guy who says he's got information about the case. He names Ronnie Willigar and says there's a metal box in Willigar's bedroom that has incriminating evidence in it. The Crime Stoppers operator asks if he wants to talk to me direct, but the caller gives a little laugh and says, 'Miller? I don't think so.' The way he says it makes the operator think the guy knows me. I've heard the thing myself—those calls are all recorded. I've listened a dozen times, and I agree, the guy says it like he knows me."

"Did you recognize the voice?"

"No."

"You're sure?"

"Jesus, Al, I've been through this all more times than I can count. I don't know the voice. But him knowing me doesn't mean I have to know him."

"True."

"Nor does it necessarily mean he even knows me personally. It could be that he knows of me. Like maybe once upon a time I jailed a relative. Or he read about me in the papers. Or he fixes my car."

"Is the voice on the tape Carlos Saddler's?"

"They say so." He shrugged. "I suppose so."

"But you have talked with Carlos Saddler, haven't you?"

"That's not how Crime Stoppers works. After the call, it's the civilian businessmen who run the system and deal with any meetings and payments."

"I didn't mean that."

Miller frowned at me.

"Saddler tends bar part-time in the Milwaukee."

"Oh. Yeah, they told me that."

"Do you still go there?"

"Sometimes. Maybe twice, three times so far this year. But I have no idea who he is."

I said, "So a call comes in and the guy seems to know you or know of you."

"The accusation—being kept entirely within the department, of course—is that I provided this Saddler creep the information that he gave on the phone to claim the reward with."

"The name, and that there was a box with stuff in it."

"Right."

"And how are you supposed to have known about these things so you could feed the information to Saddler?"

"Well, Willigar's name had just come up. What happened was, I hired a cross-referencing outfit in Atlanta to work on all the case data we'd amassed."

"What's a cross-referencing outfit? Psychological profiling?"

"A profiler's different—and it had already been tried."

"But didn't crack the case."

"No." Miller's expression seemed somehow to encapsulate both the accomplishment of what he'd done after so many had failed, and the irony that it had all gone sour.

"What do cross-referencers in Atlanta do?"

"They used massive computing power to take the data our investigation collected—which was a shitload because we'd been working on the case for years—and they ran it against a big range of other parameters."

"Such as?"

"Some of it's the obvious stuff, like known previous sexual offenses, criminal history, and so on. But they also fed in anything else they could link to. Details about the victims. Public records, like parking violations in the areas where the offenses were committed. Street maps to find overlaps in habitually used routes. All kinds of private data, like credit card records to show where people were at specific times—"

"And their favorite colors and which finger they pick their noses with. I get it. Massive cross-checking. And . . . ?"

"They turned up five names—well, they turned up two-hundred and seventy-three names, but five were rated higher probability than the rest."

"And the five included Ronnie Willigar."

"The five included Willigar. A courier delivered the full report to me on the Friday—about four in the afternoon."

"The Friday before the Monday call?"

"Yeah."

"So why didn't you raid the five guys on Friday?"

"You can't get search warrants just because a guy's name comes up on a list. Especially five guys. I had to read the report first. Work out what put these particular guys at the top."

"So you read the report."

"And the call came in on the Monday and we raided Willigar that night, but the issue was not just the delay over the weekend. It's that I took the report home to read it."

"Why did you do that?"

"The thing is over eight hundred pages long, Al. I took it home so I wouldn't have to face spending Friday night and all day Saturday and all day Sunday explaining to Janie where I was and why I was there and getting check-up phone calls every fifteen minutes while I was away."

"Helene did say something about a guy telling Janie about your girlfriend. Wendy?"

"Wendy was over nearly three years ago. She found out about Marcella."

"Ah."

"Marcella's husband—the one who was supposed to be so ex he was a joke—this asshole takes it upon himself to come out to the house . . ." Miller spread his hands. "In the middle of the biggest case of my career. At the exact time when I desperately needed a place I could go to for a little understanding. At the exact time I did not need high-volume hassle at home. I'm so fucking angry at the guy I would happily do something to him that the department *could* charge me with."

I think it was at that moment that any smidgen of doubt about my friend's innocence vanished.

He was shaking his head. "It was the worst possible timing, the worst possible bad fucking luck."

The women who'd been raped and murdered might have had a different assessment of what constituted the worst possible bad luck, but I passed on trying to get him to broaden his perspective.

"And there's more. About the same time that Helene was sent home from college."

"Sent home? But . . . why?"

"She got mixed up with a drug crowd." The rings around his eyes did an extra lap. "It's about killed me. I love that kid. I love them all, but she's always been special."

" 'Mixed up' means what?"

"She was caught in a raid when she was under the influence and in possession."

"Of what?"

"Vike."

"What is 'vike'? It sounds like either a new nickname for cocaine or something distilled from old sneakers."

"Come on, Al, keep up with your substance abuse. Vike's a happy-time prescription pain-killer. Vicodin. Don't you get out?"

"Was Helene charged?"

"College police conducted the raid. She left 'by mutual agreement.' She can go back in the fall if she completes a detox program with a counselor and then passes an interview with some Dean who will assess whether she's reformed." He put his hands over his eyes. "She's been home since Easter."

"And seeing the counselor?"

"Oh yes. Hasn't missed a session, which she can prove because there's an attendance card and Madame La Counselor signs it each time."

"Am I sensing that you don't rate Madame?"

"Don't get me started." He tried to find more beer in his bottle. "Al, what would you talk to a kid about if you were a detox counselor? I bet things like, don't do it again because stuff like that fucks with your brain and liver and heart and lungs and it's habit forming?"

"Sounds like a reasonable syllabus."

"Instead, my little girl is part of a group made up of people who would be shunned in a fucking jail. They sit and share their experiences. And they get lectures about every drug in creation—natural, artificial, imaginary. They read books about drugs that don't exist. And they do the history of drugs. The future of drugs. She's a fucking expert. Helene can tell you how long it takes each illegal substance to clear from the system, what its short- and long-term effects are, if it produces ataxia, how it's made and refined. Did you know that opium comes from the juice that seeps out of opium poppy seed cases in hot weather, because I didn't. Jesus, Al, it's driving me crazy."

Miller stood up to attract the attention of the guy behind the bar. He held up his bottle and indicated we wanted two more hits of our preferred substance.

I said, "What's Helene's behavior like?"

"She says 'please' before she leaves the dinner table. She passes all the drug tests."

"That's good."

"But then she goes out every night in an old car we keep for when the kids fly in."

"Where does she go?"

"Who the fuck knows?"

We watched the bartender, a huge guy in a t-shirt that said "Tiny," maneuver his way to where we were sitting. He put two bottles on the table. "You guys want something to eat? We got specials. We got a veal scaloppini. We got—"

Miller said, "Nothing to eat." He gave Tiny a bill and waved him away. He drank. "While Helene was at college she also ran up debts."

"How much?"

"You don't want to know."

"Don't be coy, Jerry. One of the things they say is that you have financial problems."

"The total on all the cards was a little over seventeen grand."

"Excuse me? They take plastic for this vike?"

"The biggest item she bought was an eleven grand car."

"At least selling it got you something back."

"A few days after she bought it, the car was stolen." He exhaled deeply. "She says. There was no insurance."

The Helene I'd met showed no signs of anything like this. I said so.

"She's a different person now. She says so. So does Madame La Counselor. She writes a note at the bottom of her weekly bills."

"What are you doing about the money?"

"Madame says Helene needs to see a clean start."

"You're writing off seventeen thousand dollars?"

He shrugged.

"Silly me. All you have to decide is whether to sell one of the diamonds or one of the oil paintings."

"It's a problem, but nothing we can't get past."

Then I got it. "As long as there are no other financial disruptions, like a divorce?"

The panda nodded sadly.

"You're in the shit, my son," I said.

"There's shit and there's shit."

"True."

"If only it were dry shit instead of wet shit . . ."

"And didn't have all those peanuts in it." I raised my bottle. "Old riffs."

"Old riffs."

The moment passed.

I said, "So, your cross-referencers gave you five names on Friday."

"Right."

"How come on Monday Carlos Saddler only phoned in the one?"

"I'm told that over the weekend either I or, more probably, my accomplice broke into the homes of the named people in order to pick the right one."

"Was Willigar's broken into over that weekend?"

"When we raided him, there was a broken pane in his back door where someone could reach through and unlock it. But he could have done that himself."

"Why would he do that himself?"

"Because he's a crazy fuck who wants to make my life hell," Miller said. "There was a broken pane of glass. So what? He didn't say anything about a break-in while we were interrogating him."

"Maybe he had other things on his mind while you were interrogating him."

"Al, there was nothing to suggest a break-in on the weekend in question. He had not, for instance, called the police, or reported a theft, or called his insurance company for a claim form."

"If he says in court there was a break-in but nothing was stolen, his lawyers could present it as circumstantial corroboration of his story."

"Proving nothing whatever."

Which was the essence of evidence that was circumstantial, as I understood it. I moved on. "What did you find when you searched?"

"The metal box, in the bedroom, as promised."

"What was in it?"

"Souvenirs of the victims. Drivers' licenses, union cards, family pictures, lockets, and incidental shit like tissues, and lipsticks. There was a pack of flower seeds one of them had just bought."

"Did you find anything else in the search that would connect Willigar to the crimes?"

"Lab work is still being done on a lot of different stuff."

"So that's a no."

"It's not a no yet, Al."

"But Willigar's defense will be that someone else put the box in his bedroom, right?"

"The slimeball has no defense."

"You know what I mean."

"Ronnie Willigar is guilty of the crimes he is accused of. You only have to meet the guy. You can see it in his eyes."

"Remind me, Jerry. What is the legal status of 'you can see it in his eyes'?"

"You can see it in his fucking eyes, Al. I've seen a lot of

156

killers over the years. This guy did it. It's a certainty."

Miller had certainly seen plenty of murderers. There's no shortage in a city the size of Indianapolis. A few of those killers I had delivered to him myself but I tend to recognize killers more from the knives and guns in their hands than from the looks in their eyes. Still, who was to say Miller was wrong about Ronnie Willigar? "Tell me more about these accusations against you. How did they come up in the first place?"

"I don't know."

"What's that mean?"

"It means that for the first couple of weeks after the arrest I was Mr. Cop. Strangers would say 'Way to go,' in the hallway. The press office wanted me to do PR in the schools. I was told unofficially I would get the next promotion to Commander."

"And then?"

"I came in last Monday and nobody would look at me. I figured maybe they thought I'd been getting big-headed and they wanted to bring me back down to earth."

"But . . . ?"

"I got called to the Deputy Chief's office. It was exactly twenty-three days after the Willigar raid."

"Making it a Wednesday."

"At ten-twenty in the morning. The Deputy Chief—Derrington—he's the one who does all Cohl's dirty work. I should have put two and two together but I walked in without a care in the world. Until I saw Commander Plzak was with Derrington."

"Do I know Plzak?"

"Maybe. He's one of those guys who's been around forever, worked his way up. And now he heads up internal investigations."

"Ah."

"Plzak says he's received an accusation against me through the Whistle-Blowers program. I laughed when he said it. He told me it wasn't a laughing matter. But it was, Al, because I helped set up fucking Whistle-Blowers."

"Which is . . . ?"

"An in-house Crime Stoppers. A way people in the department can report illegal activity or bad practice by other officers without being afraid they'll damage their own careers."

"Did Derrington have anything to say?"

"That he knew my record, and he was sure there was nothing in the accusation, but I had to understand how important it was in the current climate for the Chief's Office to be seen to be doubly careful, yadada yadada."

"Helene said that Chief Cohl came out to your house."

"Yeah," Miller said. "To assure me of the Department's full support, as long as I retire now. The two-faced scum. He can retire up my ass."

"Helene said Janie thinks you should take it."

"Janie could retire up my ass too if her head wasn't already up her own." He took a cell phone out and put it on the table. "She's going to call me, you know. To check where I am."

"Where does she think you are?"

"Here, talking to you."

"So?"

"She'll call anyway, to make sure." He drank. "Oh Al, I miss Marcella so much."

"You don't see her?"

"I just can't risk it. Did Helene tell you, I'm being followed?"

I nodded.

"We talk, Marcella and me. But only from public phones." He held up the cell. "This gets checked. Some life, eh? No Marcella. Crap at work. Janie at home. I never ever get to fucking relax."

Or relax fucking, from the sound of it.

"Marcella is the nicest woman I have ever known, Al. It's special, it really is. She's sweet. She's kind. Everything is easy with her."

Pity it wasn't so easy with the supposedly ex husband. I said, "Will she wait for this to blow over?"

"She says she will."

"You doubt her?"

"Doubt? No. I don't doubt. All I do is worry and drink. But it's like there are worms eating away whatever it is that's me. And it makes me wonder, when this is all over, will there be anything left of me that's worth having? Does that make any sense to you?"

"What you describe sums up how I've been feeling since I lost my license."

Our eyes locked. "Do you hold it against me, Al? What I did."

Hey, it was in the past now, right? "Of course I hold what you did against you. I'll take any opportunity I get to pay you back for it."

There was a kernel of truth in what I said. For a moment I thought he saw it in my eyes. But maybe his gift for reading eyes only applied to murderers because then he chuckled.

If only he knew.

If only I knew.

We talked for another half hour. He promised to give me details of the other four guys on the list. Maybe their places were broken into over the crucial weekend. Maybe that would prove something. For sure the cops had not investigated them. "Once we had Willigar and his box," Miller said, "who cared about anyone else?"

And he talked me through the rest of what happened after he got the cross-referencers' report. Even after the weekend he hadn't been ready to go for search warrants. Then the Crime Stoppers call came in. That made it possible for him to single Willigar out.

"So the call was critical in the arrest?" I said.

"It speeded things up a little."

"By how much?"

"Maybe a day or two. Maybe more."

"Hey, sounds a hundred and ten grand's worth of information to me."

"The reward was nothing to do with me, Al."

"So you said."

"I had to fill out a form saying what information I received and what I did with it. But apart from that—who gets money, how much, when it's paid, where it's paid—everything is completely outside the department."

"But Whistle-Blowers is completely inside the department, right? So whoever blew the whistle on you was inside the department?"

"Yeah."

"So how does someone inside the department connect up to knowledge of what information came through Crime Stoppers, and when, and from whom?"

He shook his head. "I don't know."

"Haven't you been working on who might be behind the accusation?"

"Not a lot."

"Or who would benefit from your career going down the pan?"

"No."

"Why not?"

"Because I know I'm innocent," he said with feeling. "Truth is, I can barely think at all, what with everything that's happened."

"Well, I suppose I wasn't Albert Einstein when my shit first hit the fan either."

"There's something you could do for me, that would help a lot. Would you find out what Helene is up to?"

"Helene?"

"She goes out every night. She comes back late. I don't know where she goes. I don't know what she does."

"You haven't asked?"

"Not any more. She stonewalls. But I check the car she drives and she does between sixteen and seventy-eight miles a night, all between the hours of six-thirty and midnight. And I'm afraid to push her. I'm petrified that she'll just bolt. That's what drugs is about, isn't it? Not being able to take pressure? But if I just knew what the deal is with her, then maybe I could start to get my head around this shit at IPD."

"Suppose I follow her and the news is bad."

"Anything is better than not knowing."

Well, at least it was something I could do for my oldest friend that wasn't tinged with betrayal. "I'll give it a try."

"A try. Great. Thanks. No promises. I know."

"Another beer?"

He looked at his watch.

"Curfew?"

"I have to be home for dinner, but I want to call Marcella first. I'd ask you to stop in and see her, to make sure she's OK, but . . . I know you've got a client . . ." He shrugged.

"I'll try to fit it in if you want me to."

"Maybe what I'll do is give her your number, if that's

OK. She could call you if there's an emergency."

"Give her my number. If she needs help I'll do whatever I can for her."

"Thanks, Al." There was a public phone by the door. As he got up, the cell phone on the table rang. He jumped like something had bitten him. "Fuck! Told you, didn't I?"

I picked up the phone. "Turn it on for me." He blinked, then pushed a button. I said, "Hello? This is Albert Gator, Private Eye, Ear, Nose, and Throat."

There was a very long pause at the other end.

"Look, lady, I told you what I'd do if you made another obscene call. You're gonna have the cops at your door in a few minutes now. How d'you like them apples?"

Miller made his call to Marcella and then we left. We neither shook hands nor hugged in the parking lot. An exchange of nods sufficed, for the benefit of the guy parked in a Golf who was trying to look uninterested by holding a phone to his ear.

Miller left for Wynnedale, to play happy family with Janie and Helene. And to run through the silent questions for Helene as she asked to be excused from the table and headed for the door.

He could bring himself to check Helene's odometer but he couldn't insist on knowing where she drove to . . . Families, eh?

So it fell to me—the inadequate father and inadequate son and inadequate friend—to divine what I could about Helene's nocturnal activities. Surreptitiously of course. As long as I had enough time left over from surreptitiously investigating her father.

22

When I arrived at the Elbow Room, Mary was holding the stem of a frosted glass on the edge of which an umbrella tilted precariously. A second umbrella lay on the table. I slid into the booth beside her. "Am I late? I thought I was a couple of minutes early."

"I'm getting drunk."

"Any special occasion?"

"This is the third night in a row we've arranged to meet and we've both turned up."

A lean waiter dressed in grays appeared at my shoulder. "I'll have whatever the lady's drinking." He laid a menu in front of me, replaced the ashtray with a clean one, and walked away.

"Three nights in a row," my companion said. She drank. I saw now that the frosted glass had a little straw.

"Have we exceeded some limit, or have we won a prize?"

"It's not the way adults behave, Albert. Not grown-up adults."

"It's not?"

"You may be so old that you're desperate, but I'm a young woman still, in my prime. I should be more measured. Are you having a drink, or what?"

"I just ordered one."

"I didn't have to be a neon sign-maker, you know."

"You could have been an opera singer."

"Three nights in a row." Her head sank to the table. The loose umbrella caught in her hair.

"Is there something special about the threeness. Or is it the nights-in-a-rowness?"

"Yes."

"What?"

"I don't remember. Albert?"

"Yeah?"

"Why did you order the same drink as me?"

"In case you want another but don't want to be seen ordering a third for yourself because you don't want perfect strangers who are paying no attention to think you're a lush."

"You're a nice man, Albert."

"It's my curse."

"A very nice man. Crap name though. 'Albert.' What kind of name is that?"

"Transylvanian."

"Oh yeah?"

We sat quietly for a moment. I picked the umbrella out of her hair. "How's your day been?"

"My tube bender went on the fritz."

"Are we talking he, she, or it?"

"It. Well, there are two kinds of tube bender. I'm talking about the longitudinal one. Definitely an it."

"Oh."

"Not the transverse one. She's fine."

"Good."

"But the nozzles of the longitudinal are fucked. *Way* fucked. And that means when we heat up a tube to bend it, we can't bend it evenly. Do you know what that means?"

"Bad things, I bet."

"*Very* bad things. How can you make neon signs without being able to bend tubes evenly?"

"Only with the most extreme difficulty. If at all."

"It's no way to run a business."

"Although these things do sometimes happen."

"True."

"And so you fix them. Or have them fixed."

"But do you know the worst part?"

"What?"

"While I was trying to fix the damn thing, and then, while I was arranging for the professional fixer to come out and professionally fix the damn thing, all that time, what I was thinking about was . . . Do you know what I was thinking about?"

"What?"

"I was thinking about meeting you tonight."

"And was that bad?"

"No, no. That was good. A good feeling. It was a light at the end of the dark tunnel."

"Although not, on this occasion, a neon light."

"Which makes three nights in a row."

"Or three lights, depending how you look at it."

"And that's bad."

"It is? Because it doesn't seem bad to me. In fact it seems good to me."

"Oh, it is bad. It is."

"Why?"

"*Because* I like it. Because we get along. Because I enjoy it. And . . ."

"And?"

"Because it makes me more afraid of the inevitable dark tunnel at the end of the light."

My drink came. As the waiter in grays reached for Mary's empty, I saved the straw. "A drink shared is a drink halved," I said.

She laughed. She was a generous woman made more generous by drink, just as a sad woman is made more sad.

Fuck it—what adult, what grown-up adult, isn't sad? Generosity is the rarity.

"You eating tonight or only drinking?" I asked.

"Are you trying to get me sober?"

"You could always watch me eat and decide later."

"I'll eat," she said. "Isn't it supposed to be dangerous when people start to eat alone?"

In barely a Caesar salad, an Irish stew with onion rings, and a piece of cheesecake, the previously-known, sober Mary was back. "How was your day?" she asked.

I'd decided to be cautious answering this question. I skipped the IPD stuff and told her about Miller having asked me to follow Helene.

"You're supposed to follow this girl, who knows you by sight, and she's not supposed to realize you're doing it. Have I got that right?"

"Yes."

"Is she, by any chance, blind?"

"If I'm lucky, she'll go to public places where I can blend in."

"She's what, twenty?"

"Thereabouts."

"Anywhere she's likely to go, you'll blend in like wearing a Santa suit would blend in at a bar mitzvah."

"Are you impugning my blending?"

"I suppose if she's stoned enough, she won't notice you."

"She's passing her drug tests."

"Including for alcohol?"

"Well, to look on the bright side, at least I won't have the time to do the job if I'm seeing you every night."

"Sam."

"What about her?"

166

"She's older than your friend's girl, but a whole lot more blendable than you could ever be. She helped out on cases before."

Well, long ago, when she was around for a few months. "Yeah, but . . ."

"Ask her," Mary said. "She'd certainly like to be asked."

"You think?"

"I think."

"OK. I will."

"How about now?"

"I don't know where she spends her Monday nights."

Mary fished in her bag and produced a cell phone. "She's got one of these, doesn't she?"

"Mary?" Sam said when she answered.

"No. It's me."

"You're on Mary's phone though. It comes up on my screen."

"What screen?"

"Look at the phone you're holding, Daddy. It has a little screen on it. When you receive a call, it shows what number's calling you."

I looked. "Deuced clever."

From my hand I heard Sam's voice say faintly, "Put it back to your ear, Daddy. I can't hear you."

"Oh right. Look, I don't know what you're up to, but I wondered if you'd be interested in a detecting assignment."

"Me? But I work at the luncheonette."

"It's an evening job that I don't have the time for."

"Or the blendability," Mary said.

"Sshh. Go light a cigarette."

"I better tell you where I am first," Sam said.

"I wasn't talking to you."

"Oh. OK."

"Where are you?"

"I'm in your office, using your computer. I think I may have found Mom."

23

"She's definitely in Kentucky," Sam said when Mary and I arrived at my office. "I've confirmed it to my satisfaction since I talked to you."

"What in God's name is your mother doing in Kentucky?" I asked.

"I don't know that yet."

"I mean, Kentucky . . . ? Your mother?"

"I wasn't looking there specifically, but I just wasn't getting any traces in Europe. So I did some searches in the U.S., assuming that she'd kept the admiral's last name. Fortunately there aren't many Gutierrez-Moratins and even fewer with her first name. But I found one in Lexington who has a bunch of gold credit cards, a bank account in London, and an address in just the kind of fancy suburban neighborhood that Mom would choose, as far as I can tell from one of the mapping sites."

"Do you have a phone number?" Mary asked.

"Yup."

"Are you going to call her?"

"I . . . I'm not sure," Sam said. "Before I do that, I really ought to think about why she hasn't been in contact with me even though she's been so close for nearly four months."

"Do you have any idea why your mother might have gone to Lexington?"

"Working her way through the admirals in the Kentucky Navy?" I suggested.

"Hush, Albert," Mary said. "Be a father instead of a rejected lover."

"He's probably right, though," Sam said. "For all Mom is smart and incredibly good at organizing things, she's never made a life that didn't have a man at the center of it." Then she closed the subject of her mother for the evening by turning to me. "So, what's this about a job, Daddy?"

I went through what I'd been told about Helene's return to the family home. I stressed how upset it was making her father not to know where she went at nights.

"So was it Helene that Uncle Jerry wanted to talk to you about?" Sam said. "Not about being suspended from the IPD?"

"Suspended?"

"It was on the news tonight. The reporter who used to be married to whatshisname, the politician. She said she has sources who say Uncle Jerry has been suspended."

"I was told it isn't an official suspension."

"It's about the big reward for the bodies-in-the-trunks murderer, isn't it?"

"They think he tried to get some of it, but he didn't."

"The reporter woman said there's an internal police investigation."

"That is all too true," I said.

"So how does Helene fit into that?"

"Worrying about her keeps Jerry from giving his full attention to fighting the accusations."

"She goes out every night?"

"It sounded that way."

"What else do they know? Like, does she have more money than she ought to?"

"Or less?" Mary asked.

"Jerry didn't say anything about her finances," I said. "But they're good questions."

"It could take me quite a while to figure it all out," Sam said. "Particularly if I'm not supposed to let her know that I'm investigating her."

"You're right. It could."

"But," Mary said, "you'll be paid for your time. A good rate. Right, Albert? Plus expenses. Sam will have to go to clubs if Helene does, buy drinks, bribe people, take drugs, the whole nine yards."

Just then there was a knock on the internal door that leads from my bedroom to Mom's part of the building. "I will not subsidize one inch past eight yards." I got up. "Deal?"

"Deal."

The knock was repeated. I left Sam and Mary in the office. When I opened the door it was Mom.

"Oh," she said. "It's you."

"Should I ask who you expected to open my door?"

"I, uh . . . Sam said she'd be up here."

"She is."

"I would like a word with her, please, Albert."

"Is something wrong?"

Sam and Mary appeared behind me. Sam said, "What's up, Grandma? Something computery?"

"No, no." Mom looked at Mary. "Is the young woman a friend of yours, honey?"

Sam said, "Mary, this is my grandmother. Grandma, this is Mary. She's Daddy's new squeeze."

"Thanks a lot," Mary said. "Nice to meet you, Mrs. Samson."

"Nice to meet you too, Mary. So, Sam, honey, if you're not too busy, could I have a word?"

"Is it Boris and Fontaine?"

Mom nodded, then stepped back into the hallway she'd come in from.

I said, "Are we keeping secrets now?"

Mary said, "They probably don't want to talk in front of me, Albert. I'll go to the other room."

But I wasn't having that. Being my squeeze gives a girl rights. Whether she wants them or not. I addressed my mother and daughter. "What's up with you two?"

Mom said, "It has to do with something Sam and I talked about earlier on, son. That's all. It needn't involve you."

She wanted me to leave, but I didn't want to. So I didn't. We all stood still and silent until Sam said, "Grandma?"

Mom looked at her watch. "It's Boris, honey. He's not answering his phone. Fontaine's tried him three or four times and she's worried."

"What are you going to do?"

"I'm going out to where Fontaine is, but I wondered . . ."

"Can I do something?"

"I was hoping, if you're not too busy . . . Would you come along with me?" My mother reached under a loose shirt and drew a revolver from her belt. "It's just if I have to use this, you see, I won't be able to call for help on the cell phone at the same time."

24

Sam agreed to go immediately. She and Mom walked past Mary and me while I was still trying to figure out what was going on. I followed a few steps but at my outside door Mom turned back and said, "No need for you to come, son. I know you don't approve of weaponry, and you've got your guest."

"Mom, what is all this about?"

"I have friends who need my help."

The door closed.

"Stay here," I said to Mary. "If you'll give me your cell phone, I'll call you on my line when I know more."

"If you think I'm staying behind, you're crazy," Mary said. "Just tell me who Boris and Fontaine are."

"I don't have the slightest idea."

By the time we were on the porch, Mom and Sam were on the sidewalk at the bottom of the stairs. To my left "Albert . . . gator" glowed red.

The real Albert Gator was feeling toothless. "Mary?"

She took my arm as we went down. "What?"

"I bet you thought I'd never be able to top taking you rapist hunting."

"If you arranged all this to impress me, you can stop now. I'm impressed."

"And, I want you to know how very glad I am that my neon sign is broken and that we met."

"Now you're scaring me."

Sam and Mom crossed Virginia Avenue and turned

right. We followed. They turned left on one of the streets that still heads west, though for only a few blocks now. Most of the street and hundreds of small family houses were gouged away by the city fathers to make space for 465, the multi-lane highway that rings the city.

Where once there were families and gardens and pets and kids, now there are machine-gun streams of vehicles, fired at distant targets, that pass day and night. I used to believe that such a thing wouldn't have happened if Indy had some city mothers. Trailing behind my own weapons-trained mother, I was not so sure.

"Albert?" Mary said.

"What?"

"What does this road lead to?"

"A dead end."

"Is there another way to put that?"

But ahead of us Mom had already stopped at the last cross-street. When we caught up, she was on her cell. "Fontaine? Well, where are you, honey? Over." Then, "Oh, I see you."

We all looked where Mom was looking. A dumpling of a woman stood beneath a streetlight at the end of an alley. One hand was at her ear. The other was waving.

Mom said, "We'll be there in a minute. Over."

We trooped to Fontaine. Up close I recognized her as one of Mom's collection of cronies at the luncheonette. "You brought along the cavalry, huh, Posy?" Fontaine said. "Hi, y'all. Thanks for coming out to help."

"Where was Boris posted?" Mom asked.

"He went to the other end of this here alley and turned right. He said he found him a tree right near the corner that gave good cover but still left him a good view. He told me to stay put so's I could see anybody coming up the big berm from the interstate."

"When was it you last spoke to him?"

"We checked in . . ." Fontaine pushed a button on a big black wristwatch to illuminate the dial. "It was forty-seven minutes since, Posy. We agreed fifteen-minute checks, on vibration mode, but when he didn't answer thirty-two minutes ago I didn't call you right away. I thought, you know, he might be taking a leak, or trying to, or something. But five minutes after, and eight minutes after that, and ten minutes after again, he still didn't answer."

"And there was nothing unusual happening before that?"

"Nothing," Fontaine said. "It's been pretty . . . Well, boring. You know how it gets."

"All right." Mom handed Sam her phone. "Just in case, honey. First thing we have to do is find Boris. You stay here, Fontaine, and let us know if anybody comes by."

"Roger, Posy."

Mom drew her gun, opened the chamber, spun it, and closed it again. She put it back underneath her shirt and then headed down the alley, keeping to the shadows instead of taking a straight line. Sam followed her.

What else could I do?

"Albert?" Mary whispered. "Does she have a license for that thing?"

"Of course."

"Oh."

"Why don't you stay here with Fontaine? She ought to have someone."

"You stay, cowboy. I want to know where that gun is at all times."

Ahead of us Mom stopped. In a hissing whisper she said, "Albert, you and your squeeze shut up or go someplace else. And put out that cigarette."

We shut up. We extinguished. We followed.

Whenever Mom stopped, we all stopped. When she started again, so did we, moving between the alley's pools of shadow.

In the darkness I became aware of the sounds the city was making. Sirens in the distance. Vehicles on 465. Modern urban birdsong. The only unusual thing for a city at night was that I was paying attention.

Near the end of the alley we made a false stop when the back door of a house opened with a shock of light. A man in his underwear came onto his screen porch. All he did was lock the porch door and go back in, but I was acutely aware that for him to be watched so carefully from the shadows was not a civilized thing. It was a wild thing, a wilderness thing.

We build and buy and arrange so much of our lives nowadays that we usually deceive ourselves that we're in control. But wild, randomizing forces are always out there. Things we don't know about and can't predict are always waiting to happen.

When the guy was back inside his locked box, we moved on. At the end of the alley we turned onto the sidewalk. At the next corner I saw a big willow with droopy branches. It had to be the tree Boris told Fontaine about. However, no Boris was anywhere to be seen. In a whisper Mom said, "You all stay under the tree. I'm going to look for him from the corners."

Our collective mentality was such that we obeyed her instruction without question. And fair enough. She was less likely to attract attention alone than we would as a gang of four.

Purposefully but unhurriedly Mom moved from corner to corner. She looked for all the world to be nothing more than an old woman looking for a lost dog.

And then she spotted something. She beckoned. We streamed out from beneath the branches and followed her up one of the streets.

Boris was crumpled on the curb beside a parked car. I could see blood on his face as we got to where Mom knelt beside him.

"Sam," she said, "call 911 for an ambulance, honey."

I said, "Why don't I get my car? I can probably get here quicker than the ambulance."

"Hurry, son," Mom said.

And I did. The lean, mean running machine delivered. Boris, breathing laboredly and making incoherent sounds, was in my back seat with his head on Mom's lap before there was so much as a siren in the distance. We headed for the Southside Hospital Emergency Room, leaving Mary and Sam to cancel the ambulance, collect Fontaine, and follow.

Things can go wrong at an ER. You don't hear so often about things going right. But this time a handy, helpful porter rolled Boris in on a gurney and within a couple of minutes he was being examined by a doctor. The doctor even looked old enough to be a doctor.

He decided to have Boris's head X-rayed. I went with Mom to the paperwork people. That done, we found a place to sit where the others would find us easily.

Then I said, "Tell me about it."

"What's that, son?"

"Who are these people? Boris and Fontaine?"

"Just folks who live in the neighborhood."

"Neighborhood folks who stake out alleys and street corners at night?"

"They're friends who come to the gun club with me."

"So they were going to shoot someone?"

"I'm not much in the mood for your silly side, Albert."

"Then stop flimflamming and tell me what Boris and Fontaine were out there for. And tell me why Fontaine called you when something went wrong. And tell me why the hell you haven't told me about whatever the hell is going on before now." I was not a happy boy.

"You've had so many distractions the last few years, son."

"So?"

"You've been preoccupied, and depressed. Even self-destructive."

She was referring to what happened when Adele ditched me. I said, "Well, maybe for a while, to some extent."

"It seems to me you coped with your troubles by keeping your body busy, with menial jobs and all your exercise—anything to keep from thinking about things."

"I think that exaggerates the way I've been, Mom."

"Does it? I wonder. Look at how you haven't noticed how Sam's been drifting."

"And maybe you haven't noticed that Sam is an adult. But sure, I agree, I haven't noticed some things, and I've done some other things that were stupid."

"Like drinking to excess and getting arrested."

"And I also saw a lot of very bad movies. But I'm back, Mom. I'm noticing things again. I 'noticed' how you and Fontaine use military communications terms like 'over' and 'roger.' I 'noticed' the other day when Yvonne kissed your hand. Sam told me it was some game you and your friends play, but I don't think 'game' quite covers what happened tonight to your pal, Boris. Or maybe it does. If so I want to know about the game, Mom. I want to know the rules and how to play. I want you to tell me what's going on."

Mom took a deep breath. Then she took a slow look

around the waiting room. It was a good impression of what a private eye would do to check whether anyone was close enough to hear what she was about to say.

Then someone caught her eye. A teenage boy. He was not far away with one leg elevated. His expression was sullen in the way that only teenagers can achieve.

Mom lingered on this kid. She couldn't be worried about what he would hear. So . . . what? Was she implying that's how I'd looked to her the last few years? Self-absorbed, oblivious, unaware? *Was* it the way I'd been? It was an awful thought. Could anyone show me how to roll back the clock?

Mom said, "There's no turning the clock back."

What the . . . ? I swiveled to face her, but she was still looking at the kid. I saw now that there was a woman sitting next to him. She looked to me about the same age he did. But then she ruffled his hair and he called her Mom a couple of times, in between the swear words.

My "Mom" said, "There is so much about this modern life that doesn't work right, son. Fountain Square used to be a village. A real nice place to live. Everybody knew everybody. Why, one of the reasons we started the luncheonette was I liked the idea of cooking for friends and neighbors. It was a place where if someone was in trouble, you helped out, if you could. That's just the way it was. Didn't matter whether you liked 'em or not."

I certainly agreed that wasn't how Fountain Square was these days.

Just then Boris's doctor emerged through double doors. Mom and I rose and met him halfway. He addressed her. "I've just come from your friend, Mr. Whitely. He's fully conscious now—which is a good sign, of course."

"Will he be all right?"

"We have a few more tests to do but, honestly, I can't see why he shouldn't make a full recovery. And, Mrs. Samson, he's asking for you."

"Can I see him?"

"Not yet, I'm afraid. But he had a message he asked me to pass on. Quite a character, your friend. He wanted you to know . . ." The doctor studied the back of his hand. "Hang on. I . . . Ah. He said to say, 'There were two of them.' Does that mean something to you, Mrs. Samson?"

"Yes it does. Thank you, doctor."

"No problem. And, I'll make sure they let you know when he can have visitors." The doctor left.

"Well, that's a relief," Mom said.

"Two of them is a relief?" I said.

"I meant that Boris will be all right."

"I'm glad of that too, Mom. But you were in the middle of telling me what all this is about."

"It's . . . a long story, son."

"I'll keep awake right to the end."

"It's the vandalism in the neighborhood. Until recently it's all been east of Virginia Avenue. But now it's started up on the other side."

We went back to the chairs we'd occupied. The sullen teenager was gone.

"Course there's always been high jinks. It's not like the Square was holier than thou. But it wasn't ever ugly. We can't turn the clock back, but all the vandalism, all the thefts . . . Some folks even find their own dead pets stuffed in their mailboxes. Their own dead pets. Can you imagine that, Albert? Who would do such a thing?"

"Or why?" I shook my head.

"You can't ever make it the way it was," Mom said, "but you don't have to sit still for it either. Leastways, I can't sit still. It's not in my nature. If I see a problem, I want to solve it."

Which maybe explained something about where I got the attitudes that led me into private investigation and made it so important to me to stay there.

"The way you were, for instance, son, when you lost your license. It like to broke my heart that I couldn't shake you out of it. I wanted to make you see that life is too precious to allow it to drip away each day."

"I was doing the best I could, Mom."

"I know that. I know that, son. But you're just one example. Maybe there is nothing I can do about a problem, but that doesn't keep me from wanting to, from trying. Take this vandalism. Why, I can hardly remember when I last sat down with friends without they had some new story about bad things happening in the neighborhood. A grandchild who got beat up, or a car window that was smashed in, or how somebody sprayed weed-killer on their flower garden."

"Mom, are you saying that you've been helping the people with all these problems?"

"Me? I'm just one old lady."

I was looking more carefully at the one old lady.

"But, I do know a lot of folks round the neighborhood who share my concerns."

Something clicked. Had I suddenly gotten it? Was my mother at the front of an old-age army, leading a march on the mindless marauders of Fountain Square? "Mom?"

She knew what I was thinking. I could see it in her eyes.

"Is that why you and your friends go to the gun club?"

"Pretty much."

"But you started going years ago."

"You can't rush a thing, not if you intend to do it right. Of course it's fun too. We have a real sociable time."

"So Boris, and Fontaine, and . . ." If I counted up my mother's wrinkly pals around the luncheonette, I'd have quickly run out of digits. It might not be enough for an army, but a gray brigade?

"And I tell you," she said, "it's a wonderful thing what special talents folks have, once you start looking for them. Plus what they can learn."

"This is why you've studied all the computer stuff too, isn't it?"

"You studied computers yourself, son."

"I bet there's a lot you could teach me."

"I expect so." She took a hanky out of her purse and blew her nose. "I do like to do things well. And it's always easier to learn something new if you're learning it for a purpose that will help other folks."

The Wrinkly Rangers?

Something else clicked. "Mom, were you behind the stakeout at Reverend Battle's church?"

"Oh, that was such an awful thing to do to a church. You don't have to be part of a congregation to hate something like that."

The Creaky Crusaders?

"And, son, once you told me about it, well . . ."

"But e-mailing pictures to the police? You can do that?"

The Fountain Furies?

"One of our people, Daniel, I don't think you know him, but you might recognize his face. Daniel's middle boy, Ed, has an optics business so Daniel can borrow an infrared digital camera pretty much any time he cares to. That's one of the ways we old folks have an advantage, son. We know so many people, and we have a lot of family out there, most of us. That makes a whole passel of folks we can ask to help us in some little way."

The Viagra Vigilantes?

"Of course Daniel was real lucky to get a result the very first night. A normal surveillance could take days or even weeks to pay off. But, statistically speaking, you've got to get lucky sometimes, don't you?"

What was the scale of operation of these Retired Revengers?

Mom said, "It can also help that we don't sleep so much as we used to. And we have another advantage too, son. People don't usually pay us much mind, so we're mostways to being invisible."

My own inattentiveness to all this was a case in point. But realizing just how inattentive I'd been began to overwhelm me.

It was about then that Mary, Sam, and Fontaine bustled in.

The three women had come in Sam's car, Mary told me. "Sam figured that you'll be happy enough to give me a lift back to mine."

"Yeah," I said.

"Albert, what's wrong? Has Boris . . . ?"

"Boris is conscious. He should be all right."

"You're upset about something."

"Can we get out of here, do you think?"

As we pulled out of the hospital parking lot Mary said, "Albert, just so it's clear . . . When we get back to your place, I'm going home. It's late, and I've got a lot of work tomorrow."

"Yeah. OK."

" 'Yeah, OK'? No protest? No begging? Have I lost my allure already?"

"Your allure is just fine."

She was silent for a moment. "What's up, Eye Spy?"

"I had a talk with Mom. She's been telling me about this organization she put together."

"Posy's Posse, you mean?"

"You know about it?"

"Only what Sam and Fontaine told me in the car."

"Which is?"

"That your mother and her friends help people in the neighborhood."

"We're talking about more than going to the market for a neighbor who has a cold."

"I know. They're trying to address the things that most people just complain about. And your mother and her friends are taking advantage of how much more active people of their age are now than they used to be. What's upsetting about that? It seems a good thing."

"It is a good thing. In fact, an extraordinary thing."

"What's the problem then?"

"The problem is that I didn't know anything about it until tonight."

"Poor baby," Mary said. "Mommy didn't tell Albert why she started going to the gun club."

"What upsets me most is that I didn't ask. I didn't ask myself, and I didn't ask her. For years I seem to have been a non-participant in my own family."

"You weren't paying attention to what the women around you were doing? Wakey wakey, Private Eye Guy. You're a man. You were just taking your place in a *very* long tradition."

"But she—they—have been at it, or working toward it, for years. And I never knew."

"So you know now. And, let me tell you something, pal. If you're about to embark on a self-pitying funk about things you can't change, then I'm out of here. I don't do self-pitying-funk-support anymore. Been there. Been done by that. But before I go, I do want to say thanks, what we've had has been nice."

" 'Nice?' "

"All right, 'very nice,' but that's the most you get."

"Frankly, that's not very convincing from a woman who's met a guy three nights in a row."

"You're not expecting to make that four nights in a row, I hope. It's not like I'm a kid. I've got a real life here, mister."

"I don't doubt it for a moment."

"Good."

"And we're adults, right?"

"Right."

"So we're adult about stuff. In fact I suggest we be so adult that we pick a specific place we will not be meeting at tomorrow night at, say, seven."

25

The phone woke me at the crack of dawn. What I was doing at Dawn's crack I didn't know. A guy with a new girlfriend ought to be adult enough to keep track of stuff like that, even in a dream. No matter that the new girlfriend was the kind I wouldn't be meeting at Moe & Johnny's at seven.

The phone continued to ring, seemingly oblivious to how long it had taken me to get to sleep. Felt like forever, at the time. So much to think about . . .

I finally picked up the receiver while the answering machine was playing my message. I said, "Albert Samson here. I am not a recording. Hang on."

Waiting through the message gave me time to get my brain in gear, if only first.

When the message finally beeped a man said, "This is Tom Thomas, Samson. Ames, Kent, Hardick. You called here end of last week. Spoke to our girl, Faith."

He was right. I had called Ames, Kent, Hardick. I had spoken to someone. "Yeah. I remember."

"She tells me you have your license back."

"I sure do."

"You're pumping for work, right? Any job, Faith said. No matter how small."

No doubt I said that too. "No matter how small. I have a magnifying glass."

"A creditable attitude for someone coming back into the business. And a little bird tells me you've already turned some work up."

It seemed like Tom Thomas of Ames, Kent, Hardick was building to an offer. The idea of some straightforward private eye employment was intensely attractive. Anything to dilute the weird work that I already had. Or enable me to quit it. What a pleasure it would be to throw the Perkins, Baker, Pinkus and Lestervic retainer back into Karl Benton's face.

I said, "Your little bird was right up to a point, Mr. Thomas. I have taken on some clients, but I do have room for more."

Maybe the offer wouldn't be big enough for a dramatic gesture, but if it was so big I'd be over-committed then I knew a free-lance op I could ask to take on the overspill, one I'd used before but who was another victim of my blue period. Was my blue period even bluer than Picasso's?

Tom Thomas said, "My little bird tells me you're the guy behind the Lawrence Chasson and Martin Sallaby arrests."

"Whose arrests?"

"Lawrence Chasson and Martin Sallaby."

"I've never heard those names before."

"That didn't stop you from e-mailing their photographs to the police."

"Oh, the church arsonists." He was giving me credit for that. Well, if I hadn't told Mom about Rev Battle's church she wouldn't have turned out her Posse pal, Daniel . . . "I had some involvement in that, it's true."

"Uninvolve yourself."

"What?"

"I am advising you to back off the church. It is just advice. I am not making a threat of any kind, Samson. I gave you my real name. I'm recording this conversation. Don't bother making a false accusation."

"I don't understand."

"I am giving you advice. Good advice, if you ever want work in this town."

It didn't compute. Was I still sleepy? "You want me to free my schedule so that I have time to work for you? Is that it?"

"Back off the church."

"Why is that good advice?" I asked as the dial tone came up.

I asked myself again after I'd hung up.

Then the phone rang. I picked it up. "Why?"

Miller said, "The classic conundrum of life."

"I thought you were someone else." Obviously I did. Stupid to say it. "Sorry, but I just had a call from a jackass telling me—'advising' me—not to interfere with vandals who set fire to churches."

"And do you often interfere with church-burning vandals? I hope they're over twenty-one and consent."

"It's a long story. What do you want, Jerry? Don't you know what time it is?"

"I make it . . . a quarter past eleven."

"Oh." Dawn was late today.

"Look, I'm about to go out but I have those names for you."

"Names?"

"The other guys on the list Ronnie Willigar was on. Yesterday you agreed to do some investigative work for me. And I don't care if the people bugging my phone know all about it."

Bugging his phone? Was every conversation I had recorded now? I concentrated. "Oh, yeah. Those guys. Were they broken into or not. I remember now."

"I thought we were set about this, Al. I would pay you if I could afford it. Really, I would. I hate asking for a freebie."

"No, it's OK. It's cool."

"And that other thing," he said. "You remember it?

About the young lady—who will remain nameless?"

I knew I was supposed to discover what Helene was up to, but had he asked me to do something else? About . . . What was her name? Ah, Marcella. "You mean—"

"Who will remain nameless, Al."

And then I worked it out. He meant Helene but he didn't want to say her name in case someone really was bugging his phone. "Ahh, I'm with you now, Cap'n."

"Good." Then, "Thirty-one miles last night."

"Thirty-one . . . That could encompass a lot of territory, you know. Nearly a hundred square miles."

"What the hell does that have to do with the price of co-conut shells?"

"For some reason I remembered how to calculate it. You have some names and addresses for me, I believe."

When Miller and I were done, I decided to go downstairs to confirm that Sam would be tailing Helene come six-thirty. However I had no sooner shifted myself into some clothes than the telephone rang again.

Miller calling back? I considered being cute but just said, "Samson."

"Still ain't fixed, is it?"

"Excuse me?"

"I was thinking, maybe you're hanging back because you want the name of a good sign guy. I can ask around for you."

Jimmy Wilson. The Neon Ranger. "No need, Jimmy. I've called a good sign guy."

"Hasn't done nothing for you though."

Oh, I wouldn't say that . . . "The job's in hand, trust me."

"Trust me . . . I heard a good one about that yesterday. A guy said, 'Trust me. I'm not a doctor.' "

"Yeah?"

"He's *not* a doctor, see? Get it?"

"I get it."

"Well, OK. So, how's your ma today?"

"My mother?"

"Living in the same place, like you do, you probably have breakfast together, see her all the time."

Could Wilson be one of the Posse? I'd never noticed him around the luncheonette, but that didn't seem to prove much these days. But he'd only just met Mom. Didn't he say that? "I haven't seen my mother this morning, but she had a late night last night. There was some trouble."

"She OK, ain't she?"

"She's fine, but one of her friends, Boris, he's in the hospital."

"Boris? Is he part of your ma's gang?"

Did *everybody* know what my mother was up to before I did? "Yeah," I said.

"I'm full of admiration for that ma of yours. I really am and that's no lie."

"Is that why you keep calling me, Jimmy? Because you have the hots for my mother?"

"I wouldn't say hots. That's not a nice way to talk about your own ma."

"I was talking about you, not her."

"Yeah." He laughed. "That's a good one. But I hope you're not one of them kids who can't stand it when their ma turns out to be a woman, are you? Because she's a real pistol, your ma. She is."

"She could be an automatic rifle for all I care, Jimmy. What I don't get is why you're saying this stuff to me instead of her."

"Truth?"

"If you must."

"Has she got a boyfriend? 'Cause I'd like to know that

190

before I embarrass myself. Can you tell me that? Is she spoken for?"

"I can't help you, Jimmy."

"Why not?"

"Because I don't know whether my mother has a boy-friend or not. And before you start, yeah, I'm an insensitive, unobservant oaf of a son."

I managed to shave before the phone rang again. This time it was Mary. "Hey," I said. "What's up? You changing the place we're not meeting?"

"I wondered how Boris is."

"I don't know. I haven't been downstairs yet."

"It's noon, Albert. Normal people have been up and about for hours."

"Yeah?"

"Normal people are at work by now."

"Such as yourself."

"Normal people at their normal jobs normally use morn-ings to review jobs that have been held up for some ab-normal reason."

"Are we by any chance talking about my sign?"

"What would you normally talk about with a sign-maker?"

"Make it 'Samson Investigations.' A new sign, the same size as the current one. Simple red lettering."

" 'Samson Investigations' does leave the neon door open for Sam to join the business."

"I guess it does. But she'd never want to. Would she?"

"She jumped at the job following your friend's daughter."

"True."

"Which was, let's see, my suggestion, I believe."

"Also true. You get points."

"But not enough to get you to use ransom note lettering, I guess."

"I've been so neglectful of everybody, I'm feeling pretty basic."

"I don't feel neglected, Spy Guy."

"I just hope you can say the same after you've known me for a week."

When I did arrive downstairs I stopped to look around before I marched into the luncheonette. The midday rush was well underway. Sam was at the far end of the counter taking money. Mom was not there so I watched Norman. Something I'd never really done before. And his one-armed skillet skills impressed me. The guy was good at his job. It's not that I'd thought of him as bad at it. I'd never thought about it one way or the other.

Then over his shoulder Norman gave me a look, as if he'd known all along that I was there. But he didn't say anything, or stick out his tongue, or crack wise to Sam. He just returned to his labors.

It made me think. Which I'd done a lot of in the hours before I finally slept. But none of my night-musings about Mom and her Posse had considered Norman's involvement. Now it sprang at me like a startled possum: the guy must have been a part of it all from the start. Even her first trips to the gun club were with Norman.

The Posse was conceived to harness the neighborhood's gray talent, but Norman's youth—and maybe even his motorcycle—must be useful sometimes. It was blindingly obvious—to anyone who used his eyes to see and his ears to hear.

Might the accident which cost Norman his arm have happened while he was on a Posse mission?

There was so much I didn't know.

There was so much I hadn't asked.

Norman looked at me again. This time he smiled slightly.

And I saw he knew that Mom had told me about her Posse, at last.

Why had Mom gone to the likes of Norman before she'd come to the likes of me?

Because I was not a person to depend on during my time without a license. I was a person who might go haywire.

But the gun club stuff started long before I lost my license.

Could I have been so unaware of the people around me for so long? I wanted to curl up and roll away into a shadow under the pinball machine.

"Daddy?"

Sam was at my shoulder. I never saw her coming. But I wouldn't, would I?

"What?"

"You look . . . Is something wrong?"

I studied my daughter's face. A pretty girl, my kid. An oval face with peachy skin, a few freckles, and beautiful dark brown eyes. She had elfin points at the top of her ears and ridges in her lobes. How long had her light brown hair been streaked and cut to shoulder-length?

"Daddy, you're worrying me now."

"What are you going to do with your life, Sam?"

"My life?"

"You can't muddle it away behind the counter of a luncheonette in Indianapolis. You've got so much to offer, honey. Let's make a plan."

"I've made plans, Daddy. Plenty of them."

"Tell me about them. I'll listen, I promise."

"My first plan is to follow Helene Miller tonight, but to do that I'll need the Millers' current home address."

"That's not what I meant."

"And I want expense money up front. Mary said I should ask."

"Because, if you don't get your act together, one day you'll wake up and your whole future will be behind you."

"Daddy, does this have to be now?"

"Don't aim for anything less than what you really want, Sam. You may not get it, but make sure someone else says you can't have it, not you. And there are other things . . . Like, do you want children?"

"Why, have you got one you're trying to get rid of?"

"I'm being serious. And I am listening, and thinking, and trying to understand."

"That's very cool, Daddy, so how about listening and thinking and understanding that what I seriously need right now is the Millers' address and twenty bucks, OK? Because I have three people at the cash register waiting to pay me for their lunches."

Even after Sam finished taking money, she ducked away from talking about important things. But that was OK. I understood. What's important in life can be hard to talk about, hard to share.

"Calm down, Daddy," she said at one point. "Go play the pinball machine. I bet you can break your record."

"I don't really feel like it, honey. Right now it seems like a waste of time."

"Well, isn't there some work you should be doing?"

There was. Miller's list upstairs.

But when I got to my office, the phone rang. It was Christopher P. Holloway. "I'm about to meet Karl to review the Willigar case. What have you got for us on your pal, Miller?"

"Got for you?" I'd spent time thinking about a lot of things, but my work for Karl Benton was not one of them.

"You haven't been sitting on your hands since yesterday, have you?"

"Of course not. I was just, uh, more expecting to prepare a written report rather than give a verbal one."

Quietly Holloway said, "I think we're paying you enough for both. Don't you?"

"Sure. Sure, of course. Well, I had a long talk with Captain Miller. Yesterday."

"And?"

"I was just about to head out to try to interview the other four men on the list."

"What list?"

He didn't know about the list. "Three days before Carlo Saddler called Crime Stoppers, a high-power computer place gave Miller a list of suspects. Five guys were named as ahead of the field. That list included your client."

"Our client."

"Our client. Since our defense is that the damning evidence was planted at our client's place, I want to see if the other four best-bet guys had break-ins after Miller got the list but before Willigar was arrested."

After a pause Holloway asked, "Why?"

"When the police raided Willigar, a pane of glass in his back door was broken. That's consistent with someone breaking in to plant the box."

"I didn't know about the pane of glass. It wasn't in the arrest report."

"Miller told me about it himself."

"Well, well, well."

I said, "You know about Miller's suspension, right?"

"Yes."

"And the reason for it?"

"You tell me," Holloway said.

"Miller is accused of colluding with Saddler for a share of the reward."

"Uh huh."

OK, he already knew that. "They're saying that Miller and Saddler used the list and found the evidence in Willigar's bedroom. But if we can show that only Willigar's had a break-in, we can say that the real perp had access to the list, picked a name off it, and the name happened to be Ronnie Willigar's."

Holloway thought about it. "Suppose other men on the list did have break-ins?"

"Then this line won't help us and we'll think of something else." Like that Willigar is guilty . . .

"Well, Samson, I'll pass on what you've told me to Karl."

When we hung up, I breathed more easily. He'd caught me on the hop, and I bluffed my way through. Fortunately I could tell him things he didn't know so, inadvertently, I was earning my fee. But I didn't want to be caught unprepared again.

Then, as I sat at my desk, it occurred to me to consider the possibility that Ronnie Willigar actually was innocent. I was seeing a lot of things from a fresh perspective. Why not that? To be innocent of these crimes the guy didn't have to be Snow White. Miller might have seen other guilts in his eyes.

So, suppose Willigar *was* being framed . . . Suppose somebody *did* plant the box of damning and obscene evidence in his house . . .

Cop or civilian, to have a box like that the somebody could only be the real killer. Why would the real killer give up his souvenir collection?

To incriminate someone else and take attention away from himself. But why now? After all these years? He must have been afraid he was about to be caught.

So, what made him afraid? What had changed?

The only new thing was the list. With five names at the top of it, five guys who were about to get extra scrutiny.

Was the real killer one of the five? And somehow he knew he was on the list? Wouldn't that impel him to plant the box on another of the list-guys and then arrange for the Crime Stoppers call and do it all quickly?

Miller had said it himself. "Once we had Willigar and his box, who cared about anyone else?"

I sat, unseeingly, shocked at the clarity of my logic.

If what I was supposing was true . . . If it all happened that way . . . Then a number of other things followed.

Number one, the killer was one of the four guys I now had names and addresses for.

Number two, since he knew about the list and what was on it he must—somehow—have connections at IPD.

Number three, since he'd provided the Crime Stoppers information, he knew Carlo Saddler.

Number four, Carlo Saddler knew him.

If Ronnie Willigar was innocent . . .

26

With my hypothesis in mind it no longer seemed such a bright idea to do what I'd told Holloway I was about to do. Knock on the doors of each of the four guys on the list. Not without my mother and her gun-totin' posse to back me up.

If anyone went knocking it should be the cops, but with Willigar in the bag they weren't about to.

Finding a connection between IPD and a guy on the list shouldn't be that hard, if someone at IPD would look. But who? Miller wouldn't be allowed. Proffitt? Was there any way Lieutenant Vandalism would take an interest? Powder? Such a fine collection of cops I knew these days.

Miller, however, was definitely the man to work out who could have gotten access to the list. I hit the phone. He'd told me he was about to go out, but I had his cell number.

Which did not get me through to him. It got me through to a message that said, "Say anything you don't mind the world knowing about after the tone." I considered telling him that the world, as a whole, couldn't care less about him. Instead I just asked him to call me.

It was the first time that I really wished I had a cell phone, because there was no way I wanted to sit around the office and wait for Miller's call. Two options occurred to me. One was to go out and shoot some hoops. I knew that keeping fit was a good thing. But my heart wasn't in it. I wanted something more active, more to the point. So I took the other option. I went out to see if Carlo "Chip" Saddler would talk to me.

My last encounter with Saddler had ended when Mary and I felt it prudent to leave like a rocket. How likely was it the guy would talk to me after that? Ah well. I could but ask.

When I walked into the Milwaukee, Saddler was not behind the bar. A man and a woman were. The man was the guy working with Saddler when Mary and I came in. The guy she'd spoken to first. I went to the woman.

"Get ya?" she said.

Private eyes are supposed to have snappy lines in lies that convince strangers to spill the information they're holding. My snappy line was a twenty on the bar. "I need some information."

She looked at the bill. "Oh yeah?" She was a nice looking woman in her fifties, but there was a hardness in her face that made me think she used guys like me to pick her teeth with.

"I'm a private investigator. I'm nothing to do with newspapers or TV. I think there is a chance Chip Saddler might be in serious danger. I need to talk to him but I don't have a phone number or an address."

"Chip, huh?" She pulled out a *Star* with a picture of Saddler on the steps of the courthouse. His Indians hat was slightly askew. There was a snarl on his face. "He said there'd be guys come in trying to get some of his money."

"There's been nothing in the papers to say he works here. I'm a private eye, like I said. I am not hustling for the reward money, even if he ever gets it."

She stared at me.

"Would another twenty help?"

"Yup."

I put a second twenty on top of the first.

"I don't believe you," she said, picking up the money. "But Chip's a jerk."

Karl Benton's forty bucks bought me an address and a cell phone number. I tried the cell from a pay phone. Saddler wouldn't remember my voice, surely. Especially if I raised it a little. Talked a little bit faster than usual. Tried to ingratiate myself. "Hi, Chip. *I* don't think you're a fucking retard."

I got through to a message system. I didn't want to leave a message.

So I went to the address.

What I found was a moderately run-down frame house in a moderately run-down westside neighborhood. A lot of the houses seemed to have been converted into apartments. There were several "Apt to Let" signs around. On Saddler's house there were buzzers by the front door. The place didn't look half big enough to make into four apartments, but three of the buzzers had names by them. None familiar. I pressed the fourth. I pressed it again. I pressed it a bunch of times.

Through a small pane of glass in the door I saw shadow movement. Then the door flew open and Carlo "Chip" stood before me in a vest and jeans. His face was covered with stubble. His hair was hanging loose. His eyes were puffy like he'd just woken up. "What?" he said. "What the *fuck* is all the noise?"

It took me a moment to see that he didn't recognize me. There is definitely a place in the world for unobservant men. "Mr. Saddler, I need to talk to you. I'm not after money. I'm not media. I'm a private investigator and I think you are in danger."

He squinted at me. "How did you get my address?"

"From a gal at the Milwaukee."

"What gal?"

I didn't know her name. "Mary."

He tried to compute Mary. He failed.

"I won't stay long, but I really do need to talk to you." I tried to look like I would keep ringing his doorbell until he agreed.

Maybe I succeeded. He said, "Fuck it." I followed him into his room.

He sat on the bed and shook a cigarillo from a box. I took the only chair and looked around while Saddler lit and inhaled. The room was relatively tidy. No piles of beer cans or half-eaten KFC. Nor did I see any of the paraphernalia one might expect to surround someone planning to use his reward money to further a career in music. Maybe his plan was to storm the show biz as an *a cappella* singer. Almost the only personal possessions I saw were in an open closet which was bursting with shirts and slacks and shoes.

When he was ready, Saddler said, "You said something about danger."

I said, "I think you're being set up."

He wrinkled his face. He exhaled heavily. Inhaled again. "What the fuck you talking about?"

"I have reason to believe that Ronnie Willigar did not do the bodies-in-the-trunks murders."

I gave him a moment to absorb that. He took it.

I said, "I think the real killer was the guy who gave you Willigar's name and told you about the box in the bedroom."

I definitely had Saddler's attention now. He did not contradict my assertion that someone gave him the information he'd called in.

"The guy set Willigar up to cover his own ass. He put

the box in Willigar's bedroom and then he fed you what to say to Crime Stoppers. You're the only remaining link to him. You are the only one who knows who he is. To make himself safe, he's going to have to make sure you can't talk."

I watched things well up inside Carlo "Chip" Saddler the same way they had when he was being prodded by the media people. What burst out this time was, "But I don't *know* who he is. I got a call. That's all that happened. One fucking phone call. Some guy said if I wanted to make a pile of money, I should call the number and give the name and say about the box. But I had to do it right away. He said, What did I have to lose? And I thought about it, and I figured I didn't have anything to lose. So I did it. And that's all. I don't know who the guy was. I swear."

"What about his share of the reward?"

"He didn't say dick about a share. I get the share."

"And he called on the Monday you called Crime Stoppers?"

"Maybe an hour before."

"Why did he call you?"

"I don't know. He just did."

"You didn't recognize his voice?"

"I just fucking told you that." He puffed angrily.

I said, "When you called Crime Stoppers they asked if you wanted to talk to Captain Miller."

"Man, how the fuck do you know that?"

"You sounded like you know Miller."

"Everybody in the Milwaukee knows fucking Miller. Tight-ass cop, comes in the place, big man visiting his roots. They smile to his face and drink the drinks he buys, and then they talk about his momma when he goes home."

"So the guy who called you wasn't Miller."

"I told you, I don't know who called."

"But you didn't recognize the voice as Miller's?"

"It was a voice. Who can tell?"

An aspiring musician might. "So how'd he get your number?"

"I don't know," Saddler said.

"Lot of people have it?"

"Some. A lot maybe." Then he said, "Maybe he got it the same way you got my address."

I left Saddler where he sat. I went out to do some sitting of my own.

He'd confirmed one link in my speculative chain—that someone fed him the information he called in. A someone who didn't seem to be in it for the money. That alone should be enough to exonerate Miller, once the IPD investigation got around to talking to Carlo "Chip."

But, who had made the call? Someone who knew Saddler . . . Someone who knew the box was at Willigar's on the Monday . . . Were the someone's actions triggered by the delivery of the list to IPD?

The whole thing suddenly felt scary to me. And real.

I needed to know who had access to the list. I drove to a public phone. Then I found another that worked. I called my own number to see if there were messages on the machine. None, except the one I'd recorded in the morning by not getting to the phone quickly enough, the one in which Tom Thomas tried to warn me off catching church vandals. I erased it. Then I tried Miller's cell. Got his message. So I tried Miller's home.

After several rings a woman's voice said faintly, "Hello?"

At least it wasn't Janie. "This is Albert Samson. Is that Helene?"

"Oh, hi Mr. Samson."

"I need to talk to your father about something important, Helene."

"They went to Terre Haute again. Gramma's in the hospital."

"I'm sorry to hear that." Then, "You didn't go with them, huh?"

There was a pause before she said, "No. I have things I have to do here."

Let Sam sort all that out. I said, "Well, tell your father I need to talk to him, OK?"

But when I hung up I didn't want to wait around. I really didn't.

As I drove to Leroy Powder's house I wondered if I was on a fool's errand and just the man for the job.

There was no real reason to believe Powder would listen to me, but compared to Proffitt there were fewer reasons why he wouldn't.

Of course, I had no idea whether he'd even be home.

But he was. "Powder, I've got a once-in-a-lifetime opportunity for someone to become a better cop, and I've decided to give it to you. Congratulations."

The glare he gave me would have curdled milk. Fortunately I was not lactating. "You what?"

I was about to go through it again, but he rubbed his face and said, "I was in the middle of something." He turned his back on me. And left the door open.

I followed him to his kitchen. There was string on a plate, with a fork and a spoon. "What you up to today? Practicing for spaghetti because you've got a dinner date with a Chinese girl?"

"Nope." He dropped onto the plastic chair in front of the plate. "She's Japanese." I pulled out a chair across from him but he held up a hand. "How about you tell me why you're here before you make yourself to home?" He picked up the fork.

"It's about the bodies-in-the-trunks. I'm working on whether Ronnie Willigar actually did the crimes."

Powder put the fork down again. "Don't you know what they found at Willigar's?"

"I'm examining whether that stuff was planted there."

"By who?"

"One of these guys." I showed him my list of names and addresses.

He glanced at it. "What phone book did you get this from?"

I explained where the list came from. "And there was a broken pane of glass in Willigar's back door when they arrested him."

"This is because of a broken pane of glass?"

"The guy who named Willigar to Crime Stoppers says he got the information that morning from an anonymous caller. I think it was the list coming in to IPD that pushed the real killer to set Willigar up in order to keep the police from investigating the other names."

Powder stared at me.

"If I'm right—*if*—then the guy has enough connection with IPD to find out about the list. And he has some connection with the Crime Stoppers informant."

Powder still said nothing.

"Ordinary cops," I said, "close cases when they find incontrovertible evidence connecting murders to a suspect. They drop other lines of inquiry. Miller did. But your *better* cop goes the extra mile. Your better cop says, 'Yeah, but . . .' and he keeps working until the other doors are closed too. You're much better placed than I am to check out people's connections to IPD, to find out who might know Saddler, to connect the dots to the guys on this list."

Powder held up a hand. "I get your drift, Samson." He rubbed his face. Then he fished around in his jacket for a cell phone and made a call to someone called Toki.

27

I got to Moe & Johnny's at about twenty past seven. "Let me guess," Mary said. "It wouldn't be another flat tire . . . A flat battery?"

"I know better than to think flattery will get me anywhere with you."

"You do know the only reason I'm still here, don't you?"

"Uh, because you were late too, and you wanted to find out whether I was here on time and left, or whether I'd be even later than you?"

Her face said that I'd got it exactly right. She drank from the glass of beer in front of her. "We've been together too long."

"I'm just having a good day for unexpected perceptions."

"Yeah?"

I counted them up. Norman as part of the Posse. The Ronnie-Might-Be-Innocent stuff. Figuring Powder for someone who'd pick up the gauntlet and do what I couldn't inside IPD. "Seems like. Maybe you should let me give you some Lotto numbers."

"OK. Number me."

I gave her the first set of numbers that came into my mind.

She drained her glass. "Come on, big boy. I got me a ticket to buy."

We took her car and headed north on College. They sold Lotto in a drugstore across the canal in Broad Ripple. I waited outside.

I found myself thinking about Powder. Funny guy. About a hundred years old now, but still ambitious. Not the ambition that piles up honors and cash. The ambition that wants to change things to be more like the way they ought to be. That much he shared with Mom, but Powder's fervor for policing verged on the religious. So he'd ditched Toki and the spaghetti in order to go into IPD to examine the heretical notion that Ronnie Willigar might be innocent.

Could Willigar be innocent, really? The guilty stuff was in his house. The simplest explanation was that he put it there. So he's guilty, according to Occam's Razor, the ancient precept that the simplest explanation of something is the most likely to be true.

Yet things aren't always simple. Sometimes they're not what they seem. And *if* Ronnie Willigar was one of those times . . .

In any case it was amazing that Powder was working on it. It had been an amazing day. I was having a run of amazing days.

Mary got back in the car and said, "So, Samsdad, what now? Still feeling lucky?"

"I feel lucky to know you."

"Excuse me?"

"You're an unusual and special woman."

"You're not getting any of the prize money. That may seem bitchy, but you gave me those numbers freely. I didn't twist your arm or anything and a girl doesn't get an opportunity to secure her future very often."

"I'm being serious."

"So am I."

"It's . . . I just feel really good about you."

She turned in her seat to face me. "If you don't lighten up, you'll be feeling good on your own. You're sounding like . . . Like you're about to go somewhere dangerous and you're dishing the shit in case these are your last words to me."

"I'm not going anywhere."

"Then shut up, OK?"

"It's just that today I've been understanding all these things I missed before. Seeing things I never noticed. Putting stuff together."

"Well, don't worry about it. Men get moments of lucidity, but they pass. You'll be back to seeing what you want to see and hearing what you want to hear in no time. In the nicest possible way, of course, because you're a nice guy."

I pondered that.

She sighed. "You've been to my place, right?"

"Yeah."

"There are important parts of my life that we haven't talked about yet. There are clues to some of them where I live. So tell me what you saw at my place."

I thought about where Mary lived. A frame house, three stories, 1920s, a porch wrapped around three sides. A hanging swing at the front. Not much land, no garage or driveway visible from the front. The most unusual feature was a turret that projected from the attic above the second floor. It made the house look gothic. It was an unusual place for a woman to live alone, but I did know it was the family home that she'd inherited.

Inside the front door a hallway opened to an austere living room on the right. Polished wood floors, widely spaced furniture. On the left there were double doors, but they'd been closed. I hadn't asked where they led. We'd never lingered long downstairs.

"How about photographs, Samsdad? Like by the bedside."

Her bedroom was at the top of the stairs, on the right.

There were lights by each side of the bed that came on from a switch by the door. They were not bright. I tried to visualize the bedsides. There *was* a framed picture, on the side where her things were: ashtray, glass of water, book, phone, clock. And picture frame. There were two figures in the picture. Young? Old? Male? Female? I couldn't remember enough to put together, to understand. And I had not asked.

She said, "So don't pat yourself on the back too hard about your newfound perceptivity just yet, eh? Where we eating? Someplace near, I hope."

The Midtown Grille was little more than across the street. Mary glanced through the menu before we accepted a table. "This will do nicely," she said.

"Sorry about being . . . unsettled," I said once we'd ordered drinks and food. "It's just I had trouble sleeping after the revelations of last night. And the rest."

"How is Boris?"

"I . . . I don't know. I didn't see my mother."

"Did you try to see your mother?"

My face showed that I hadn't. "It's been an odd day from the start. A phone call woke me up and—"

Her vodka tonic arrived. "Better bring me another one of these," Mary said to the waitress. "He wants to talk me through his whole day to justify why he didn't talk to his mother."

"Oh honey," the waitress said. "Let me make that a double."

Mary took out her cell phone. "What's your mother's number?" But all she got was Mom's voice mail. "What's your mother's cell number?"

"I don't know."

Mary sighed. "Sam will know. Does she have a home number?"

"Just her cell. But you might have trouble getting her, depending where Helene Miller has gone."

"Sam's out there alone and you don't know where she is?"

I frowned. "Well, sure."

"With whose number to call on her cell if she gets in trouble? Not yours, because . . ."

"I don't have one."

"Even though you have no idea where the Miller girl will lead her."

"That was the whole idea, wasn't it?"

"Even though Helene Miller was busted out of college because she was in with a drug crowd."

"Yeah, but she's passing all her drug tests."

"With whose urine?" Mary fiddled with her phone, then put it to her ear. "Hello? Sam? You all right . . . ? Yeah . . . I'm here watching your father squirm because he hasn't arranged back-up for you in case of trouble, even though last night he saw how your grandmother backs up her people . . . So where are you now? Really?" Mary turned to me. "She is outside our favorite bar, the Milwaukee."

"She's *where?*"

"Yeah, honey, we know the place. We were there only a couple of nights ago. I loved it."

Any bar was bad enough since Helene wasn't old enough to be served. But . . . Helene had connections at the Milwaukee?

Mary said, "The Miller girl parked in front of a hydrant and went in . . . While you're waiting, Sam, could you give me your grandmother's cell phone number? He doesn't have it . . . OK. OK. Thanks. Oh, wait. The Miller girl's out again . . . There's a man and a woman with her.

They're getting into the Miller girl's car . . . OK, Sam. Sure. I'll leave my phone on. You call me about where you go and what the girl is doing and for any damn reason whatever. Your father will pay your bill. And mine. Bye."

Mary did whatever one does to finish a cell phone call. "Maybe Sam borrowed a gun from her grandmother." Mary dialed another number, held the phone to her ear for what seemed a long time, then put it down. "Your mother's not answering."

The waitress brought the double vodka tonic. "We've got a little problem," Mary said.

"Honey," the waitress said, "if you want me to call you a cab, just say the word. I'll get a couple of the boys to make sure he don't follow. 'Cause once they turn bad, honey, there ain't no going back. Take it from me."

"The problem is that we're going to have to leave. Can you pack the food I ordered, maybe with a plastic fork and knife? Not the gentleman's however. He'll be driving."

28

While the food was being packed, Mary tried Mom's number again and then she called Southside Hospital. There someone confirmed that Boris was still a patient. "We're going to see him," she told me. "He might know where your mother is."

On the drive she smacked her lips a lot as she ate.

Boris was more than conscious. "I don't know why these dingbat doctors have went and kept me here," he said from inside his bandages. "Don't make no danged sense. I got hit on the head. So what. I been hit before, plenty of times. Never done me no harm."

The nurse we talked to on the way in had offered a different opinion. "Are you family?" she asked.

"We sure are," Mary said. "Poor Uncle Boris. I hope he's gonna be OK."

"We're not certain it's as straightforward as it seems. Doctor Raphael has some more tests he wants to do tomorrow and then he'll review the case. But what's already certain is that Mr. Whitely is severely concussed."

The cussed part was obvious as soon as we got to the bedside. Boris Whitely was a handful in anybody's popcorn box.

"They say I got a headache," Uncle Boris said, "but there's headaches and headaches. Who knows best how inside of my head feels, them or me? Hey babe, pass me that box of tissues. Yeah, that one. I got clobber in my throat I want to clear. The food here sucks. It really does. You a good cook, babe? You look like a good cook."

Mary passed the tissues. Uncle Boris took three, put them to his mouth, and practiced his death rattle. "That's better. Yeah." He leaned back on his pillow. "Hey, you're a cute one, babe. I see from present company you got a thing for older men. How about you make some time for me, eh? I own my own house and I got a heart condition. What do you say?"

For once, just for a moment, Mary seemed at a loss for words. I said, "We're here to find out if you know where my mother might be, Mr. Whitely."

"Not with your father I bet. Heh heh heh heh. But do you mind? I was having a conversation with the young lady."

"Yeah," Mary said. "D'you mind? A house, you say?"

"I figure I can get myself sprung tomorrow for sure. What about tomorrow night? You like line dancing?"

"About my mother," I said. "Posy Samson . . . ?"

Boris stopped in mid-come-on. "You're . . . Posy's boy?"

"Yes."

"Little Albert, what lives at home with her?"

"She's not answering her phones."

"That's because she's on surveillance, boy. We don't talk to civilians when we're on duty."

"On surveillance where you were attacked yesterday?"

"Somewheres out there. Can't sit by just cause one of your troops goes down. Not with a new outbreak of vandalism."

"That's the spread to the west side of Virginia Avenue?"

"You got it, Little Albert. Till last week the scum stayed east of Virginia. East and north. 'Course what's also new is banging folks on their heads. Wouldn't of happened if I seen there was two of them, but I only saw the one busting up some car windows, and I figured he was on his own. But then his pal come up and held me for the first one to bang me around. Didn't just knock me out of the way and run for it, no no. That would be too easy. Like I told the cop that came here to talk to me, soon as I get out of here I'll be looking for those two misfits. I got me a score to settle. But it's OK, babe," he said to Mary. "I can still handle a social life. Pass me that tissue box again, will you? I feel another gob coming up."

We spent another ten minutes with the patient. It felt like an hour. As Mary and I walked down the hospital corridor, I said, "My mother is out patrolling where a guy got smashed on the head last night. And she's not answering her phone."

"You don't buy that they only take calls from each other when they're on patrol?"

"It's possible."

"If I was saving the world, or one of its neighborhoods, I wouldn't want to stop what I was doing because a friend with a phone decided to call me for a gossip."

"Sure, I get that."

"On the other hand, your mother could be lying in a pool of blood even as we speak."

"Thanks for that image."

"Or standing over the corpses of a dozen bad guys she's just gunned down."

"Her gun only fires six shots."

"So, what you want to do, Samsdad?"

"I want to go to where the trouble was last night."

"Because . . . ?"

"I've been a shit son for so long."

"That you're willing to be a shit boyfriend . . ."

I knew she was making a point, but I faced her with another. "Is that what I am now? Your boyfriend?"

"Four nights in a row? I hate to be the one to break it to you, Little Albert, but we're engaged."

"Oh."

" 'Oh'?"

"Cool."

"Whew. For a moment there I thought you were losing your enthusiasm."

"So what do you want to do? Drop me off west of Virginia Ave?"

"And miss the chance to spend another evening walking in dark alleys?"

"I can take a taxi from here."

"You don't get rid of a fiancée that easy, Little Albert. And while you drive I'll find out what Sam's up to."

Mary's end of the conversation with my daughter was not overwhelmingly informative. "Yeah . . . Uh huh . . . Really? What are they doing? . . . Yeah? . . . Yeah. Uh huh . . . So are you going in? . . . No, I can see that . . . Uh huh . . . Uh huh . . . OK. Sure . . . Yeah. Bye."

"Was her end of that as fascinating as yours?" I asked.

Mary, however, was silent for a time.

"What?"

"Something Boris said."

"What?"

"Why *do* you live with your mother at your age, Albert? Because it's not entirely normal, is it? Have you been there ever since your marriage broke up?"

"I'm only there while the builders finish my palace."

"Oh."

"What's up with my daughter, Mary?"

"Helene and her friends are at a place called Sunshine Bridge. Do you know it?"

"No."

"Neither do I. But she says it's somewhere way the hell out on the northeast side and that it's a retirement home."

"A *what?*"

"Helene Miller and her two friends have gone to a retirement home."

"To do what? Strip the place of its plaster do-dads and moth-eaten sweaters?"

"She could be there because she wants to help members of the senior community."

"Did they actually go inside this retirement home?"

"About ten minutes ago. Sam doesn't think she can follow without risking that the Miller girl would see her."

"But what the hell are they doing in . . . ?"

"The Sunshine Bridge Retirement Community. Could the Miller girl have a relative there?"

"There's a sick grandmother in Terre Haute, and Jerry's parents are both dead. I don't know about the other grandfather."

"An aunt? An uncle?"

"Could be, but I haven't heard new information about other members of the Miller family for years. Family was never top of our agenda, even in high school."

"Honestly, men."

"Hiding from family stuff, including siblings, was one of the things we shared in those days."

"You have siblings?"

"In theory, if not in practice. Don't you remember the picture by my bedside?"

"You don't have a picture by your bedside," she said. "But I always figured you for an only child. Living at home at your age and all."

29

We parked near the big willow that had been Boris's lookout post. For a couple of minutes we sat in the car just looking around for whatever there was to see.

The time was only a few minutes earlier than when we'd trailed behind Mom the night before. As then, the neighborhood was quiet. A few lights. A stray dog. A van passing through. Not much going on. An urban residential area at rest.

"What now?" Mary said.

"We get out and check under the tree. Then we walk around, sticking to the shadows. Being two of us, we take shapes like we're talking to each other."

"What does *that* mean?"

"It means that if we're looking up and down a street, you look one way over my shoulder, and I look the other way over your shoulder. To a casual observer we're a couple out for a walk and a talk rather than a pair of highly trained investigators."

"Cool. I'll even hold your hand, as long as you remember that it's just business."

We got out of the car. We went beneath the willow. I looked for signs that someone—Mom, say—had spent recent time here. However the willow leaves blocked the streetlight so effectively I wouldn't have seen anything darker than a lighted cigarette.

Mary lit a cigarette. Her lighter showed up nothing on the ground. Quietly I said, "Let's start where Uncle had his little accident." Mary took my hand. We headed out, and crossed the street unhurriedly.

Boris had interrupted a guy who was breaking the windows of a car. We found glass chips in the gutter and for a minute we stood looking over each other's shoulder. There wasn't much to be seen.

"It would be nice to know if last night it was kids, or whether they were older," I said. "And what the police attitude is. I wish now I'd talked to my mother."

"You didn't know you'd be out tonight playing Posse."

"At the hospital Mom did say that there have been these acts of mindless vandalism for months now."

"All cars?" Mary asked.

"Cars, house windows, pets killed. Ugly things."

"But *why?* What's up with that?"

"I . . ." I was about to say that I didn't have any idea, but then I wondered. Could it . . . ? Was it possible . . . ?

"What?"

"If this was going on in your neighborhood, how would you feel about it?"

"Well, I'd hate it."

"Mmmm."

"What do we do now, Samsdad?"

"I think we should walk back up the alley we came down last night."

"Because . . . ?"

"It's the area where Boris and Fontaine were on duty last night."

"OK."

We headed for the mouth of the alley. "Would you hate it all enough to want to move out?"

Mary said, "Do you think that's what it's about? Someone trying to get people to move?"

"Or drive prices down, or . . . I don't know. But what I'm thinking, if random acts happen too often, they stop being random. If mindless things happen a lot, maybe there's a mind behind them. If what happens seems to have no pattern, then maybe the lack of pattern is what it's about."

"I am, like, *so* horny now."

"Yeah, yeah. And, yes, it could just be kids who've run amok. But I'm having a put-it-together day, and my feeling is that it's about making people less happy to live in the neighborhood." I stopped. I'd just remembered the call from Tom Thomas trying to back me off catching church vandals.

"Albert?"

"I had a weird call this morning. Maybe that fits too." I began to walk again. "It doesn't have to be about trying to make people sell up. Maybe it's just making the community less likely to oppose development because the area's going downhill and needs some kind of change."

We said nothing more until we reached the alley. "It looks dark down there," Mary said.

I led her to the closest deep shadow. I put my arms around her waist. "You are an unusual and special woman . . . I'm lucky to have found you."

"What?"

"As it happens, I am about to go somewhere dangerous and—"

"Fuck off."

I led. We weren't as meticulous as my mother had been, but we did use the shadows and we did not move quickly.

Somewhere ahead I heard something—a thuddy bang. It was not loud. I stopped us. We listened. It happened again. "What's that?" Mary whispered.

"Dunno." It didn't sound threatening, but . . .

I began to move forward again, but there was more thudding and she tugged my arm. "Are you sure this is what we should be doing?"

"What option do we have? The police aren't going to be interested if we call in a report of strange sounds in a spooky alley. Sure, I'd call in the Posse if I knew how, but I don't."

"We don't have to *do* anything."

I thought about that. Do nothing . . . It seemed to summarize my months, my years, of not reacting to what was going on around me.

I said, "I don't want to ignore it. Why don't you stay here?"

"Alone? Not in this lifetime."

We moved forward. The thudding repeated and began to sound like somebody hitting something with a big stick. It stopped. It started again.

Then glass shattered and there was a high-pitched shout and there was different thudding and somebody moaned.

I ran ahead into the darkness. I passed one garage, and another, and then I saw a candle, flickering in the back window of a house. Something blotted out the candle for a second. Someone was in the yard.

I turned toward the candle, but after only a couple of steps my right leg crashed into something hard and immovable. I lost balance, spun around, and fell on my back.

From the alleyway behind me Mary called, "Albert?"

The ground was the last place I wanted to be. I twisted to get up and I smacked my head on the corner of something hard. I fell back again.

With one hand on my head and the other on the ground I tried to get my bearings and turn—more carefully this time—in the direction of the candle. I got to my knees, wondering if there was enough clear space above me to stand up. I moved the hand from my head and stretched it upwards.

Then I heard running footsteps. They came my way. They were fast steps. They were thundering hooves. A hoof crushed my right hand.

I felt fingers snap.

I cried out. There were shouts. There was a roar. Near me a motor started. Lights exploded on. There was a motorcycle. It was the immovable thing I'd run into.

A figure was on the bike. A second figure passed inches from me and jumped on the back. A spinning wheel kicked stones into my face. The headlights caught Mary's startled face.

The bike screamed into movement. It ran her down.

30

"Mary?" I scrambled to where the headlights had frozen her. "Mary?" She wasn't there anymore. "Mary? Mary?"

In the distance a roaring red tail light left the alley. Surely she couldn't have been carried on the motorcycle's horns. "Mary?"

I was desperate for some light. All I could see in the darkness was the image of Mary's face, caught by surprise. She'd followed me. Coming to help. "Mary?"

I heard a telephone ring.

It was a cell phone. The tune was "Don't Be Cruel." "Mary?"

I followed the sound and found her at last. She was crumpled against the garage I passed before turning into the candle yard. I threw myself down beside her. "Mary?"

Faintly she said, "Hi, Samsdad."

"Are . . . are you all right?"

"I . . . don't know."

"Do you hurt?"

"I . . . Not really. It knocked me down . . ."

"As long as it wasn't out." With my good hand I touched her face. I touched her shoulders.

"Not without a condom," she said.

"I was afraid . . ."

"Do me a favor?"

"Anything."

"Answer the damn phone?"

It was glowing on the ground beside her. I pushed buttons and put it to my ear. "Hello?"

"Answering each other's phones now, eh?" Sam said. "*Very* intimate."

"This is not the best time. Are you all right?"

"I just called to update you. Helene Miller and her two friends are still inside this Sunshine Bridge place. Boring isn't the word."

"So you're OK?"

"Of course I'm OK. What else should I be? Well, I'll let you get back to whatever you were doing. Give my love to step-mommy. Bye-ee."

I pushed some buttons, but couldn't make the phone's light go out. "Mary, how do you . . . ?" Then I saw that her head had dropped. "Mary?"

"Just resting. But . . ."

"But what?"

"I don't feel so good."

A sheet of panic enveloped me. I wanted to speak, to help, to do what was right. But I was as frozen as she'd been in the headlight.

"Albert?"

And then I was all right again. I said, "I'll go get the car but first I need you to show me that you can move your arms and legs and stuff."

She said nothing.

"Mary?"

"Don't like your women passive, huh?"

"If something's happened to your back or neck then moving you could—"

"I know, I know. Just joshing." Then, "There."

"There what?"

"I'm moving my feet."

I reached to where I figured her feet ought to be. I

couldn't find them. "Where . . . ?" Then one hit my right hand. "Ow!"

"What?"

"You just don't know your own strength. Now, move your hands."

"You want cartwheels? Get the car, please, Albert."

I wasn't certain I should give up on proof she could move her arms.

"Please, Albert, get the fucking car."

31

At the Southside ER I grabbed the first porter I saw to get him to bring a gurney out to the car. He recognized me. "You again, man?"

I recognized him. "You did so well last night, I thought I'd bring you another emergency."

"I see somebody smacked your head."

"It's not me. There's a woman in my car who was run down by a motorcycle."

"Keeps you from getting in a rut, I guess."

"Could you step on it, please?"

"If I step on it, brother, I'm not going to be able to push it, now am I?"

"She's in a bad way."

"I didn't figure you brought her here to party."

I tried desperately to think of something that would get him to hurry up. But finally he was beside the car. "She awake?" he asked me. "You awake, sweetie? Can you tell me your name?"

"Sweetie," Mary said.

"Hey, I guessed right. It's a gift. OK, Sweetie, I'm going to lift you out. I'll be as careful as I can, but we need to get you up on this gurney, OK?" He lifted her out. "That wasn't so bad, now was it?"

"I've had more fun at the dentist."

"Careful, Sweetie, you going to hurt my feelings. Now we're going inside. May be a bump or two, but I need you to keep talking to me. I need to know you ain't lost consciousness. Got it?"

"Sweetie Pie," Mary said.

"What's that?" The guy began to roll.

"That's my whole name. Sweetie Pie."

"That's great, Ms. Pie. Let's keep hearing from you."

Once Mary was on a bed in a curtained cubicle, I went to the desk to give them what information I could. I knew where she lived, what her phone number was, and her last name. But not her birth date, or insurance details or whether she was allergic to penicillin, or who her next of kin were. "I've only known her a few days. Sorry."

The receptionist was pale with a long neck and no smile. She hailed a passing nurse. "Cubicle four, Howard." She passed Howard a clipboard.

"Meanwhile," I said, "I need some treatment of my own."

"Oh yes?" She squinted. "Your head doesn't look that bad to me."

I showed her my right hand. It was swollen and purple. Not a pretty sight.

She frowned. "You didn't beat up that woman you brought in, did you?"

I did better providing my own details for the receptionist with the smilectomy.

"Sit over there, Mr. Samson. We'll call you when a doctor's available."

"Can't I wait where my friend is?"

"This is a hospital, not a dating agency. Take a seat, please."

I moved away from the desk. I wanted to be with Mary but my hand did not look good. Neither did the odd angle of my little finger. And it throbbed. While I stood looking at it, the throbbing got worse. My hand felt like the thudding in the alley had sounded.

The thudding . . . The *moan* . . .

I suddenly remembered that I'd heard a moan when I was in the alley listening to the thudding. It was a clear sound in my memory.

And . . . I must be the only person besides Mary who knew about the moan. Had the guys who ran Mary down injured somebody else?

It couldn't be my mother, could it?

I made my way to cubicle four as fast as I could. An ER doctor was saying, "Tell me if this hurts. Or this. Or this."

"Do I get a discount for all three?" Mary said.

"Excuse me," I said.

"Please go away, Mr. Pie," the doctor said. "I'm examining your wife now, as you can see perfectly well. Wait outside. I'll be with you as soon as I can."

"Mary, I'm sorry, but I have to leave."

"Albert?"

"I think . . . Someone might be lying injured in the yard where the motorcycle was. I have to go back and see."

She said nothing.

"Mary, did you hear me? Do you understand?"

"Don't think less of my husband because he's leaving me here all alone, doctor," Mary said. "He's squeamish. He can't cope with anything medical."

"I'll be back as soon as I can," I said.

"Mary?" the doctor said as I left. "I thought your name was Sweetie. Have I got the right patient?"

32

The closer I got to Virginia Avenue and the alley, the more I feared that a life was in my hands. Or that a life had slipped through my hands. Not a very secure place at the moment, my hands.

There was no reason to think it was my mother. She was out somewhere, that's all. I refused to think it might be her.

Instead I worried that I should have called the police from the hospital rather than come back myself. But would it have saved time to try to explain why I thought there might be an injured person? Or to try to explain where this injured person might be? Or this body. Much quicker to check it out myself.

The weight of my unasked-for but unavoidable responsibility made my head hurt. Or was it just because I'd banged my head on something?

I parked near the end of the alley. It crossed my mind that Mary might have a flashlight in her car. But where would she keep it?

I looked in the glove compartment. No joy. I found the release latch for the trunk. Walking to the back of the car, I startled myself by wondering if I was going to find a body in the trunk.

Stupid thought.

There was no body, but there was a flashlight. Its light was dim but it was light. Tell Mary to change the batteries.

Mary . . . She would be all right, wouldn't she?

I didn't want to think about that either. I tried to concentrate on the dark alley I was about to enter.

The flashlight wasn't the long kind you could hit baseballs with, but it was blunt and heavy enough to be a weapon if I needed one.

A weapon against who?

My hand hurt.

Fuck it. I foreswore the shadows and went down the middle at a quick walk.

I'd thought it would be easy to go straight to where it had all happened, but the deeper in I got the less sure I became. I found myself looking for the candle. And then I saw it, still flickering in the window. A symbol of life?

There were so many imponderables. The person who moaned might not have been badly injured. Maybe he or she returned to the house and called for whatever help was needed.

The moan I heard might even have come from one of the evil bastards who ran Mary down. In which case there would be no one lying injured in the yard at all.

But I didn't believe any of those scenarios. I felt in my heart that someone was there, hurt. That someone needed to be found, by me.

I turned the corner of the garage. Carefully I made my way toward the house, sweeping the yard with the dim light.

When I was about three quarters of the way to the candle, I saw him. Or her. What I saw was a pair of feet sticking into the grass, toes down. The feet were attached to legs. But the legs disappeared under a bush. It was as if someone had crawled there and then stopped.

"Hello?" I said. "Hello?"

Nothing.

Using the flashlight, I pushed branches aside. Not far up the legs I discovered a skirt. *Please,* not my mother.

I lunged at the bush and tore the rest of the branches aside to reveal the rest of the skirt, a back, and then a head that was twisted away from me. The hair was gray and it was matted by something dark. I couldn't see the face.

"Be breathing," I said aloud. "Please be breathing." But I was breathing so hard myself I couldn't hear. I needed to get closer to her mouth and nose, but the positioning was awkward.

Using my left hand, my right elbow, and my bulk, I maneuvered to get my ear near the woman's head. It felt like it took me forever but it couldn't have been more than a few seconds.

I thought I heard something. Could she be breathing and alive after all? I strained to hear.

And then I was flooded with light.

I jerked up. I lost balance. Desperate not to fall on the injured woman I pushed against some branches with my right hand. That hurt like hell, but I did roll backwards and onto the ground. It left me looking into what seemed like the sun. A man said, "Gotcha!"

I said, "This woman—"

"Don't you move a muscle, now. Not a single muscle, cause that's all it's gonna take for me to pull this trigger on you."

"She's hurt."

"And I can see who hurt her."

"I did not—"

"Shut up, hear me? You just drop that flashlight and back off her. Hit her again and you're a dead man."

"I didn't hit her."

"And I'm the Pope. Didn't I see you hit her?"

"No, you didn't."

"Or about to."

231

"I came here to help her."

"Sure you did. Help her meet her maker. I may be old now, young fella, but I've never been stupid."

I lifted my hands slowly where I was sure he could see them. "Mister, call an ambulance now." Then, I realized . . . This guy must be one of *them*. "I think it might be Posy."

"What would you be knowing about Posy?" he said.

I was about to tell him when a telephone started to ring. A Posse pal calling him to check in? "Are you going to answer that?" I said.

Then I realized that the tune was, "Don't Be Cruel." Mary's phone was in my jacket pocket. Without thinking, I reached in with my right hand. "Ow! Fuck! Shit!" I cradled my right hand with my left. The phone continued to ring. Finally I got it out and fiddled with its buttons.

If I'd been the old guy I probably would have shot me. Fortunately I'd said the magic word—my mother's name. "Hello?"

"Hi Daddy. Finished with what you and Mary were up to when I called before?"

"Sam, this is not a good time."

"Daddy . . . ?"

"There's an injured woman here who I think . . ." But I didn't want to tell her what I thought. "I need to call an ambulance."

"Are *you* all right?"

"Yes. Well, no. But it's not important."

"Is Mary all right?"

"Yes. Well, not exactly. She's in Southside."

"Is that where you are?"

"I'm in some bushes and one of your grandmother's Posse guys is pointing a gun at me."

"Daddy!"

232

"You're OK, aren't you, Sam?"

"Yeah. Just bored."

"I'll call you back when I get a chance." I wasn't sure how to hang up, but I pushed buttons until the phone beeped and flashed.

From behind the old guy's flashlight I heard movement. I said to him, "Look, pal, if you have a phone, call an ambulance, will you?"

There was no response.

"Call a fucking ambulance," I shouted.

"Albert?"

A new voice. Female. Authoritative. "Mom?"

33

I told my mother I was going to leave.

"No," she said. "It's a murder. You need to tell the police what you heard and what you saw."

"I told you. You tell them. If I remember anything else, I'll call you." I showed her Mary's phone.

"What's wrong with your hand, son?"

My right hand now looked like a balloon animal. "It got stepped on."

"The paramedics can take a look when they get here."

"I'm going to Southside."

"I'm sure your new friend is in capable hands there."

" 'Hands' is a bad joke just now, Mom."

"I wasn't—"

"I know. I know. But Southside is where I'll be if the cops need anything else from me."

"If you insist on leaving . . ."

"I do."

"Then first try again to remember a license number for the motorcycle."

I visualized the moment the bike leapt into life and its lights came on. All I saw was Mary's startled face. Mary, who was only there because of me. "Nothing, sorry."

I walked down the alley. In the distance I heard a siren.

The Southside receptionist saw me before I saw her. Maybe long necks are good for that. "Back again?" she said.

"The woman I brought in earlier . . ."

She saw my hand. "Ooo, that looks painful."

"The woman . . ."

"I think they're just finishing with her. I'll see what I can find out, and I'll get a doctor to look at your hand. Take a seat and I'll call you."

I didn't take a seat. I walked to the cubicle four. Instead of Mary I found a nurse putting stitches in a teenager's cheek. "What?" the nurse said without looking up.

"The woman in here before. Hit by a motorcycle. Where is she?"

"I don't have the slightest idea." The teenager made sounds of pain. "Well, if you're going to move your head around, what do you expect?" the nurse told him.

Outside the cubicle I looked each way along the corridor, unsure where to go next. I had about resigned myself to going back to the receptionist when a door opened up the hallway and a nurse backed out pulling a wheelchair with a patient in a neck brace. I headed for them.

As I approached, the nurse turned the chair my way. Her patient was Mary. I ran to the chair and knelt.

"See that, Dorinda? It's the effect I have on all the men," Mary said.

"Lucky you," the nurse said.

I said, "Are . . . are . . . are . . . ?"

"In my presence no man can utter a coherent sentence," Mary said. "It seems neat, I know, but, honestly, it's a curse. Imagine trying to hold a conversation."

"Mary, are you . . . Are you all right?"

"Ready to rumba."

"What?"

"Oh, get it together, Albert. I have a bunch of cuts and bruises but the worst is whiplash."

Without meaning to, I looked at the chair.

"Oh, and I'll never walk again. So I'm your responsibility now, darling. I'll move my stuff in tomorrow."

My jaw must have dropped.

"Close your mouth, Samsdad. Just a haha."

I stood up. "Ha ha."

Frowning, Dorinda said, "Sir, if you don't mind my asking, does your hand usually look like that?"

While a guy who looked like a wrestler splinted my broken fingers, I went through what happened at the candle house.

"And this woman was dead?" Mary said.

"Mom said so. I guess that stuff is something else she's learned about. And the woman was a friend of hers."

"Oh dear." Mary looked thoughtful.

"Ow!"

"What?" Mary said.

"Not you. The Hulk on my hand."

"Did I hurt you, sir?" the wrestler asked.

"Yeah."

"What did I do? Was it like . . . that?"

It was exactly like that. "I just discovered the body of a murdered woman, but you're doing a good job of taking my mind off it."

"We aim to please."

Mary said, "This woman . . . Do you know when she died?"

"As in whether she'd still be alive if I'd remembered her sooner?"

"Well . . ."

"I don't know." I thought about how she looked when Mom examined her. "I have to say, her head looked pretty battered."

The Hulk stopped what he was doing. "You mean that murder stuff was on the level?"

"It doesn't matter now, Albert," Mary said. "What's done is done."

"Yeah," I said to her. "Yeah," I said to him.

"What are you going to do when the kind man is finished working on your hand?" Mary asked.

"I . . ." I'd been about to say that I wanted to go home, but I had a feeling that there was something I should be putting together. What was it?

"Albert?"

I couldn't work it out.

"We get murdered people in here sometimes," the Hulk said. "But there's not much we can do for them."

"Are you finished?" I asked.

"Just about, but remember, when the swelling goes down you'll have to have these re-bandaged."

To Mary I said, "Let's go home."

"What about talking to the police?"

"I'll call Mom and ask her to tell the cops where we'll be. I think I have your phone in a pocket somewhere."

She patted my pockets and found her phone, but when she began to push buttons the Hulk had conniptions. "You can't use that in here. There are rules. There are signs."

"How about cutting us some slack?" Mary said. She pointed to her neck brace and then to my bandaged hand.

"You'll find all the slack you need outside the front entrance."

"Fascist. Come on, Albert."

When we were well on our way to the outside door and the Free World, I said, "It was a nice try. I'm proud of you."

However, Mary's response was drowned by Sam's

shouting. "*There* you are. I've been looking everywhere." She jogged toward us down the corridor.

Together we followed signs that promised a cafeteria. However because of the time of night the only food on offer was from vending machines. I didn't mind. Even mechanical hot chocolate comforted me.

"You guys have been in the wars, huh?" Sam said as she unwrapped a Twinkie.

"I always wondered who eats Twinkies," Mary said.

"You can't get them in France, you know."

"What barbarians."

I sipped.

Sam said, "Daddy said on the phone that you were in here. I was going to come straight over but, naturally, that was the exact moment Helene Miller and her buds chose to come out."

"We were fine," I said. "I told you."

"That is *not* what you told me."

Mary said, "So did you stick with the Miller girl?"

"She headed back to town anyway. I stayed with them until she dropped her friends off at Illinois and 38th Street. She headed west then and I let her go because that's the direction of her parents' house. But it will all be in my report."

I sipped.

Mary said, "Do you know yet what she was doing at a retirement home?"

Sam shook her head. "But I could go out there tomorrow during the day and ask. If Daddy will authorize the expense."

"He'll authorize the expense. Won't you, Albert?"

"Sure," I said.

"He'll do anything I say because of this." Mary fingered the collar. "It's all his fault, so he kneels at my feet . . ."

Sam looked from one of us to the other. "Am I looking at the product of a kinky date gone wrong?"

"No," I said.

"Not Mr. Whip," Mary said. "Mr. Whiplash."

"A guy stepped on my hand on the way to his motorcycle."

"Just after he and his pal murdered a woman."

"And before they ran Mary down."

"More knocked me aside, really."

"Wait, wait," Sam said. "A murder? Really?"

"Really."

"How awful. Who did they kill? Do you know?"

"It all happened at a house that backs on the alley we followed your grandmother down last night," Mary said.

I said, "Mom says her name was Rochelle Vincent."

"Rochelle Vincent?" Sam said. "Oh no. Not Rochelle." She shook her head. "I only saw her a week ago."

"Did you know her well?" Mary asked.

"No, but Grandma talked to all the people she knew west of Virginia Avenue when the vandalism began to happen over there and I went along sometimes."

"How . . ." I was going to ask how long it had been since the first incident west of Virginia Avenue, but I stopped. I'd had an idea. An insight.

"Daddy?"

"Albert?"

34

I called Mom on Mary's phone before we set off. "Where are you?" she asked.

"In Mary's car, about to leave the hospital."

"Stay there, son. The police want to talk to you."

"They can talk to me at home. Is that where you are?"

"Yes, but . . ."

"Could you call them? Let them know I'll be there in a few minutes?"

"I guess so. Son, do you know where Sam is?"

"Right behind us."

"And she's all right?"

"Of course she is. What else?"

"On a night like this, one is afraid to ask."

"Was Rochelle a good friend of yours?"

"A good friend and an old friend. I've known her for more years than I can remember."

"I am sorry about what happened to her."

"This business . . . What's been going on around here . . . It has got to stop."

"Will you be up when we get back? There are one or two things I'd like to talk to you about."

"I may never sleep again."

The emotional impact of the murder, catching up with her. "Could . . . Is Norman around?"

"He's a good boy, Albert. His heart is in the right place."

"I just thought he might keep you company."

When I'd hung up, Mary asked, "Is your mother all right?"

"Not really."

"What—" she began, but the opening notes of "Don't Be Cruel" interrupted her. "Get that, will you?" she said instead.

My daughter was not pleased with me. "Why are you letting Mary drive? She's wearing a neck brace. She has whiplash, for crying out loud."

"She's driving because it's her car, and also because she said she wanted to. I think she's one of these modren women what likes to be in charge of its own destiny."

"Or," Mary said, "I was stupid enough to think you might be grateful to be driven, what with your broken fingers."

"However," I said to Sam, "it's more likely that Mary is a nurturing, caring woman who took on the driving because of my broken fingers. But as a nurturing, caring father I'm going to hang up on you now because you shouldn't be talking and driving at the same time."

After another silence Mary said, "What is it you want to talk to your mother about?"

"Just a couple of questions, about her friend. No big."

"Did you just say, 'No big'?"

"Although it just might turn out to be a big."

"What *are* you talking about?"

"Nothing."

"Then could we not talk?"

"It's just that, given the kind of day I've had, all the fresh perspectives and new understandings, who knows."

"Let me concentrate on my driving, OK?"

"See, it struck me there was something else, something that might not be what it seemed to be. And then—"

Mary began to sing. "Not listening. No-ot listen-i-i-i-ing. Listening, I am not."

But I was. Mary's voice was lovely, low and rich. Even the few nonsense phrases reeked of quality and character. "You sing," I said.

"Not anymore. These days I smoke instead."

"That opera singer stuff was real?"

"Hush now, Little Albert, eh?"

I hushed. I had much to learn about this woman.

Mom was in my office when we arrived, but she was not alone. "Albert, this—"

"I know who this is."

Sitting on the corner of my desk was Homer Proffitt. "I oughta be arresting you, Albert, for leaving the scene of a crime, but your mom here says you suffered some kind of serious injury." He rose as if to look at my hand. "That's it, huh?" He turned to Mary. "Miss, you would be?"

"Rich but not famous."

Mom said, "This is Albert's friend, Mary. Mary, this is Lieutenant Proffitt."

"Hi, Lieutenant."

"I hope that neck brace isn't indicative of a serious injury, ma'am."

I said, "Rochelle Vincent's murderers ran Mary down with their motorcycle as they made their getaway."

"It's just whiplash," Mary said.

"Oh, don't say 'just' whiplash," Proffitt said. "Why, one time an armed robber I was chasing turned around and crashed head-on into my car. At first I thought I was lucky to walk away from it, but my neck still wasn't right after a whole year."

"Go on. Cheer me up."

And at that point Sam came in. "Oh, hi, Lieutenant Proffitt. Are you working on Mrs. Vincent's murder?"

"I am, and now that I've tracked down your dad and his friend I can get their statements and we can get on with finding the killers."

"You always knew where we were, Proffitt," I said. "I kept Mom up-to-date each time we went somewhere."

"And now you're here." He opened a notebook, though he wasn't reading from it when he said, "I understand from your mother that you're the one who discovered the body."

"That's right."

"Well, we need to go through all that." He looked around the room. "Alone, please, folks."

Mom said, "The girls and I will leave you to it, Lieutenant."

"Mary," Proffitt said, "please don't go far. After I'm done with Albert, I'll need to speak with you."

"Just whistle," Mary said.

The sudden image of Proffitt alone in a room with Mary made my stomach turn. I said, "I don't think Mary's up to being interviewed." The way I said it made everybody look at me. "What? She's been through a lot."

"Albert, it's a *murder*," Mom said.

"Mary?" Proffitt said.

"I'm fine. Nothing that a chair and a glass of water won't fix."

"Come on, girls," Mom said.

So it was me and Proffitt. I didn't like that a whole lot either. Still . . .

I sat at my desk. He pulled up my Client's Chair and flipped his notebook to a new page. "I gather you discovered Mrs. Vincent's body the second time you were at her house tonight. Is that right? The second time?"

That's not where I figured the story began, but it was up to him to ask what he wanted to know. "Yes."

"How long after the first time was it when you decided to return?"

"I don't know how long by the clock. After the motorcycle ran Mary down, I drove her to the hospital. When I was sure she was being taken care of, I went back to Mrs. Vincent's. That was before I had my hand looked at, by the way."

"I'd agree that a dying woman is more important that a sore hand . . . But tell me, Albert, why didn't you stay at the house in the first place and call for an ambulance?"

"I figured Mary would get treated faster if I took her myself."

"What about Mrs. Vincent?"

"I didn't know she was there."

"You sure about that?"

"Of course I'm sure."

"Because if you didn't know Mrs. Vincent was there, how come you went back?"

It was a perfectly reasonable question.

"Well?" Proffitt said.

"At the hospital, I half-remembered having heard somebody moan behind Mrs. Vincent's."

"You half-remembered?"

"Yes."

"And that's why you went to the house the second time?"

"Yes."

He wrote in his notebook, then asked, "How well did you know Rochelle Vincent?"

"Not at all."

"You didn't, say, half-know her?"

"What the hell kind of question is that?"

"One that tries to address why you went to her house in the first place if you didn't know her at all."

"I didn't set out to go to her house specifically. Mary and I were walking in the alley and we heard sounds. Bangs and thuds, aggressive stuff. That's what drew us to her backyard."

"Mary's your current girlfriend?"

"Yeah."

"And the two of you were out for a walk, in an alley?"

"I recommend it. Maybe you should take your wife to an alley sometime, Homer. You might find she enjoys it, if I remember correctly."

With passion I hadn't seen coming, Proffitt said, "A woman was murdered tonight and you screw around. I'm trying to give you the benefit of the doubt here, Albert, but you make it hard. All that matters right now is finding these killers. Any kind of history we have with each other doesn't matter a damn."

He was right. But the closest I could bring myself to saying I was sorry was, "Yeah. OK."

"The only reason I didn't cuff you when you walked in and take you downtown is that your mother is such a fine lady and she's real upset about her friend. But leaving the scene of a murder is something we take very seriously, believe me."

"Everything I did tonight was for a good reason."

"So tell me the good reason you and your girlfriend were walking in that particular alley tonight."

I took a deep breath. "Do you know about the man who was attacked a block or two from Mrs. Vincent's last night?"

He tilted his head. "Go on."

"Boris Whitely. He was walking down the street and he happened to see a guy breaking the windows in parked cars. Boris stepped up to stop it, but the guy had a friend. Instead of running away, the two of them made a point of beating Boris senseless. Boris is in Southside, with a bad concussion. Maybe worse. He told me there'd been an officer out there to take his statement."

Proffitt said, "I read the report. Albert, are you saying that because two guys attacked this Boris Whitely last night, you think they're the same two who killed Mrs. Vincent tonight?" He shrugged. "Even if they are, Whitely couldn't give us a description that would help us catch them."

"I'm telling you why we were in the alley. Boris Whitely is a pal of my mother's. After what happened to him last night, I decided I would spend some time walking around that part of the neighborhood."

"You hunt for vandals at night with your girlfriend . . . ?" He stared at me as if I was from a different planet.

Maybe I was. "Look, Proffitt, will you listen to an idea? I've been on a roll the last few days and I'd like you to consider something."

"What?"

"There's been a lot of vandalism around here. Some of it really nasty, and it's been going on for months. Yes?"

"Yes."

"But two things have changed recently. Before the last week or ten days, none of the vandalism was west of Virginia Avenue. And no vandalism has left people injured, until Boris last night."

He nodded.

"Well, I'm asking, Why the changes?"

"What are you getting at, Albert?"

"Maybe somebody wanted Rochelle Vincent dead and decided to use the vandalism nearby to mask his intentions."

"You're suggesting the murder tonight was premeditated?"

"The idea came from what they did to Boris. He says the two guys made a point of beating him up."

"Even so."

"If different things are happening, I'm suggesting they're being done by different people with a different objective. What objective? Well, look at what happened. Rochelle Vincent is dead. I could be wrong about all this, of course, but I think you should check who benefits from Mrs. Vincent's death. You'd do that eventually, but I think you should do it now."

Proffitt studied me.

"Like I said, Homer, I've been on a roll recently. And when someone's on a lucky streak you should bet with him. And my bet is that somebody out there will benefit a lot from this death. I'd guess it's somebody pretty young and pretty desperate and pretty stupid, because this is a pretty dumb idea. But I'm also betting that if you find him—and his friend—quickly enough, you might even find Mrs. Vincent's blood still on them."

35

Proffitt didn't stay much longer. He called Mary in, but left once we both promised to be available in the morning.

"Why did he go so soon?" Mary asked when we were alone. "What did you say?"

"I confessed."

"I was perfectly capable of talking to him tonight."

"I'm too tired to protect you, kid. Proffitt left because I gave him some ideas he wanted to pursue right way, that's all."

"What ideas?"

"Things . . ." I really was tired. My fatigue piling up on my shoulders. It was about to drop me in my tracks. "Things."

"You're being uncharacteristically uncommunicative."

"Does it add to my allure?"

"Are you worried about your allure?"

"Not enough that it will keep me awake."

"Because your mother and Sam told me who Lieutenant Proffitt is. I mean, with respect to your ex."

"Tonight he was just a cop trying to find out who killed my mother's friend." My mother . . . "Is Mom still up?"

"They're in her sitting room."

Sam was sitting with her arm around her grandmother's shoulders.

I said, "Mom, are you all right?"

"Not altogether, son." And I could see she wasn't. She

looked old. She looked feeble.

"Proffitt has gone."

She nodded.

"He'll do everything he can to catch the killers."

"Poor, poor Rochelle." Mom looked up at me. "Do you remember her, son? She ran a nursery for years and years."

"I remember her," I said because it sounded like she wanted me to.

"Not a nursery for children. Plants and trees and flowers. Wyatt, her husband, his family had a little farm. But when the city grew out to them, they figured a big nursery was a better bet than a small farm. Beautiful things she had out there. Norman took me out there sometimes, on his bike. That was before his accident of course."

"Is Wyatt still alive?"

"Wyatt? Not for years. And their boy died in Vietnam."

"Did Rochelle still run the nursery?"

"No no. Managers did that. But Rochelle kept busy. Like with the library when there was talk of closing the Fountain Square branch a few years ago."

If Rochelle Vincent had owned a farm's worth of land on the edge of the city, had I just been told the motive for her murder?

Or was I just so tired that I had a one-track mind?

I was fiercely tired.

When I tuned in again, Mom was speaking to Mary. "You're a nice young woman, very nice."

"Thank you, Mrs. Samson."

"I just hope he's treating you right."

"No complaints so far."

"And I do wish you didn't smoke."

When Mary and I had retreated to my part of the house,

I said, "You are staying here tonight. That's an order."

"Albert, I just said that."

"You did?"

"Poor tired baby." She patted me on the head. "So who's first in the bathroom?"

"You."

I dropped onto my bed to wait.

The next thing I knew, it was morning. With very bright light.

My mouth tasted like it was lined with the scum off water in which potatoes had been boiled with their skins on.

Somewhere close, Mary said, "Our first all-nighter. How romantic."

With no more communication than was absolutely necessary, we followed minimal ablutions with a glissade down the stairs to the luncheonette and its prospect of coffee.

Norman looked up from his griddle. "Hey, it's the lovebirds."

"Do you feel like a lovebird?" Mary mumbled. "I don't feel like a lovebird."

"Coo," I said, but even to me it sounded more like a caw. Maybe because my claw hurt. How much morphine do they allow you for broken fingers?

Sam appeared before us. She looked obscenely healthy and pink-cheeked. Not a single sign of having been through anything hard or late or unusual the night before. Had my only child reached a crossroads in her life and chosen to make a pact with the devil? Was it a consequence of your standard devil-pact to scream when you say things like, "Good morning, Mary. Good morning, Daddy. Coffee?"

Pact or no, it was diabolical. I covered my ears. "I hate loud children. Do you hate loud children?"

"I hate all children," Mary said.

We fell onto chairs at a table.

Something nearby smelled bad. It was me.

I looked at Mary to see if she'd noticed. She was moving her head around. Sometimes pain showed on her face. Oh yeah. The whiplash. "Where's your neck brace?"

"I hate neck braces." She moved her head again, then winced.

"Jim Bouton says that baseball players suffer more injuries from testing whether their injuries have healed than they did from getting injured in the first place."

"Mary says that private detectives suffer more injuries from quoting Jim Bouton than from all other causes put together."

I hoped she'd interpret my silence as delight in this observation.

Sam arrived with cups of coffee. "I thought you guys would like to know," she screamed, "when the rush finishes here, I'm going to Sunshine Bridge."

"Don't forget to jump," Mary said.

"Hey," I said, "that's my kid, remember."

"Did I say that out loud?"

"Sunshine Bridge . . . ?" Sam said. "The retirement home Helene Miller went to last night . . ."

"Oh yeah," I said.

"More coffee?"

"Yes," we both answered. Quite possibly in an excessively loud fashion ourselves.

Sam poured. "Honestly, the two of you look awful." She left.

Mary looked at me. "She's right about you."

"To me you look beautiful."

"Now open your eyes."

★ ★ ★ ★ ★

Once the coffee hit, we became more human. Mary offered me a lift to Moe & Johnny's—and the car I'd abandoned there when we set out to get her a Lotto ticket little more than half a day and twenty lifetimes ago.

But I declined. I wanted to shower and change clothes before I went anywhere.

"Call me," she said, and then she was gone.

I lingered long enough to eat some toast one-handed. Then I sentenced myself to go upstairs and get clean.

Which felt good.

I was me again.

36

There were messages on my machine.

The first was from Miller. "She did sixty-two miles last night, Al. So, do you know where she went? Call me on the cell. Leave a message if I'm out of range, but careful, remember. God, after all the worrying, now I'm scared about finding out."

How scary would Sunshine Bridge be, I wondered. Were Helene and her friends scoring old-people drugs from the staff, say? Or stealing jewelry?

When I called Jerry's cell, I got the message service. "The young woman in question picked up two friends and they went to a retirement home called Sunshine Bridge. They stayed inside something like three hours. Do you know what she was doing there—checking it out as a place to park her parents, say? If so, let me know. But that's where she was last night. Where are you today?"

The second message on my machine was from Christopher P. Holloway. "I shouldn't have to chase you for the daily reports Karl wants."

When I rang back, Delilah put me straight through. "So, what did you get for us about the men on that list?" Holloway asked.

"Nothing, yet."

"You saw them and got nothing, or couldn't see any of them, or what?"

"I didn't try. When we got off the phone yesterday I got a new idea. See, I figured that—"

"You changed a plan we had agreed on without talking to me first?"

"It occurred to me that the Crime Stoppers informant, Carlo Saddler, ought to know which of the guys on the list gave him the information. So I decided to try to see him before anyone else. It was just a different approach to the same thing."

Holloway sighed. "What did you get from Saddler?"

"Nothing, unfortunately. He got a call less than an hour before he contacted Crime Stoppers. He has no idea who from."

Holloway was silent.

I said, "That timing is consistent with the theory the stuff was planted at Willigar's."

"But proves nothing."

"Then, I managed to get an IPD detective to take the names on the list and agree to investigate them, based on the hypothesis that Ronnie Willigar is innocent."

"The police have reopened the case?"

"Not the police. One guy. It's not an official departmental investigation. It's . . ." Well, you have to stretch a point or two with a client sometimes. "He's a friend of mine."

"Who?"

"I can't tell you that."

"Not Miller, surely."

"Not Miller."

"Karl will want the name."

"Sorry, I can't. I won't."

"This wouldn't be another black guy, by any chance?"

"What kind of question is that?"

"Never mind. So, your nameless cop friend . . . What exactly is he doing for us?"

I was about to try to spin an answer when I heard noises at Holloway's end of the phone. "Hang on, Samson," he said. Then, "What?" to someone in his office.

I heard a woman's voice, and the rustling of paper.

Holloway returned to me. "Samson, what the hell is this story in the *Star*?"

"What story?"

"It says you discovered a body last night. Some old woman. A murder victim."

"It's in the paper?"

"Because you'd better not have been working on any other case. Karl laid that out from the start. You work for us and only us."

"It was strictly accidental. I was out for a walk and—"

Maybe it's typical of lawyers not to recognize the truth because they don't hear it very often. "God help you when Karl hears about this," Christopher P. Holloway said. "I think your next move should be to get your butt down here."

"That's a bit of a problem, because I don't have my car." See, my girlfriend, who I wasn't meeting, decided she wanted a Lotto ticket because I was having such a lucky day, and . . . "It's a long story."

"I don't want to hear it. Get yourself a cab. Walk. Steal a skateboard. Whatever it takes."

There was a knock on my internal door. I wasn't expecting anyone. "Hang on a sec, Mr. Holloway."

Sam came in. She was followed by a police officer.

"Mr. Holloway," I said, "it seems that I've got the police here."

"To arrest you for murdering the old woman?"

"Don't be absurd."

"Because I think Karl might just help them prosecute

you." I heard noises at his end again. "Speak of the devil."

I said, "I have to deal with this. I'll call you back or come down to your office as soon as I get the chance." I hung up and turned to Sam.

"Daddy, this is Officer Garlick."

Sam ushered in a uniformed policewoman with long black hair and her gun still in its holster. Given that I'd half-expected Homer Proffitt this morning, Garlick was a welcome alternative, in the if-you've-got-to-have-a-cop-at-all sense. "Seat?" I said.

"Thanks." She sat, and then adjusted herself on the chair.

To Sam I said, "Are you heading off soon?"

"In a couple of minutes."

"Give me a call when you've talked to them."

"Verbal report? Sure, Daddy." She left.

Officer Garlick said, "Does your daughter work with you?"

Might there be an issue about a license for Sam? "Not really."

"Even so, it's nice that she's around. I never really knew my dad."

"No?" I didn't quite see how this was going to lead to the events of last night, but . . .

"He left my mom when I was seven. Sometimes I think that explains a lot."

I waited for her to move on to business, but instead she looked around the room. Of the two of us she seemed the more nervous. That's not how it works when you're with cops. I wondered if maybe she hadn't been at it all that long, although she looked in her thirties. "Well, Officer Garlick, let me take a wild guess what your visit here this morning is about."

"All right." She smiled. Nice smile.

"Rochelle Vincent."

She waited. Good technique. Let the interviewee make the running. He might give something up that you don't already know.

I said, "You're here to take a formal statement about last night. The timing of my various trips to the alley. When exactly I found the body. And so on."

Nothing for a moment. Then she said, "I don't have the faintest idea what you're talking about, Mr. Samson. Or is it OK if I call you Al?"

"If I can call you Betty."

"Betty?" She frowned. "My name is Marcella."

Marcella?

"I know Jerry told you about me."

This was Miller's girlfriend, Marcella. Marcella! "Of course, Marcella. Hi there."

"Hi."

"So you're not here, like, officially?"

"Not at all. Oh, I get it. It's because I'm in uniform. No, see, I'm on nights right now and I stopped here on my way home."

"OK, I'm with you now."

"I was late finishing, because we had an arrest just before I was due to sign off. If I did finish on time you probably wouldn't of wanted me to stop by. Not everybody is up at eight in the morning. Jerry says you sleep late sometimes."

"Sometimes, that's true."

"What happened to your hand, if you don't mind my asking."

"It got stepped on."

"Ew!" She made a face.

"It'll be all right. The swelling's already down." Which reminded me I was supposed to have it re-bandaged today. Ah well.

"So," she said. She changed her position in the chair.

"So."

"I bet you're wondering why I'm here."

"Hey, I'm not going to play poker against you."

"What?"

"It . . . It's just my way of saying you're right. You win your bet. Yes, I am wondering why you're here."

"Oh yeah. Jerry told me you're a joker."

What Miller told me was that she was the nicest woman he'd ever known. That she was sweet and kind and everything was easy with her. He hadn't claimed she was the brightest spark in the campfire. But, hey, who needs bright sparks? Especially after all those years with Janie, the kind of woman who could ignite a campfire just by gnashing her teeth.

Miller also neglected to tell me that his Marcella was a cop. "So," I said, happy enough to take her away from whatever business had brought her here, "how did you guys meet?"

"I was civilian secretarial staff and I got a temporary assignment to Homicide, only it was my first assignment after training, so I made a lot of mistakes. Jerry was the only person in the whole department who was nice to me and told me it didn't matter, so I noticed him right away."

"Homicide is not known for its mensches," I said, and regretted it immediately. "So, now you're in uniform."

"Yeah. One day I said how boring it was to be stuck behind a desk and how I'd rather be out at the sharp end, and Jerry encouraged me to try for it. He's been real supportive, which I have to say I have not ever been used to from a man before."

"How long have you been in uniform?"

"It'll be four months since I graduated from the Academy next week."

"Well, congratulations. They say the first four months are the hardest."

"Do they? I didn't know that."

Neither did I, God forgive me. "When Jerry and I talked, he said real nice things about you, Marcella. He's very very fond of you, and he hates not being able to see you."

"I hate it too. So, is . . ."

"What?"

"Is he all right?"

"Well, he's got a lot of things he's trying to deal with and it's hard."

"Like his daughter. I know."

"His daughter . . . His job . . . His wife . . ."

"She must be the stupidest woman in the world," Marcella Garlick said earnestly. "Not to appreciate Jerry, I mean."

"Right."

"Because he is such a kind man. Such a good man."

"You had some trouble with a husband yourself, didn't you?"

"You can say that again."

In most other company I would have. I am not a kind man or a good man.

She said, "Harry hates it that I have a boyfriend now, even though him and me were divorced more than three years ago. Three years . . . I mean, like, get over it, duh. But not Harry."

"Did the divorce happen before you went to work for IPD?"

"Yeah, but because I already knew people there it made

it easier for me to try for an IPD job."

"You knew people at IPD?"

"Because of Harry. He's a cop too. A sergeant out on the westside."

"Oh."

"And Harry never let me work while we were married. Even the very idea would set him off."

"Set him off?"

"Yeah . . . Well . . ." She looked away, which seemed as clear as giving me a blow by blow.

"I'm sorry," I said.

"But then, when I finally got shut of him, a couple of the wives I knew, they said knowing the job from having been married to a cop might help me get in on the civilian support side."

"And I guess it did."

"That and I was lucky at the time because they were trying to recruit more minority women. So it was a good fit."

"Minority?"

"I know I don't look anything but my grandfather was Chinese and my mother is from Salvador. I say, I'm my own Rainbow Coalition." She smiled her nice smile.

I smiled back. "And I guess you didn't know what you were getting into when you got married."

"You can say that again. But Harry had a steady job— hey we're always going to need cops, right? And he wanted a wife. Also, it helped my mom with the others that I could leave."

"One of those things that seemed a good idea at the time, eh?"

"But it really wasn't, yeah. That's exactly right. Jerry says you're sensitive, when you're not joking."

"I guess I don't have any secrets left. So, how long were you married?"

"Too long. Twelve years. And I owe my freedom to Oprah. She saved my life. I wouldn't be here without what I learned from her show. I owe her everything."

"That's quite a testimonial."

"I'm not the only one. She's helped lots and lots of us. I write to thank her about every month. You can e-mail the show, you know."

"I didn't know."

"Well, you can."

She nodded until I said, "Did you and Harry have any kids?"

"No, thank the Lord. He wanted some bad, but I think there's something wrong with him, even though he always said it was me." She lowered her eyes and then looked away.

I'd bet the subject of children set Harry off too. Whatever creaky baggage Miller might come to Marcella's table with, he had to be a real improvement on Harry Garlick.

I said, "At least no kids made the divorce easier."

"There was nothing easy about that divorce, Al, believe me."

When Miller talked about Marcella, he'd referred to her "supposedly ex." "Am I remembering right that it was Harry who told Janie Miller about you and Jerry?"

"Yes."

"How did he know about the two of you?"

"By following me."

"Harry follows you?"

"He thinks I still belong to him. Crazy, isn't it? I've told him, over and over, 'Find yourself another girl, move on, get some closure.' "

"You talk to him?"

"I have to. If I don't, he calls me in the middle of the

night until I do. If I take the phone off the hook, he just comes to the door and wakes up the neighbors."

"The law can keep him from doing things like that."

"I guess, but I worry that would make it harder for him to get a job someplace else."

"He's going to leave?"

"Oh, he knows things aren't right the way they are, and as soon as he can get enough money together, he's going to move away to make a fresh start."

"But, somehow, he never has enough saved up, right?"

"Not so far. But he is trying. I'm sure he is."

If Marcella still believed anything Harry Garlick said to her, Oprah's work was not yet done. And if any fresh start was going to be made, Miller and his Marcella would have to be the ones to make it.

She was about to say something else when my telephone rang.

I hesitated before answering it, thinking my caller would probably be Karl Benton. But it could also be Sam, or Mom, or Proffitt. Or Mary. So, "Albert Samson."

Miller said, "The young woman in question went to a retirement home?"

"With her two friends. Jerry, there's someone—"

"What the hell did they go to a retirement home for?"

"I hope to know more about that later today." Having heard me say Jerry's name, Marcella leaned forward.

Miller said, "What's the place called again?"

"Sunshine Bridge. It's out on the northeast side."

"Who are the friends, Al?"

"Dunno. A male and a female."

"Well, where did she pick them up from? Did you get the address?"

"Not from a residence."

"Well where was it from?"

"She picked them up outside a bar."

"She's too young to . . ." After a moment, "What bar?"

"Just a bar. She was only there a couple of minutes and then all three of them went to this Sunshine Bridge. Do you know any reason why she would spend three hours in a retirement home?"

"Was it the Milwaukee?"

"You're not answering my question, which does seem at the heart of the matter."

"It was the Milwaukee. Fuck."

Well, I'd tried.

"Fuck fuck fuck."

"Speaking of which, I have a police officer here in the office at the moment."

"Tell him the job ain't jackshit any more. Tell him to quit now and become a paperboy."

"Why not tell her yourself?"

After a moment he said, "Her?"

"In uniformed person."

Behind me Marcella said, "Hi, Jerry!" and waved.

There was a pause. I could just see Miller looking around to see where Janie was. Then thinking about the wiretap on his phone. But he said, "Put her on."

I passed the phone to Marcella and made myself scarce. I didn't expect them to have a long conversation, but I wanted it to be a private one.

I sat on my bed and pondered what I wanted to do next.

I ought to go to the offices of Perkins, Baker, Pinkus and Lestervic and make peace with Benton and Holloway. So I'd found a murder victim . . . Serious work was still being done on their case. OK, maybe not by me, just at the moment, but I'd be the one reporting whatever Leroy Powder discovered. So come on, guys, how's about patting Al on the back? Give him some credit.

Or maybe I should see how Powder was getting on before I talked to my clients.

And there was my car to pick up.

And—

Miller's Marcella knocked to let me know she was done. Marcella Miller . . . The name had a pleasing sound. But when I returned to my office she looked upset. "Are you all right?"

"Fine. Yeah."

"Are you sure?" Even I could see she wasn't fine.

"It's all . . . so complicated. I have got to go now, Al."

"You know, Marcella, we never did get around to why you came here."

"It was . . . I just thought maybe you could give me some advice about something, since you've known Jerry so long. But it doesn't matter anymore."

"I'm happy to talk."

"I have to go. Is that a way out?" She pointed to my outside door.

"It leads down to the street."

"Great. OK. Thanks, Al. Nice to meet you."

"Any time you think I might be some help, call or come back."

But she left without speaking again.

37

I wanted my wheels back. Before anything else. Top priority. Even a lean mean private detecting machine needs his wheels.

I phoned for a taxi, then went down to the luncheonette hoping to catch a word or two with Mom about how Boris was. I wasn't going to make *that* mistake again.

But Mom was not there. Norman was on his own behind the counter and, for once, he was sitting on a stool instead of griddling. He was reading something in a notebook, and I realized how rare it was to see him sitting down. Mr. Personality or otherwise, the guy worked hard. You had to give him that.

Was this going to be the day I saw his good side?

Should I try for some civilized conversation with him? If he responded . . . Well, we'd never be best buds, but it would be nice not to taste bile every time I walked by the guy. He did have genuine concern for my mother. Wasn't that worth some effort? I could try something he'd be interested in. Hey, how about those new Harley-Davidsons . . . ?

On the other hand, it's not polite to interrupt someone who's reading.

I turned instead to the pinball machine, but when I got to it, for some reason, I didn't feel like playing. So I headed for the street, to wait for my cab.

"Out of quarters?" Norman called after me.

Asshole.

I'd been standing outside the luncheonette for three or

four minutes when a green car coming up Virginia Avenue made a U-turn and pulled over to the curb beside me. I opened the back door and got in. "54th and College," I said.

The driver started laughing and turned around. I found myself looking at the grinning, oval face of Jimmy Wilson. "Hey, if it ain't Albert Gator out on the street looking like a lost dog. I see you still don't got a new sign."

"I thought you were a taxi, Jimmy. Sorry." I moved to open the door again, but I used the wrong hand. "Fuck!"

"What's with the hand? Cut it trying to fix the sign yourself?"

I reached across to open the door.

"Don't get out. You want 54th and College? I can take you. I got time."

"I called a cab. I left my car up there last night."

"I saw it not here. I thought maybe you crashed it."

"Thanks."

"Well, I noticed the bandage, see. I notice things."

Which made one of us. How could get I into a car without realizing it wasn't a taxi?

Jimmy said, "That's Moe & Johnny's up there at 54th."

"Is it?"

He chuckled and we pulled away from the curb. "Tell me what company?" He held up a cell phone. "I'll tell 'em you're coming with me."

I was about to decline again but then I couldn't think why I should.

He called the cab company and I looked out the window. Just before crossing the interstate bridge we passed the turn to Timothy Battle's church. That put me in mind of a question I'd failed to ask myself—or someone who might know the answer. How did church arsonists come to have legal representation of the caliber of Tom Thomas at Ames, Kent, Hardick? I didn't know Thomas, but the firm was a big one.

"There you go," Jimmy said after a few words on the phone. "Everything kosher and bacon-crisp."

His voice reminded me of another overdue, if less important, question.

I said, "What exactly do you do that has you driving up and down Virginia Avenue every day?"

"I go other places too." He shrugged. "I give guys rides. And deliver stuff. And pick stuff up. Errands. That's what I do."

"Who for?"

"Lots of people. And they don't expect me to advertise."

"That's how come you pay attention to neon signs? You yearn to advertise but they won't let you?"

He checked out my unsmiling face in the rearview mirror. "You're a funny guy, you know that?"

"But you do go up and down Virginia Avenue a lot, right?"

"I sure do."

"And other places in the Fountain Square neighborhood?"

"Yeah. It's a busy place."

"So you must have noticed the graffiti and vandalism that's been going on lately."

He was quiet.

"You notice things, right?"

"Yeah, I've seen some of that."

The overdue question . . . "Jimmy, why did you come to my office last Friday?"

"Because I saw—"

"And don't say it was because of my neon sign."

"Sure it was. You turned it on and it didn't make no sense."

"There are other broken signs around. Do you stop and talk to those people too?"

He was quiet again.

I said, "That would be easy for me to check."

He snorted.

"Friday was the first day after I got my license back."

"Oh yeah?"

"And when you came to my door you knew about my mother. You said she was a neat lady."

"She is a neat lady."

"How did you know about her, Jimmy?"

"She runs Bud's Dugout. People know her."

"So, you eat in there sometimes, is that it? When you're in the neighborhood?"

"Sure, yeah. Sometimes."

"How long you been doing that?"

"Quite a while now."

"A year?"

"Maybe. Sure. A year or so."

"My mother hasn't run the luncheonette herself for a lot longer than a year, Jimmy. She's almost never behind the counter these days."

"No?"

"And you knew her first name. You also said you'd never met her but would like to. Why did you come to my office instead of going into the luncheonette if you wanted to meet my mother, Jimmy?"

"You got a good memory. You go to college for that?"

"Yeah, with a Masters in Sticking To The Subject. We've just crossed 22nd Street, Jimmy. If you don't get your story straight by Fall Creek, I'm going to jump over the seat and grab the wheel and run us into a tree."

"Naw, you wouldn't—"

"You better fucking believe it."

He went quiet again. It seemed like he did believe it. Just as well. I was losing patience. Not only with him, but with ongoing vandalism, and arsonists with good lawyers, and honest cops accused of corruption, and kids who beat women to death in their backyards, and grandmothers who have to organize vigilante groups to make a neighborhood nice enough to live their years out in.

And my hand hurt. Jimmy did well not to mess with me. I wasn't far from losing control.

He said, "I can see why guys would hire you. If any do, I mean, what with you having a sign outside your place that don't mean shit. You really stay with stuff. Like one of them . . . whatchamacallits, that terrier with a bone. What kind of terrier am I thinking of?"

"A bone terrier. What's this all about, Jimmy? I can see the Fall Creek Bridge coming up."

"Well, let's see. How'm I gonna put this?"

"In English will do nicely."

"What happened was, I don't know the name of the guy. I don't drive him all the time, but more than once. And he was talking on the phone. What is it with lawyers, huh? There ain't one I drive who don't talk on the phone in the car. And it's like I'm not there at all. Some of these guys, they even talk dirty to their girlfriends while I drive 'em. And I mean dirty dirty. It's like I'm deaf and dumb to them. It's like I'm fucking invisible."

My mother claimed old people were invisible. Was I seeing invisible people now because I was becoming more observant?

I said, "Let's pretend for a minute I believe you don't

know the guy's name. What did he say, Jimmy?"

"You ever been in a war? Overseas, front line?"

"No."

"It ain't all it's cracked up to be, believe me. Don't lose no sleep over it."

"Jimmy . . ."

"OK, OK. This guy is a lawyer and I've drove him before, like I said. And he's always on the phone. So I've heard him talk about a lot of things, but then recently I heard him say your mother's name a few times. Which I did already know, however. And this guy, it's not like he says her name with respect. And then I'm driving him last Thursday and what he's talking about is you and how you have your license back and he says that might be a problem. Your mother's just an old bitch, but with you in the picture it might be something they have to deal with. That's what he says, 'Something to deal with.' "

"Deal with how?"

"I don't know, but that's why I asked if you were ever in a war, because it was the way they talk about things there, that hard edge in the voice. And to tell you the truth, I didn't like the sound of it. And that's why I came to your office. I don't plan to lose my job over any of this but I thought maybe I'd keep some tabs, you know? And then you were nice to me, so I was glad I did it."

"What about since Thursday?"

"I haven't drove the guy since then."

"Are you sure about what you're telling me, Jimmy? That it's accurate?"

"I'm sure. Hey, you know, I got a English uncle who's a curate."

"What?"

"It's some kind of church thing."

I looked at his face in the mirror. It broke into a smile and I realized that I should have liked Jimmy all along.

He said, "Hey, I got a million of 'em."

"Do all these guys you drive ignore you?"

"I could be made by Ford with the rest of it." He patted the dashboard. "But you, you gave me a cup of coffee."

"And I owe you another one. Look, at 54th Street there's a coffee place on the corner, Cath's."

"Yeah. OK. Why not?"

Cath's' armchairs weren't as deep and comfortable as those at Roxanne's, but we were on the northside and people up there don't know how to live. The coffee, however, was acceptable. Jimmy also accepted a blueberry muffin.

"So how'd you get the hand?" he asked when we were settled.

"A guy stepped on it after he murdered someone."

"That true?"

"Look in today's *Star*." I sipped from my coffee.

He studied my face. "How can you drink that stuff without you got no sugar in it?"

"Who was talking about my mother and me, Jimmy?"

He shook his head. "They know my name but I don't know their name."

"You know where you pick him up and where you drop him off."

"Where I pick him up is where I pick them all up because I'm on call for a whole building. I come with the rent." He showed me his cell phone again. "That's me, just a phone call away."

"I'm going to get one of those."

"Get your sign fixed first."

"Where's the building, Jimmy?"

He shook his head.

"All I have to do to find out is follow you around."

He tasted his coffee and then stirred more sugar into it.

"And then I go into the building to find out which lawyers work there." I drank from my own cup. "In fact, suppose I guess the name of a law firm. If I get it right, all you have to do is nod."

He picked up his blueberry muffin.

"I think your building houses the offices of Ames, Kent, Hardick."

The muffin stopped just south of his mouth.

"Is that a good muffin? All you have to do is nod."

The muffin returned to a saucer. "You been checking up on me, Albert?"

"An Ames, Kent, Hardick lawyer named Tom Thomas called me yesterday. He said bad things would happen to my career if I continue to help a church in my neighborhood that's been attacked by vandals and arsonists."

"The one near the interstate?"

"You know about that? Some of your passengers been talking about the church?"

"Hey, I know all kindsa stuff. You know why a tank is called a 'tank'? Ever think about it?"

"No."

"I forgot, you was never in a war."

"I feel like I'm in a kind of war now, Jimmy."

He was silent for a moment before he said, "I've helped you about as far as I can go."

"Burning churches, killing pets, damaging people's houses . . . Those things are wrong."

"Bush finished second but won the prize. That ain't right, but it's how things are."

"Are you afraid? Is that it?"

"I'm afraid I got a wife at home in a wheelchair that's only got me to provide for her."

Which was not a small matter. I said, "OK. Let's leave it there for now. But I may have to come back to you, Jimmy. You know stuff."

"I know whoever said there's no such thing as a free muffin, I should of listened."

"Thank you for coming to my office last Friday, Jimmy. You're an island of humanity in a sea of greed." I really felt it. Talking with him had brought me back from the brink of something.

He lifted his coffee cup as if acknowledging a toast. "You're welcome."

Winston Churchill commissioned the first tanks around the time of World War I. They were a big secret. In the factory that made them, the official order form said they were "Water Carriers for Mesopotamia." But the guys on the factory floor referred to them as water tanks, and then tanks.

I got all that, and more, while we finished our coffees. "You want I should walk you to your car to make sure it starts?" Jimmy said as we left Cath's.

"It always starts."

"But does it finish?"

I stood in Cath's lot until he pulled out. Then I crossed College to where my car was parked on 54th Street, across from Moe & Johnny's. "Fun on a platter" was how their logo read. Not Mary's and my experience of the previous night as a whole, but that wasn't Moe's fault. Or Johnny's.

I wondered how Mary was coping. With a cell phone I could have called to find out. There was a public phone outside the supermarket next to Cath's, but the car took priority.

Even in a neck brace Mary was probably feeling better than I was, being as how she was a mere sprig and not an old trunk like me.

I unlocked the car door, still thinking about Mary, wondering if she would win anything on her Lotto ticket. Then I noticed that my car wasn't quite level. Had I parked in a pothole?

I walked around and I saw that the offside front tire was flat. Not just flat—it had been cut. Above it on the paintwork someone had scratched a face with a tongue sticking out and the number nine.

"Fuck," I said. Then I remembered the spare was already on the car and all I had in the trunk was an unrepaired flat.

I sat on the curb beside the leery face. "Fuck fuck fuck fuck fuck."

I'd been sky-high since getting my license back. On a roll. Now suddenly I was in the pit again, feeling the way I felt for so long. Attacked by the world. Nowhere to go that didn't lead me straight into a black wall. Why *my* car?

A part of my brain said, Keep calm. It's just a tire. No big.

But it was a big. Every time I try to take a fucking step forward, something gets in my way, something keeps me immobile. It was like my arms were pinned to my sides when all I wanted to do was stretch them out and grab on to something, someone . . .

It was hard to bear.

I didn't want to bear it. I'd hoped I'd never feel this way again. How can things change so fast?

Get a grip, Albert, the calm side of my brain said. Be a grown-up. Call someone. But who? Mary had a business to run, and whiplash. Sam was already out on an errand. Mom?

When Norman's name occurred to me I accepted that the car was screwed, and so was I, and all for no better reason than to provide entertainment for some bored fucking kid who signed himself Nine. Or herself.

I got up and pounded the roof of the car in frustration with my good hand. Then with both hands. Fuck fuck fuck fuck fuck *fuck*.

I sat down on the curb again.

My right hand hurt, so badly. All I could do was cradle it in my left. And hum to it. For whatever reason.

And, somehow, I moved on.

I realized that my feelings now were *not* the same as those that plagued and engulfed and attacked me during the dark years without my license. Then I was cut off from anything that made it worth getting up in the morning, worth going to bed at night, worth doing any fucking thing at all. Then I felt numbness.

This was pain.

That was depression.

What I felt now was anger. Pure, personal fucking *rage*.

I felt like Nine had let my blood, not air, out of the tire. I felt like the face had been carved in my skin. I might not be able to do anything about Nine, but that didn't mean I had to sit still for every fucking thing like it. I'd sat still, dumb, and blind for too long. Far too long.

So I got up. I unlocked the trunk and took out the dead tire that lay there. I carried it back across the street to the public phone. I called a cab.

Vandals in the abstract are one thing. You can think rationally about them. This was not abstract. This had happened to *me*.

38

The cabdriver showed no surprise at picking up a passenger who was carrying a flat tire. The surprise came when I told him I wanted to go to Maryland Street. "I don't remember no garage down there," he said.

"It's a lawyers' office."

"Oh," he said. "Gimme the tire. I'll put it in the trunk."

I hesitated. "I don't want to get out and forget it."

"I won't let you forget it."

I gave him the tire.

As I rode downtown I grew calmer, and purposeful. There is a strength that comes from being clear about what you want to do next.

When we turned onto Maryland Street the driver asked what number I wanted. "Anywhere along here will do." I didn't remember the number. I was pleased to have remembered the street, since when I looked up all the lawyers in town it was their phone numbers I was interested in.

"You sure?"

"I'm sure."

I paid him, collected my tire, and walked along the sidewalk until I saw a sign across the street that said, "Ames, Kent, Hardick." Not in neon.

As I crossed, a car honked at me. I gave it the finger. Which one of us was in a big comfortable car and which one of us was walking around humping a tire? Jerk.

The four office doors of the building were made of security glass. The kind it would take a sledgehammer to break a hole in. Or maybe a car driven at speed.

Inside, a short corridor led to an elevator. A display board listed several firms. Ames, Kent, Hardick, Attorneys at Law, occupied all of the second floor.

The elevator opened to more glass doors, with Ames, Kent, Hardick logos on them. These doors looked easier to break than the ones downstairs. They probably wouldn't take more than your average claw hammer.

At a desk a young woman wearing earphones typed in front of a computer screen. She smiled as she caught sight of me and took the earphones off.

I said, "You're Faith, aren't you?"

"Yeah, hi. Do I know you?"

I rested my tire on the floor. "You forget how heavy these suckers are. Yeah, we talked last week."

"Can I help you, Mister . . . ?"

"I can see you're busy, Faith. Just remind me where Mr. Thomas's office is. He's expecting me, and I'll make my own way."

Faith glanced to her right, but said, "If you'll give me your name, sir, I'll let Mr. Thomas know you're here."

By the time she got to the "sir" I'd already picked up my tire.

Tom Thomas had his name on the door in big letters. Surprise surprise. I managed to turn the handle with my damaged hand and I barged the door open with the tire. The door flew open so hard it bounced off the inside wall.

I stepped inside and kicked the door closed behind me.

Thomas had a phone in his hand, but he was standing by his desk—probably alerted by Faith. He was a big guy, either muscular or fat. I couldn't tell which because of the suit. "Hi, Tom," I said.

"Who the hell are you?"

Behind him a large window overlooked Maryland Street. I had an office on Maryland Street, long ago. I got evicted, because some money-crazed property fucker had other ideas for the place than letting the likes of me make a living.

"I'm Albert Samson, Tom. Posy's boy, the one who's been making trouble about the church near Fountain Square." I dropped my tire on his desk.

"Are you crazy?"

"You gave me some free advice. I'm here to return the favor."

"Get out. I don't have time to see you now."

"Yes you do." I pulled his phone out of its socket. "Sit down, Tom. Sit down and you won't get hurt. Not that that's in any way a threat."

He hesitated.

"Sit the fuck down."

Bullies understand bullying. He sat.

I moved to his side of the desk. He rolled his chair back but that only made space for me to sit on the edge in front of him. "See my tire?" I said. "If any tires get sliced within a mile of Fountain Square, your tires will get sliced."

"What?"

"If any windows get smashed, yours will get smashed."

"What?"

"Do you have a problem with English, Tom? Isn't it your first language?"

"Are you threatening me? Because if—"

"Did you threaten me? I'm making you a clear and definite promise. But let me take the specific and generalize it. From now on, *anything* that happens within a mile of the fountain will happen to you. I don't mean the plural you, Tom, you and your buddies in this deal you're putting together. I mean the singular you, Tom Thomas, you your-self. Do you yourself understand the point I'm making here? Anything that happens there, happens to you."

"You are threatening me."

"I'm connecting the dots for you, Tom. I am showing you the picture. Think about it for a minute. I'm a private eye. I can find your car. I can find your house. I can find your mother—if you ever had one. I can find where you party. I can find where you take a dump. And I can put it together. And what I'm putting together here, Tom, can be-come your personal nightmare. And don't think you can stop me. Because there are lots of us. For instance, it wasn't me who took the pictures that put your arsonist clients in jail. Other people did that. People you can't even see, be-cause people like you don't see people like them."

I could see he didn't like what I was saying. I'm defi-nitely becoming more observant.

"But none of this needs to happen, Tom. You don't have to have a personal nightmare. You can have your sweet dreams back. All it takes is for the vandalism and malicious damage and arson to stop within a mile of Fountain Square."

"It's about that church, isn't it?"

"It's about what will happen to you. Haven't you been listening?"

"The guy wants to do the deal and you can't stop it."

"I don't give a fuck about stopping a deal."

"Then what—"

"But I do give a fuck about how deals are done. I give a fuck when people find their pets dead, when they find their walls defaced, when they have to sing hymns through a hole in the wall. Those things aren't abstractions, like owner-ship, or development. Those things are personal to the people they happen to, Tom. And if they happen again, they'll be personal to you too."

"You can't prove—"

"I don't need to prove. This is not a negotiation. This is not a trial. It's a promise. I've told you what's going to happen. Go ahead and conduct business in Fountain Square. You want to buy something? Offer a price. But you will not drive any more people in Fountain Square to sell up or sell cheaper. Not without knowing what being intimidated feels like. Personally."

I stood up. I was done. I picked up my tire and left.

39

When I emerged onto Maryland Street I was no longer anyone's personal nightmare. I was just a private eye with a
sore hand who was carrying a flat tire around in downtown
Indianapolis.

I was still angry. Of course I was, but I was elated too.
I'd taken on something vague and general, and I'd made it
specific.

I still didn't know what was going on in Fountain Square
or who was involved. But I'd made my point and a promise
to someone who did. I hoped for his sake that Tom Thomas
understood that I'm a man of my word. Otherwise he was
in for some hard times.

It's not that I was trying, personally, to prevent Thomas
and his cronies from doing whatever they had it in mind to
do. I cared, and probably wouldn't like it, but I'm only one
resident with one opinion. The rest could care or not, express or not. Maybe the Posse would mobilize community
opinion. Maybe they already had. It's not like I knew a frac-
tion of what they'd been up to in the last few years. Yet.

The world we live in here says people can buy and
people can sell and people can build and people can tear
down. What I do feel passionately about is that the process
should be an honest one. Say what you want, and then get it
or not. But no bullying. Especially not of the weaker, the
poorer, and the older.

Does being against bullies make me a revolutionary in
capitalist America? If so, my revolution will be restricted to

Fountain Square. Cities get big but communities don't.

My hand hurt a lot. Had I really pounded on the top of a car with a broken hand? Funny how when you're revved up ordinary things get lost. Adrenaline, the pain-killer of choice.

And now I was hurting, walking down the street in the middle of the day, carrying a flat tire.

Coming out of Ames, Kent, Hardick I'd turned east. It wasn't part of a plan. I was just trying to get away from Tom Thomas as fast as I could. But I saw that I was now in sight of the City-County Building. Home of IPD. Maybe my subconscious guided my steps. Well, who was I to ignore my subconscious? A lot of times it seems to be about all the conscious I got.

When I got to the main entrance, I asked for Proffitt. He came down to escort me up himself. In the elevator he said, "We arrested Robert Hicksen this morning."

"Who's Robert Hicksen?"

"Rochelle Vincent's nephew." As that sank in, he added, "We expect to arrest the owner of the motorcycle sometime today."

Well well well. "That means I'm a hero, right?"

"It means I'm going to let you off the hook for leaving the scene."

"Gracious just isn't the word for you, Proffitt. Where's all that southern charm shit you lay on for the ladies?"

"Hicksen shat himself during the interview."

"Before or after he gave you the name of his friend?"

"He gave us that before we finished reading his rights. He was shaking from the moment he answered the door. He couldn't give up his friend fast enough. He says he never wanted to harm his aunt. He says his friend suddenly went nuts."

"Remind me to cry."

We got out of the elevator and seemed to be heading for the same interview room we'd used before. I said, "Homer, are you not even going to ask me why I'm here?"

"To give your statement. What else?" He stopped outside the interview room door. "I left a message."

"I haven't been home for what seems a lifetime." I looked at my watch. I'd been out for considerably less than two hours.

"Well, why did you come in?"

"I thought you might reinflate my spare, what with you being full of hot air and all."

"I saw you're carrying a tire."

"Can't slip anything past you, can I, Lieutenant?"

"What's it for? You saving up for a whole car?"

In the interview room he took out the form for taking witness statements.

I said, "I don't want to talk about last night yet."

"Don't screw around, Albert. I am not in the mood. I got very little sleep."

"That Adele, she's a hottie."

He stood up. "I'm going to get someone else in here to do this."

"It's you I want, Homer. Nobody else will do. But before we talk about the past I want to talk about the future."

"What kind of game are you playing now?" He glared down at me.

"The one where the vandalism in Fountain Square suddenly stops."

"What?"

"I solved your murder for you yesterday. So I had time to sort this out for you today. I am on a roll, Homer." Although it was possibly a moot point whether a guy carrying around a flat tire can be on a roll.

With a deep sigh he sat. "Make it simple. Make it direct."

"I've just had a chat with a guy. If he wasn't behind the malicious damage himself, he knows who was."

"For Christ's sake, Albert, if you have evidence about who—"

"I don't have the kind of evidence that would make anybody shit his pants. But for various reasons I think there's a good chance that my persuasive arguments and cogent reasoning convinced this guy to make sure all the bad stuff around Fountain Square stops."

Proffitt shook his head slowly.

"But I need to know if the bad stuff doesn't stop, Homer. That's why I came in, to ask you to let me know if there are more incidents in the neighborhood. It's important. So important that I came to see you even before I got my tire fixed. Did you notice my tire? It's flat."

I made my statement and signed his form. Usually I'm fussy about giving a witness statement. Sometimes the interviewing cop changes what I say, thinking he's making it clearer. The result is language I would never use. I mean, it's *my* statement, right? It ought to be in *my* words.

But today I made nicey nicey. There was something else I wanted Proffitt to do. "I've got a favor to ask you," I said when I gave his pen back.

"Is that a joke?"

"You owe me. I put you on course to arrest a couple of murderers."

"We'd have gotten them anyway."

"But not so quickly. Last night you had your nose

pointed in the opposite direction."

He leaned back with a long-suffering expression on his face. I wondered if God's face looked like that when He, or possibly She, settles down to work through a backlog of prayers. "What?"

"My mother is very upset about what happened to Rochelle Vincent. Would you call her and tell her you've arrested one guy and know who the other one is?"

"That's the favor?"

"Yes."

"I'll do that."

"Thanks." We stood. I picked up my tire. "You don't happen to know where there's a garage around here, do you?"

40

If Proffitt left a message for me while I was out, Mary or Powder or Sam might have done the same. I went to the phones in the IPD entrance foyer. About the time I picked one up, I remembered Christopher P. Holloway.

Holloway was odds-on for having left more than one message. I didn't want to hear what he had to say, so I just dialed Mary's cell. "Hey," I said, when I got through to her.

"Hey."

"I'm returning the call you might have made after I went out this morning. I'm still out."

"I didn't call you."

After a moment I said, "That's all? No joke? No warmth?"

"My neck hurts, Albert."

"Ah. Sorry, kid, sorry. Hey, they've arrested one of the guys who ran you down. They expect to get the other one later today."

"I heard."

"Oh yeah?"

"Your lieutenant friend told me, when he called to arrange for me to make a statement. I'll probably do it tomorrow. He didn't insist on today. Just as well."

"As well as hurting, are you maybe kinda tired?"

"Can't hide anything from a detective of your caliber, can I? So where are you?"

"At IPD. You hear the background noise? That's all the felons and the misdemeanies they're bringing in to question."

"They brought you in?"

"No. I came to see Proffitt about something else."

"I thought you couldn't stand the guy."

"Work is work. It's not like I intend to date him."

"Myself, I thought he was sweet. And have you noticed his buns?" She laughed but it turned into a cough.

"Smoking's going to kill you one day," I said.

"If hanging out with you doesn't do it first."

"Fair comment."

"By the way, we're about ready to start on your sign. My guys took down your old bits and pieces in this morning and brought them in. You decided on, 'Samson Investigations,' right?"

"Is that what I said?"

"You seemed to want to keep the possibility open that Sam might join the family business."

"You don't think she might want to? She jumped at the work on Helene Miller. She's even out at that retirement place now, asking what Helene was doing there last night. And look how she found her mother on the computer. She's obviously interested in the work. So maybe I should make the sign 'Samson and Daughter.' "

There was a long hesitation before Mary said, "I think you ought to talk to Sam before you commit the sentiment to neon, Albert."

"You're so wise. How did you get that way?"

"They teach it in Crone 101."

It took me twenty minutes and directions from three passers-by to find a service station, but when I found it I found Muddy too. Muddy, a tire-mending knight in green cotton twill armor. Muddy who said, "That tire's flat, ain't it? Want me to fix it?"

Yes! Yes! Yes, Muddy, oh yes! "If you would, please."

"OK."

Muddy, the man.

In less than an hour the repaired tire was on my car. Its slashed predecessor went back to town in Muddy's pickup. I would buy a new spare later. Muddy I would date.

And I was behind the wheel again with the motor running. It was *good*. Who cared if I had a leering face on my fender? Not me.

I went home. I wanted to make sure that Mom, like Proffitt, would let me know if things continued to happen in the neighborhood. But as I entered the luncheonette Mom was not to be seen.

Normally I would have looked in her part of the house, but I was in a hurry. I had things to do. There were places I was overdue. So I took a breath and asked Norman, "Is my mother around?"

"She went out a little while ago. I'll tell her you're looking for her if she comes back."

No crack. No tone. And he'd done the speaking-civilly thing before. What was the deal?

"Thanks," I said with care. I moved to the curtain that was portal to the house and my office.

"Albert?"

"What?"

"Nice work on Rochelle Vincent's killers. That cop called your mom. He told her you gave him the idea who they might be."

"He told her that?"

"He said because of you they had less time to run or cover their tracks. Nice work."

"Thanks." We held each other's eyes for a moment.

Then Norman returned to his griddling.

Proffitt not only keeping his promise to call but saying more than I asked him to . . . Norman being civil . . . It was positively unsettling. Was I going to have to see good sides to everyone I hated? Maybe grow up a little bit?

The phone-message indicator was going crazy. I flopped a pad open on the desk and sat down. My finger was poised, genuinely poised, over the play button when the phone rang.

I hesitated, but decided to be a big boy and answer. "Samson and Daughter." Might as well see how it sounded.

"At last." Christopher P. Holloway. "Why don't you have a cell phone, or at least a pager?"

"They're on order. Look, I know you asked me to come in this morning but a police officer arrived here and—"

"I don't know how you do it, Samson. I really don't."

Do what? "What exactly are you unclear about?"

"You don't give us the reports we expect. You don't come to the office when we ask you to. You spend time—our time—finding bodies. As far as we can tell, you're doing nothing. But then something like this . . . I don't know how you do it, but you deliver."

What had I delivered? "I work in mysterious ways, all right."

"You're not taking on a little too much self-regard there, are you?"

"But, as you say, I deliver."

"You certainly do."

"Would you care to tell me which of my deliveries you're talking about?"

"Miller's resignation of course."

"Miller resigned?"

"Surely you knew that."

"Well . . . It was just a matter of time . . ."

"I only heard a few minutes ago. Apparently he gave them his letter about noon. Then he cleared his desk and *adios amigo*."

Miller quit IPD? I coughed for time. "And you're pleased?"

"That the officer who arrested our client and who was accused of corruption then resigns? You bet we're pleased."

"The accusation related to the reward, not the arrest."

"Don't bet on the jurors being able to make that distinction once Karl finishes with them."

I didn't know what to say. I wanted to be talking with Jerry, not Christopher P. Holloway. I said, "Well, well."

"Not meaning to pressure you, in the circumstances, but have you heard yet from this other cop friend of yours? The one who is looking for the real bodies-in-the-trunks killer?"

"There may be a message on my machine. I've only just come back to the office."

"You've been with the police all this time?"

Marcella at the beginning, Proffitt at the end. "Pretty much."

"Well, if there is news . . ."

"I'll let you know."

I sat with the phone in my hand and breathed fast and beat my heart fast. Miller, no longer a policeman . . . ?

41

Miller joined IPD instead of going to college. Even in high school he knew all about cops and the law. When we shared petty and not-so-petty criminal activities he could quote the statues we were breaking and the sentencing options if we were convicted.

It's not that he had relatives in the force. People in his family did not have much faith in the fairness of law enforcement. Maybe he became interested as a way of distancing himself from his family. Or maybe he just believed that being a cop was a way to help people and that helping people was a good thing.

Whatever. He joined. And, despite the racial bias and corruption that were endemic when he signed on, he worked hard and he persisted and gradually he made his way up the IPD ladder. Whenever shake-ups gave honest cops and pre-tanned cops a better deal, Miller benefited. He rose to the rank of Captain slowly, considering his talents, but he rose. There was a time when he figured if IPD ever had a black Chief it might as well be him. It wasn't, but as far as I knew he'd still harbored ambitions for the department's top spot.

Only Miller was a cop no more.

I called his cell phone. The message system cut in immediately, meaning the phone was turned off. I tried his home number, bracing myself for an exultant Janie who'd wanted him to resign. But in Wynnedale too the answering machine cut in quickly.

Well, they probably had the drawbridges up, against a media assault.

The idea of media made me think of Veronica Maitland, the television reporter with the teeth. She'd known about Jerry's suspension before I did. She must have good sources in the department.

But I couldn't think of a way to get her to talk to me.

A more practical option was to call Marcella. It seemed a long time since she was in the office. "I bet you're wondering why I'm here," she said. Instead of letting her tell me, I took her off in other directions and we never got back because Jerry called.

After which Marcella bolted from my office.

What sent her clattering down my stairs? Jerry'd just found out from me that Helene had a connection with the Milwaukee Tavern. Did that make him think it was Helene who'd fed the information to Carlo Saddler, maybe for a share of the reward and because of her debts? I knew Saddler got Willigar's name from a man, but Jerry didn't. Could that be it? Had Jerry resigned to protect Helene?

The phone rang. "Samson and Daughter."

"*There* you are, Daddy."

"Here I are. Definitely."

"Why didn't you call me back?"

"I've only just come in and I haven't listened to my messages yet."

"Hey, what was that you said when you answered the phone?"

"Just seeing how it sounds. Do you like it? I know I said you ought to do better with your life, and you should, but if what you really want is to make this a family business . . ."

"I . . ."

"Give it some thought, Daughter. So, where are you? What's up?"

"Well . . . I just left Helene, at the Millers' house."

"You've been with Helene? What happened to not letting her know you were following her?"

"It's quite a tale."

"Before you start wagging it, tell me, was Jerry there?"

"No. She's alone."

"Does Helene know where her father is?"

"He left sometime this morning to go downtown."

Downtown. Of course. To IPD to resign. It hadn't crossed my mind to try Miller at his place of no-longer-work.

"Daddy, are you going to let me tell you what I've found out or not?"

"Fire away."

"Well, you know there were two people who came out of the Milwaukee to go with Helene last night?"

"Yeah."

"Well, the guy is Marvin Hadder and the girl is Lorraine Brickman. Helene, Marvin, and Lorraine were friends before the Millers moved to Wynnedale and now they're all doing volunteer work at Sunshine Bridge one evening a week."

"They're doing *what?*"

"They talk to the residents, help put people to bed, make food if somebody wants a snack, play games. Anything, everything. That's what Mrs. Sweeney, the Director, told me. She says they've been a great help since they started, and very reliable. And Daddy?"

I was nearly too open-mouthed to say, "What?"

"I know where Helene goes the other nights too. She has a whole round of facilities where she helps out. One's for geriatrics—that's Sunshine Bridge—but there's a psychiatric place, a pediatric, a disabled, a youth club, a substance rehab place, and a halfway house for parolees. One for every night of the week."

"But . . . why?"

"I know that too, but you have to promise not to tell her parents."

"I can't do that. Jerry's crazy with worry about her. That's why you're involved in this."

"I know that. After I found out that Helene wasn't doing anything bad at the Sunshine Bridge place, I thought Uncle Jerry would want to know as soon as possible. That's the reason I went to the house when I couldn't get you—or him—on the phone. And then Helene answered the door and, well, we got talking."

"And she told you what she's up to."

"She only told me because I promised I'd let her tell her parents in her own time. But, I'm sure that'll be soon. She didn't realize they were upset about her being out so much. They never said anything."

"Tell me, Sam."

"I guess I'm going to have to trust you here."

"I guess you are."

"Well, Helene wants to change her major to social work when she goes back to college. She's doing the volunteer work to get practical experience and convince them at college that she's serious about it."

"Helene is . . . She's going to become . . . a social worker?"

"You sound the way she thinks her parents will."

"I have my own difficulties about social workers, but why does Helene think her parents won't like it?"

"It's her mom especially. Her mom thinks Helene is too

smart for teaching or social work. Her mom thinks African-Americans with the talent have a duty to be, like, lawyers and doctors and Ph.D.s. But I don't get that. Isn't social work a way to help people?"

"Janie Miller prefers people connected with her to help themselves."

"But it's got to be Helene's decision. Children can't do stuff just because their parents want them to, can they, Daddy? Did your mom and dad want you to become a private detective? I don't think so. What's important is that the child does something constructive in life. Something constructive that satisfies the child."

I told Sam to return to Bud's and I returned to my answering machine. The first message was from Don Cannon, the lawyer who batted for me in the game to get my license back. He thought he might have some work to put my way. He hoped things were going well. And was the story in the *Star* right?

The next was from Holloway, asking where the hell I was.

Then Sam, urging me to call her.

And Holloway, leaving only his name and a tone of voice.

The fifth message was from a woman named Brenda. She asked if she could make an appointment to talk about Otis, her cheating scum of a husband. She saw my name in the newspaper and decided she'd better do something about her feelings now, or it would be Otis I'd be finding in the bushes next.

Holloway again.

Then Sam, saying, "Daddy, why aren't you checking your messages? You are soo frustrating sometimes. Call me."

And that was it.

Nothing from Miller. Nothing from Powder.

I called Cannon. The job he wanted to talk about was an industrial theft case being handled by a partner in his firm. Employees were stealing from Amtrak, allegedly. Amtrak didn't like it. Did I know that the biggest train repair yard in the country was on Indy's southside? Would I be willing to go undercover? Meanwhile, what's this about finding a murder victim?

It was good talking with Cannon. Calming. By taking my mind off my immediate concerns for a few minutes I came back to them clearer, more focused. I knew I wanted to talk with Powder. Then I could devote myself to finding Miller. I was a man with a plan.

Powder wasn't at home but he answered his cell phone. "Oh. You."

"Me. Yes, and—"

"Be at my house in . . . half an hour. Otherwise this is going to have to wait, because I have to go somewhere." And he hung up on me. Gracious as ever.

At least if I was going to see Powder soon, I ought to be able to meet Mary about the usual time—if we were meeting. I was about to call her when the phone rang again. I'm such a popular boy. "Samson and Daughter."

"You're still there." It was Christopher P. Holloway.

"I am, and as it happens I've just made an appointment to see my police contact. I'll call you as soon as I'm finished with him, but you might want to give me a number for after-hours in case I have to go somewhere with him."

"Forget it," Holloway said.

"Sorry, I'm not quite sure what you're saying. Call you in the morning?"

"Don't bother calling at all."

"I still don't get it. What do you mean by 'don't bother'?"

"I mean," Holloway said, "you're off the case."

"What?"

"It's no complaint with you. I'm off the fucking case too."

"You're going too fast for me. Has something happened? Did Ronnie Willigar top himself, or decide to plead guilty, or what?"

"Karl has just informed me that the people funding Willigar's defense have pulled out."

"Just like that?"

"Just like that. Karl says he got the call a few minutes ago. And I'm not any happier about this than you are, Samson. In fact, I'm fucking furious. I've been busting my ass on this case. I've . . ." He stopped himself. "What's the point? It's just the way it is. You can't change it. I can't change it."

"Who are they, these people who've pulled out?"

He hesitated. Was his anger being measured against his discretion? He said, "I can't really tell you."

"I'm the guy who lost his license rather than give up a source, remember."

"There is . . . No. I can't tell you."

"Well then, how about telling me what, exactly, you can't tell me?"

"What I can't tell you?" He gave a snort. "I can't tell you that there's a group of businessmen and professionals who get together for things like this, and . . ."

"And?"

"I can't tell you that Karl's one of them."

"And what don't they do when they get together?"

"They don't fund . . . situations like this one."

"And what kind of situations would those not be?"

"Ones that . . . Well, the truth is that these people are

. . . Well, they think of themselves as the ultimate guardians of how things ought to be. They are . . . uncomfortable . . . about the prominence being achieved in Indianapolis by members of certain . . . groups."

"Do you mean some of the secret societies?" Indiana is secret society heaven.

"No."

"Well, what sort of groups?"

"The p-c sort. No, I can't say any more. I can't tell you this."

"Certainly not. And you already haven't told me a single thing. I'd swear to that on a Bible, or a checkbook, or anything else held sacred. But I'm trying to understand what you haven't told me, Mr. Holloway. Is this something to do with Gerald Miller?"

"Of course it is. We told you that when you were hired."

"I mean the fact that he's African-American."

"Give the man a prize." I heard a nervy laugh.

"So the issue is race?"

"I could never say that."

"I know, and you haven't."

"They don't like it when the blacks—or the others—get too much success. There, I've said it."

"No you haven't."

"No. I haven't. You're absolutely right." Then, "You're not recording this, are you?"

"Certainly not. I'm not wired. I'm not plugged in. I'm not transponded. I'm barely breathing. All I'm doing is trying to understand what you're telling me."

"I'm telling you that a group of influential business and professional men in this city puts together a fighting fund whenever they think they can undermine the high-profile achievements of minority professionals. Your pal Miller cracked a huge case, the most media-intensive and media-sensitive case we've had in this city for years. He cracked it after a string of white officers failed and as a result his big smile was all over the papers and the TV. So you and I were paid to defend Ronnie Willigar and bring down your pal. This morning Miller resigned, under a cloud of accusation and suspicion. So the group funding the defense figures they've achieved their goal, that to spend any more money would be pissing it away. So you're out of a job and, if I had a shred of dignity, I would be too. I hope you took all that in, Samson, because I'm not ever going to say it out loud again."

"Thank you, Mr. Holloway. For not telling me that."

"You're welcome."

"Does this group call itself anything?"

"I can't possibly tell you that they call themselves The Guys. Do you like that? The Guys. And don't forget, it's not just the blacks and the yellows and the reds they hate. It's women too. And Jews. And gays. And the disabled." He forced a chuckle. "In fact they hate everybody except themselves."

"It always works that way, doesn't it?"

"It does."

"How do they decide who to go after? Do they have meetings?"

"I don't know. I only know this much because Karl trusts me, up to a point."

"Karl struck me as an asshole."

"I couldn't possibly agree with you, enthusiastically."

"Mr. Holloway, why do you work with him?"

"Why did you take a job undermining your friend? For the money, of course. Because I've got a wife and kids and a lifestyle. And because I've got a better job here than I'd get

anywhere else. Because I'm no star. I just lucked into it."
He gave a laugh, though not a funny one. "Samson, I hope
you banked the check we gave you, because they're stopping any that haven't cleared."

"I banked it."

"Good."

"If you're off the case now, does that leave Ronnie
Willigar with the public defenders?"

"No no. Karl still represents him. There just isn't any
money. Karl will cut a deal for the poor sap if he can, and if
he can't, he'll send me to watch the execution."

"Does that mean Willigar did it?"

"I don't have the slightest idea, Samson. Do you?"

42

I sat by my phone in a kind of suspended animation. It was
as if any movement would shake the new information and
new understanding out of my head.

A secret society to whitewash society . . .

Could it be real?

Could it not be real?

I should have asked Holloway—and Benton—more questions. I should have demanded to know how an isolated figure
like Ronnie Willigar came to have high-budget legal representation. I did ask eventually, but never pursued an answer. I
had my big check. I was excited to have a big job so soon.

I was disappointed in myself.

I was grateful—very grateful—to Holloway for telling me
what he had. I was also sorry for the guy. Would he find the
shred of dignity that would enable him to quit?

I got up and went to the basin in my bathroom. I washed
my hands and face.

Who were The Guys? How long had they been oper-
ating? What other "situations" had they influenced? Who
had they undermined?

Could all this be true?

Could it not?

I washed again.

What about Willigar? With the stroke of Miller's pen on
the resignation letter, Perkins, Baker, Pinkus and Lestervic
washed Ronnie Willigar away. Should I be feeling sympathy
for a man who had a box of obscene souvenirs in his bed-

room? *Was* it possible that Ronnie Willigar'd been framed?

Maybe I'd have a better feel for that when I knew what Powder had managed to glean. I dried myself. I got my stuff together.

Influential men who combine forces to undermine . . . It was enough to give substance to anybody's feeling of paranoia. Did Jerry have a clue?

I tried his IPD number. There was no answer. I tried his civilian numbers again. I left call-me messages this time.

Of course he didn't have a clue. He'd barely confronted details of his situation within IPD, much less an outside effort to get his scalp.

Which had succeeded.

I felt unsettled. It was like I had awakened from a sleep of years. So much had happened so fast. The only calming part of it was . . .

I called Mary. "Hey," I said. "About tonight."

"Let me guess. We've been together so long things are getting stale for you."

"That is so far from the truth . . ."

"Don't go soft on me, big guy."

"We never said whether we're meeting."

"Do you want to?"

"Yes."

"All right. But could we skip the rapists and murderers, just this once?"

"I'll try to get all them out of the way this afternoon."

"That won't get you out of feeding me."

"I wouldn't want it to. In fact we could go to an all-you-can-eat place. Unless you're barred everywhere."

We fixed on a downtown bar. We fixed a time.

I set out for Powder's via Virginia Avenue. Passing the

turn to Timothy Battle's church reminded me I wanted to talk with him too. I'm not *au fait* with how reverend persons spend their non-Sunday time, but I resolved to call when I got a chance. It would have been convenient to have a cell phone . . .

A watch I have, and I decided there was just enough time to stop and see my own personal Savior, Muddy-the-Tire, and pick up my new spare.

However, my calculations didn't allow for a Muddy sermon about everything He'd done, and how the new tire should go straight on the car, and how He should rotate the others and rebalance them. This was a Man who took His tires seriously—which was why I loved Him—but all I had time to do was put an offering in the collection plate.

I was only seven minutes late for Powder. I wouldn't have been surprised to find the cranky old bat had gone. It was Powder, after all. Not someone normal. However he stood at his door as I parked. I was relieved to be wrong.

"I don't have all day, Mr. Investigator," he said as I walked up the path. "Some of us have places to be."

"Don't tell me. You've got a date with a lady of Mexican origin who you're taking for a Korean meal?"

"Don't be silly."

"Oh. Right."

He led me to his kitchen. There was a notebook and an open file folder on the table. "What's with the bandages?" he asked as we sat.

"Couple of broken fingers."

"Shouldn't chew your nails." He held up a hand. "Just my little joke. I heard about what happened last night."

"No rest for the re-licensed private eye."

"If it was me, you'd be locked up for leaving the scene."

Powder's casual aggression made me feel tired—and I

had a lot to feel tired about. I just waited for him to get on with whatever he had to say.

He picked up the notebook. "Now let's see. You asked me to find out if any of the people on this list have contacts inside the department."

"Yes."

"It was the wrong question, Mr. Gumshoe."

"It was?"

"Think about it. If you saw somebody in the street, how long would it take you to find out who their good friends are? Days, weeks . . . Well, what you did was give me a list of four people on the street. Hopeless. And your question wasn't even what you wanted to know."

"What did I want to know?"

"I'm trying to help you become a better gumshoe here. You could sound a little more grateful."

"Thanks."

"What you really wanted to know was who had access to Miller's list. Do you see? Establish access, then look for a connection to one of the names."

I waited.

"And access is also a much better question to ask *me*." He rubbed his face. "You people outside the department have grandiose ideas about the amount of information cops can get. I probably wouldn't do much better with the friends of a person on the street than you would." At last he picked up his notebook. "Well, yes I would, but the point is that when it comes to tracking access to a document within IPD—"

"Who had access?"

"Do you see now? If you think it through and ask the right question—"

"Who had access?"

"You'll be a better gumshoe. I'm trying to help you here."

"I've had a hard day, Powder. In fact a lot of hard days. Who had fucking access?"

"Nobody."

"What's that supposed to mean?"

"It means the report arrived on the Friday afternoon. It came by courier. The secretary to whom the courier reported was told it had to be delivered into Miller's own hands. Which it duly was, once they found him down at the soda machine. The secretary saw Miller receive the report about four o'clock. She saw him put it into a briefcase on his desk. She saw him close the briefcase and lock it. When he left for home about an hour later she saw he was carrying the briefcase. No one else went into the office between the report's arrival and Miller's departure. The secretary in question happens to be a friend of mine. I trust her on this matter completely."

"You're saying no one had access."

"Listen up. I'm saying no one at IPD had access."

If no one at IPD had access . . .

Powder leaned back in his chair. "Miller himself says he took the report home and didn't come back with it until the Monday. I suggest that the next question you ask is who could have had access to the briefcase over the weekend, and I suggest that you put that question to the former Captain."

"Well, where does this leave us?" I said.

"Us? *Us?* You plopped yourself down here with a theory that Ronnie Willigar was maybe being framed with the help of someone in IPD. I've examined your hypothesis and found it sucks. That leaves *us* nowhere. That leave *us* with you about to haul your sorry ass back to your car so I can

305

get on with something more important, like trimming my toenails. I only have seven toes, by the way. Did you know that?"

I left Powder to his feet. I was more concerned with my fingers. They were throbbing and hot and uncomfortable.

Powder was right about access to Miller's report. It was something I should have asked Jerry myself. An area I should have pushed. Private eye on a roll has another flat. Well, I would repair the omission when I finally got access to Jerry.

But I didn't feel like finding a phone to try his numbers yet again.

Something different was in my head. Something I wouldn't be able to do for much longer if I put it off now.

43

The facility where Indy's accused are detained is in the Marion County Sheriff's Department, one door to the south of IPD. It has cell blocks on the second, third, and fourth floors and, generally speaking, the accommodation is not felicitous. I know. I've spent nights there. More than once.

This time, at least, I went in through the Sheriff's Department door rather than through the connecting passages from IPD. I made my way to the officer who controls visitation to inmates. The nametag on her chest read "X. Orbaum." She sat at a desk covered with potted plants and pictures of children. "Sir?" she said.

"I am an investigator working for the defense counsel of Ronnie Willigar. I need to see Mr. Willigar, please." I gave her the letter on Perkins, Baker, Pinkus and Lestervic stationery that confirmed my status.

X. Orbaum read the letter carefully. "It says here you're an investigator."

"Yeah."

"License, please."

I pulled out my old one. "I was suspended for a while, but I was reinstated last Thursday. I don't have the new actual license, but I am legal."

"Not here, you're not." She gave my old license back.

"Perkins, Baker, Pinkus and Lestervic wouldn't have hired me if I wasn't legit." She looked bored. "You don't want to be the cause of a mistrial, do you?"

"I won't be. Not for denying entry to someone without the right paperwork."

I didn't want to ask her to call Holloway. The only thing I could think of to say was, "Call Homer Proffitt at IPD. He'll vouch for me. Lieutenant Homer Proffitt. This is urgent."

Officer Orbaum stared without moving for so long I was about to give up and go away. But then she said, "Sit over there," and pointed to a couple of chairs.

I sat over there.

She made a call. She read from my accreditation letter. She glanced my way and looked like she was trying not to smile. When finally she hung up, I began to rise, but she held up a hand and then made another call. At last she beckoned me over.

I couldn't have been more like a dog begging for a bone if I tried.

She pointed to a door. "Knock on that door and go through. Officer Jarlett will search you and then show you where to go."

"Thank you." I turned but hesitated long enough to say, "May I ask what the 'X' stands for?"

"It marks the spot."

"What spot?"

"Where you find my heart if you dig deep enough."

X. Orbaum was, no doubt, a bundle of laughs. Officer Jarlett was not. He was big, rough and thorough. He took his time. When finally he was finished I felt so *searched*.

Lawyers—and lawyers' representatives—meet their clients in small rooms not unlike the interview rooms in IPD. They have a table and chairs. There's a glass panel in the door.

I sat where I would see Ronnie Willigar as he entered. The idea of meeting him face-to-face felt necessary, while I was outside. The guy's legal defense was, effectively, gone. No one at IPD was considering anyone else for the bodies-in-the-trunks rapes and murders. I'd wanted to see the guy for myself. See him with my own eyes. The new ones that saw things. I needed to know if he needed me to bat for him when so many others had struck out. At least that's what I needed before I got there.

Now, the longer I waited for him, the less comfortable I became. The guy had probably killed five women . . . At least five women. I wanted to be alone in a room with him . . . why?

Willigar was brought in handcuffed. He was about my height but thin, with dark stubble and short, black hair slicked back. His prison uniform looked too big, but he moved easily, athletically. He sat in the chair across the table from me.

"I'll be outside," Jarlett said. "Give you about half an hour. Knock if you want out sooner." He left and closed the door.

Willigar flicked his head in the direction of the departing guard. "He don't like me much."

"No?"

"He don't say it, but I can tell."

"Yeah?"

"You want to know something?" He bent toward me across the table.

It was all I could do to keep from jumping back and running for the door. "What?"

"I don't care much for him neither."

"Oh."

Ronnie Willigar's face stayed close to mine. It tilted

downward slightly but he kept me fixed with his light brown
eyes. "That fella has secrets," Willigar said of the guard.
"Bad secrets." He winked confidentially.

"You think so?"

"I know so. I can see that in people. I can see their secrets. It's a gift." He nodded. He smiled. "People don't
care much for it, 'cause they can't hide what they want to
hide. All I have to do is look them in the eyes and I can see
it all."

"That sounds . . . disconcerting." I picked the word because I was disconcerted.

"I got the gift, all right, but you don't have to worry. I
don't see nothing bad in you, not bad out of the ordinary
way."

"No?" I shook my head.

"It's true," he said. "I'm right."

But that wasn't why I was shaking myself. I was trying to
get a grip. I was trying to get control of the conversation. I
wanted—needed—to find out if he was a killer, and a rapist.
I said, "Tell me something."

He scratched under his chin with a finger. "Fire away."

"Tell me what you see when you look in a mirror." Did
he see what Miller saw in Willigar's eyes? Guilt? Undeni-
able rape-and-murder guilt?

But instead of answering, the man before me rocked
back in his chair and loosed a bunch of short, loud hoots.
They caught me by surprise.

And then he tipped himself forward again. Both his el-
bows were on the table and he was almost out of his chair.
"Now *that* would be telling, wouldn't it?"

"It would." I nodded.

"I couldn't do that."

"Why not?"

"Wouldn't be secrets then, would they?"

"Then tell me something else," I said. "When you look into a woman's eyes, do you see her secrets too?"

For just a moment his face went dead. Was that when I finally lost belief in the possibility of his innocence? He said, "Sometimes."

"Good secrets, or are they always bad secrets?"

"Most secrets are bad." He twisted in his chair, though without losing eye contact.

"I didn't know that."

"They are. Most of them."

Willigar and I stared at each other. He and Miller both believed they could see truths in people's eyes. Did that make them the same?

Willigar smiled.

Fuck it. They *were* different. Jerry was right and Willigar was crazy. In any real world, that difference mattered.

Willigar scratched the back of his neck and the way he looked at me changed. It was as if he was focusing on the man in front of him instead of trying to see inside my head. "Who the hell are you, mister?" he asked. "They said you're my lawyer, but you ain't Chris and you ain't Karl."

"I'm an investigator. I've been working for Chris and Karl."

"But not any more?"

How could he tell? I didn't answer.

"You're not going to get me out of here then, are you?" He leaned forward again. "Are you? Are you?"

44

When I emerged into daylight I walked to the end of the block where there's a little park with low walls that enclose flower beds. I wanted a spot where I could sit in the sun. A spot out of the darkness of Ronnie Willigar's soul. I sat on a wall, Willigar's fate no longer my business.

I lifted my face to the sun. I closed my eyes, though that hardly seemed necessary considering how little I'd used them for so long. I'd failed to see what was in front of me for years, decades. Not just recently.

Take The Guys. A revelation in the specific case, but also no more than a manifestation of attitudes that have been powerful in Indianapolis all my life. Attitudes I'd opted not to see. Stuff I'd closed my eyes to.

But I saw The Guys now. And Tom Thomas and his cronies. What was different?

I was different.

I got into private-eyeing by accident. Circumstance buffeted me a little and then it seemed like a good idea. A way to make a living and help some people with their problems and keep some independence.

I was never a raging success, but I managed to meet my needs. And I was happy doing it, even if I didn't quite realize that till I lost my license. No-license equaled un-happy-bunny. And now I was sitting in the sun, a private eye again, ready to hop. I just wanted to do it right this time.

But what's "right" and what's "doing it"? Making

money, if it meant I had to take orders from the likes of
Karl Benton? No no.

As I sat I felt an urge to call Brenda, the woman with a
faithless husband. Maybe that kind of job was more my
speed. I was going to have to learn to see myself, along with
seeing everybody else.

I used the excuse of a wispy cloud passing across the sun
to get myself moving again. I got up and headed for the
mall that has transformed Indy's downtown. I wanted to
transform myself. I bought a cell phone.

Emile, the salesboy, went through what was necessary to
make it active. Then he showed me what was necessary to
make a call. I practiced in front of him. I called myself at
home. I wasn't in, so I left a message. "This is me, you
high-tech devil."

"Good job," Emile said, sounding like he'd never said it
before. He popped a thick instruction book into a plastic
bag. He all but patted me on the head as he sent me on my
way.

Once on the sidewalk I stopped to make a call by myself
while I still remembered how. I didn't have Brenda's
number, but I did have Timothy Battle's.

After a few rings I got a system-voice that said, "This
call is being forwarded." Had Battle been pulled away from
sermon-writing to preside at a shotgun marriage, or expel a
demon, or administer last rites to someone worried about
his wrongs? Then Battle, speaking through an echoic
acoustic and a lot of background noise, said, "Sonia?"

"Not Sonia. This is Albert Samson." There was a pause.
"The private investigator, Joe Ellison's friend?"

After a crackle he said, "I remember perfectly well who
you are, Mr. Samson."

"I'd like to come by for a talk. Do you have a few minutes?"

Pause. "When did you have in mind?"

"Now, if that's possible."

Pause. "Not possible at the moment, Mr. Samson. I'm at an altitude of a little over two thousand feet."

"I didn't realize reverends got high."

Pause. "In my plane, Mr. Samson, in my plane. Look, I have some stops to make after I land, so I won't be back at the church until seven or seven-thirty. I can see you then or, if it's urgent, you could always come out to the airport. I'll be down in about twenty minutes. Hopefully not much sooner."

Everything in my life felt urgent. "I'll need some directions," I said.

Greenwood Municipal Airport is about ten miles to the south-southeast of the city center. It seems to rise up out of cornfields and comes complete with a housing development, a hospital, and a golf course.

Battle was waiting in the lounge. He sat at a table by a rank of vending machines and got up as I approached. "Care for some coffee? Or a sandwich, or a cup of soup?"

"I don't see you with anything." I sat. "Eaten here before?"

"They're a bit short on soul food."

"I'll pass, thanks."

He gathered some papers that were spread on the table and put them into a leather bag as he sat again. "What's so urgent?"

"Some things have happened recently." Could my showdown with Tom Thomas really have been only this morning? It seemed a lifetime ago.

"I read the newspaper report about you, if that's what you mean. Shocking for such a tragic death to occur in our neighborhood."

"I'm talking about the vandalism."

"We've had no more incidents at the church."

"If you do, I'd like you to let me know about them as soon as you can."

Battle studied me. "Why?"

"It's a long story, but I believe the vandalism in the neighborhood and at your church had a purpose behind it."

"Everything happens for a purpose, Mr. Samson."

"I'll leave the ecclesiastical generalities to you. My thinking is more specific. I believe the damage at your church has been aimed at getting you to sell the building and land."

"I see." His face showed no new expression.

"The house next to your church is empty. Are there other unoccupied properties on the block?"

"I couldn't say."

"But there is a lot of land on the church's site itself. Much more than you've paved for parking."

"We enjoy the bounty of ample space. We use it for community events."

"Reverend Battle, has there been an approach to buy the church and the land?"

"Not since I've been on the scene, Mr. Samson."

"That's about a year and a half, if I remember rightly."

He nodded. "Yes."

"I had a talk with a lawyer this morning," I said. "The lawyer representing the arsonists who attacked your church. And he said something interesting. He said 'The guy wants to do the deal and you can't stop it.' "

"What deal would that be, Mr. Samson?"

315

"I figure it's the deal to purchase your church and its land."

Battle and I sat staring at each other. I'd seen his poker face before, but he hadn't seen mine. And whatever the power of his stare, he had nothing on Ronnie Willigar.

He spoke first. "A sale would not be up to me. Such things are entirely in the hands of our Board of Trustees."

"Would you oppose a sale?"

"That would depend on the terms."

"How about the Trustees?"

After a moment he said, "Many of the current Board helped raise the funds to build the existing sanctuary twenty-eight years ago. It was a mammoth task. A blessed achievement."

"So they have emotion and sentiment invested in the place and might never sell," I said. "Unless . . ." Pennies were beginning to drop. "You're an ambitious man, aren't you?"

"I'm not sure my ambitions are your business, Mr. Samson."

"Since you arrived at the church has the size of the congregation increased?"

He said nothing, but for once I felt he was uncomfortable.

"It has, hasn't it? And you want a bigger church."

"It's no secret that the scope of our ministry is restricted by the size and design of the current building."

"And if you sell the existing property, with its access to the interstate, to a commercial enterprise, say, then chances are you'll have enough money to build a bigger church elsewhere."

"More space, more people, more activities, more worship."

316

"You already knew who was behind the vandalism, didn't you?"

"Did I?"

"Because you're working with them. You told them the only way to get your trustees to sell was to make staying put hell. That way, when the offer comes it will seem like the solution to a terrible problem. Almost a Heaven-sent solution."

Battle said nothing.

And then another dawning. "I am so innocent," I said.

"Are you?"

"It costs a lot to run a plane, doesn't it? You're in for a cut."

45

I surprised myself by being upset as I drove back to town. Why should I care if a church guy was cutting himself a deal? Did I really expect the church business to be any different from any other business in a buy-and-sell world?

It seemed that I did because people like Joe Ellison and Juice Jackson expected better of people in Battle's position.

Still, if Battle did really well and became a prominent civic figure, at least there were always The Guys to bring him down to earth.

A sick joke for a pilot if there ever was one.

I laughed, but only a little.

And then I wondered if I was being innocent about The Guys as well. Holloway said they put money together to undermine people. Might they also make more active interventions?

It was a scary thought. I wondered how to follow it up. Could I try to contact Veronica Maitland, the TV reporter with the teeth, about The Guys? She had political contacts and good sources inside IPD. And she was not a guy . . . It was something to consider. Another day.

I was nearly home when I remembered my new cell phone. It gave me the technology to pick up my messages on the move. But I was too close to bother.

Nor did I bother with messages as I passed the flashing lights on my machine. I was looking for my mother.

I found her in the small room where she watches TV.

She was playing Scrabble with Norman. "Norman is looking after me, son," she said. "I'm feeling a bit blue. Identifying Rochelle . . . Making arrangements . . ."

I sat next to her on the couch. I put an arm around her. "I'm so sorry about your friend."

She seemed to shrink into my chest. "Me too."

"Posy," Norman said, "there was something you wanted to say to Albert."

Mom sat up again. "Was there? Oh, of course there was. I'm so proud of what you did about those killers, son."

It had been a very long time since I heard my mother express pride in me. "Thank you. Thanks for saying so."

"That policeman told me how you helped. Oh . . . you know the one."

"Proffitt."

"That's him. Homer Proffitt. Adele's man. I clean forgot his name."

It wasn't like my mother to be vague with names. But she didn't have a friend murdered every day either. There was something I was overdue to say to her too. "I'm proud of you too, Mom."

"You are?"

"Getting people together the way you have. Doing what you do. It's a hell of a thing."

"Well . . . Thank you, son."

Which also reminded me . . . "How is Boris doing?"

"Boris? Oh, he's fine. They released him."

"Vagrant," Norman said, adding three letters to "rant." "Fifteen." He fished in the tile bag.

"Let me see now." Mom studied her letter rack. "I'm not doing very well today."

I said, "I'll let you get on with your game, but I want to ask a favor."

She looked up. "A favor?"

"If there's more vandalism in the neighborhood, I'd like to be told about it."

"I . . . What was that again, son?" Mom looked so old, sitting there.

Norman caught my eye. I didn't look away. He said, "You'll be told."

"Thank you," I said to him, possibly for the first time in my life.

He nodded. Then he said, "Posy? Have you got a play?"

"What? Oh. Well, it's not very good." She laid four letters out and made "rover" on Norman's "v." "How many is that?"

"Too many. You're still way ahead."

"Really? It doesn't feel like it." Mom ran a hand through her hair. She looked up at me again. "It's good news about Sam, isn't it, son? Maybe things like that run in the family and I never knew it."

"What news, Mom?"

She covered her mouth coyly. "Did I do an oopsie?"

I left Mom and went to the luncheonette. Sam could tell me the good news herself.

Except she wasn't there. Martha, who usually only works at lunchtimes, was clearing up. "Hi, Mr. Samson."

"I'm looking for my little girl."

"She had some business thing." Martha waved her hand, successfully conveying vagueness. "Norman said to close up."

"Great. Thanks."

I went up to my office. I had enough time to check my messages before I left to meet Mary. None was from Sam, and I saved the first three without hearing them out—from

Cannon's partner, from Brenda, and from Flossy McCardle, the *Nuvo* reporter.

The last message was different. I listened to it twice. "Not there, huh?" Miller said. "Well, I'm not entirely here either. I . . . I don't know, Al . . . Give me a call. On the cell."

I dialed the number. It rang until the message service clicked in. I said, "Jerry, call me back on . . ." I found the scrap of paper I'd written my new cell phone number on and read it to him. "Anytime."

When I got to Mary, she was already there and nursing a cup of coffee. Beside it was a nearly empty plate of wings.

"Is that *coffee* coffee," I said as I slid into the booth beside her, "or is there something stronger in it?"

"I'm only here because I don't want to be the one who breaks our record of consecutive meetings, Albert. I'd much rather be at home in bed." She held a finger up. "*Don't* even say it."

I didn't. "If I hadn't had an extraordinary day, I would have collapsed five times myself." I took her hand with my good one. "I'm running on pure adrenaline."

She picked up a menu. "Can I get adrenaline here?"

I put my new phone on the table.

"What's that horrible purple thing?"

"Emile told me it might not be the prettiest, but it works the best."

"It's yours?"

I bowed.

"Wow." She looked at me. "It must have been quite a day. But, honestly, that's about all the excitement I can stand tonight. OK?"

"You got it." Then, "Where's your neck brace?"

"Where's the new dressing for your hand, Mother?"

"I'm going to the bar to see if they have one there. You want something?"

"More coffee and some food."

"Here?"

"Is here where I am?"

I came back to the table with coffee and a beer.

She said, "An extraordinary day, huh?"

"Yeah."

"Well, why don't you pick one thing and tell me that."

It was hard to choose but, "The worst part was not being able to talk with Jerry Miller since he resigned from IPD."

"He resigned?"

"This morning."

"Why?"

"I don't know. I picked up a message from him before I came out and he sounded completely adrift. I left him a message back, with this number." I patted my new phone.

It rang.

"Is that something I did?" I asked.

"You have a call, Samsdad."

I panicked. "I . . . I . . . I don't remember how."

She picked it up, pushed a button, and said, "This is the new technology of Albert Samson. One moment, please." She held it out.

"Jerry?"

"What was that about?"

"My new secretary. They sell them with cell phones these days. Amazing what a little competition will do, eh?"

After a moment he said, "I guess you heard."

"Yeah. Can we talk about it?"

"What's to say?"

"Quite a lot, I'd have thought. Where are you?"

"At home. I'm packing."

"You're leaving?"

"Damn right."

"Jerry, is this to do with Helene?"

"Helene? How could . . . Oh, do you mean the social work stuff? Hell, whatever makes her happy."

So the resignation was not because of Helene. "Where are you going now? Marcella's?"

"I won't be doing that just now. But I'm sure as hell going somewhere."

"You don't have any place in mind?"

"The world is full of places."

"Stay at mine." He didn't respond immediately. "No one will look for you there." More silence at his end. "Finish your packing. Get something to eat. Be at my place at . . ." I looked at my watch. "Nine? Nine-thirty?"

"You're sure? Given the circumstances?"

"The circumstances? Oh, our recent history . . . I'm sure," I said.

"Thanks, Al," he said, and hung up.

As I sat wondering what Jerry would have to say, Mary took the phone from my hand and pushed some.

"Now, now, Little Albert," she said, "don't you know better than to invite your buddy for a sleepover without asking permission?"

We finished eating in time to be at my place a little after eight-thirty. I wanted to get Mom's spare room ready, either for Jerry or for me. Mary even volunteered to go without dessert.

We drove in tandem but as I parked I saw that Miller was already there, waiting on my stairs beside a garment bag.

323

"Hey, Jerry," I said as I crossed the street.

He stood up. "I appreciate this. I really do." He stepped back to let me go up first.

"Hang on a sec," I said. Mary was with us a moment later. "Jerry, Mary. Mary, Jerry. She's the secretary who came with the phone. Say, 'Hi.' "

"Hi."

"Hi."

I headed up the stairs. In my office we found Sam, working at the computer.

"I didn't realize you were having a party," Miller said.

"You remember my baby girl," I said.

"This is Sam? Wow. Well well."

"Hello, Uncle Jerry."

I said, "Why don't you stow your stuff in the next room."

"Is this a good idea, Al?" He glanced at Mary.

"I'm not staying," Mary said. "I disappear when he turns off the phone."

"Did you eat?" I said.

"No. I . . . I wasn't hungry."

"Dump the bag. We'll go down the street to Peppy. The girls can play girlie computer smoking games."

"Don't underestimate how much grrrrr there is in girls, Daddy," Sam said.

I led Miller out and we left them to it.

Open 24/7, people come to Peppy Grill from all over the city. It draws an altogether different clientele from Mom's neighborhood breakfast and lunch crowd. The only thing against taking Miller there was that Peppy is a cop stop. Once a prospective robber pulled a gun on the cashier only to find three cop guns ringing his neck in less time than it took him to say, Just kidding.

I guided Miller to one of several tables in a porch annex. I figured we'd have a better chance for privacy out there. "I'm still not hungry," he said as we sat.

"Eat anyway. When you're under stress you have to keep your blood sugar up."

"And my cholesterol down. And my arms out sideways."

"The chili isn't Mom's, but it's edible." He shrugged as a waitress duly appeared at the table. "Chili for my friend and two regular coffees."

"Sure thing," she said.

Miller said, "Sam's all grown up now."

"Been married and divorced and everything. How long since you saw her?"

He shook his head.

"She's probably joining the business, you know."

"The luncheonette?"

"The private eye business."

He opened his eyes wide, but I didn't think it was a joke.

I said, "The kid's got a taste for detection. Can't you see it? 'Samson and Daughter' in neon? She's the one who found out what Helene's been up to at night, you know."

Miller took out his wallet. "I owe you for that. One or the other of you."

"No, you don't."

We looked at each other. He put his wallet away.

The coffees arrived.

When we were alone again I asked what I wanted to know. "Jerry, why did you resign?"

He blew on the coffee surface and sipped. "Because I behaved unprofessionally."

"What's that mean?"

"It means I took the bodies-in-the-trunks report home to

read." He took a deep breath. "Doing that inadvertently provided the opportunity for stuff to be copied from it, in particular the list of prime suspects."

"Who by?"

"Marcella. She copied the names and gave them to her husband."

"She *what?*"

"She tell you about her ex? Harry the Asshole Garlick?"

"Yeah . . ."

"Well, Harry the Asshole convinced the dumb bitch he'd leave us alone and go to Alaska if only he had enough money."

"She told me something like that."

"So as soon as this hundred and ten grand reward was announced, he was on her like a blanket for inside information, from me."

"But he's a cop. He can't collect a reward."

"He can if he finds a front man. Enter Carlo Saddler."

"I talked to Saddler myself. He said the man who gave him the Willigar information didn't talk about splitting the reward money."

"Maybe Garlick intends to deal with that once it's paid. If it's paid."

"Might it not be?"

"There is a list of conditions that have to be met. But I don't know about this case." He threw his hands up. "Not my business. Not now."

"But you are certain Garlick got information from you through Marcella?"

"Yeah. She gave him the list. Then he must have broken into the guys' houses until he found Willigar's box."

"But I thought you took the report home to work on that weekend so Janie would know you weren't seeing Marcella."

"I stopped at Marcella's on my way home." He sighed. "For weeks I'd been talking about what I hoped the report would give me when it came. How I thought it could make my career." He shook his head. "I hung myself out to dry. It's my own fucking fault."

"How did Garlick pick Carlo Saddler to work with?"

"Marcella thinks he knew him because he arrested the dumb fuck once. Then, when he followed me to the Milwaukee and saw Saddler behind the bar—"

"I thought Garlick followed *her*."

"Me too sometimes. When he saw Saddler he must have worked out that he could cause trouble for me at the same time as going for the reward because of the Milwaukee connection. Marcella says it's Harry who called Whistle-Blowers and started their investigation of me."

"Great."

"Yeah."

"OK," I said, "so Marcella was the source of the information. Why resign? Get them to break Saddler down, and bust Garlick out of the job—and maybe into a jail."

"I can't," Miller said. "Anything I do puts Marcella front and center."

The chili came. "Give him fries and some pie with that," I said to the waitress. "He needs building up."

"What kind of pie?" the waitress asked.

"Cherry because it rhymes with Jerry."

That was enough to get us some privacy again.

I said, "Marcella would testify against Garlick, wouldn't she?"

"All she could testify to for sure was that she gave him the list. What if they don't believe the rest of it? What if they prosecute her as an accessory to the fraud?" Miller shook his head. "You know how hard they come down on cops. At least the ones who aren't connected."

"You guys gotta be whiter than white these days, huh?"

"Droll."

Which reminded me about The Guys. I thought about asking Miller if he knew anything about them. But I decided to leave it for another time. He had personal business to concentrate on. The Guys would keep. In fact, maybe eventually we could go after them together. My sign could always read "Samson and Daughter and Best Friend."

"What?" he asked.

"Nothing. Eat."

He ate. He ate more. "Not bad. But—"

"Not as good as my mother's."

"How is your mother?" He hesitated. "She is still . . ."

"Alive? Yes."

"Good. Good." The fries came.

He salted them, ketchupped them, and pushed the plate between us. We each took one. We'd shared countless plates of fries as kids. We couldn't afford two plates back then.

He said, "Marcella only found out last night what Harry the Asshole did."

"Yeah?"

"That's why she came to see you this morning. She wanted advice. Because, pathetic as you are, you're still my best friend."

"That makes you pathetic too."

"I can't argue about that." Miller wiped his mouth. "Maybe I'm the one who should be asking you for advice."

"About . . . ?"

"Her. Marcella. What she did."

I thought about Marcella and what she did. "She made a mistake," I said.

"More than just a 'mistake.' " The fierceness with which he said it underlined—as if it was needed—how big a deal it was for him to quit IPD.

"I didn't say it was a little mistake, but her intention was to make things better for the two of you. And all she did was get manipulated by someone who's known how to manipulate her for years."

He studied his chili.

"We all make mistakes, Jerry," I said. "Even you."

Our eyes locked. He knew full well what I was referring to. He said, "It was not a mistake for me to have your license pulled, Al. I don't regret it. I'd do it again."

"In that case, my best advice is that you shoot Harry Garlick and try to get off by pleading sanity."

"You got a gun I can borrow? I had to turn mine in."

"Mom has guns. She'll lend you one."

"Your mother has guns?"

"She goes to a gun club. She probably has certificates and medals."

"Quite a woman, your mom."

"Yeah," I said. "She is." But this was no more the time to tell him about Posy's Posse than it was to talk about The Guys.

Suddenly I was struck by the similarity between what the Posse was doing and what The Guys were doing. Both pooling resources of the like-minded to restore a world gone bad as they saw it. But there had to be a difference. Didn't there?

"Al?"

And what about what I'd done with Tom Thomas? Wasn't that a personal version of the same thing? But there was a difference, wasn't there? Between what I'd done, what Mom did, and what The Guys did. We did good, they did bad. Right?

"Al?"

"What? Oh, sorry." More stuff to work out another time. "So, what's going to happen with you and Janie?"

"We'll do something about Helene's debt—maybe sell the fucking house—but after that . . . Nothing. Nada. Kaput."

"Will you see any capital from the house?"

"Not if Janie has her way."

"But there's your pension."

"She'll have half of that too."

"You could always put your half on a horse." And then I remembered Mary's Lotto ticket. It was Wednesday night.

"Al?"

"What?"

"Just a mistake? That's what you really think?"

"You don't doubt her good intentions, do you?"

"No."

"Then what's important is how you feel about the woman."

"Yeah." He sighed. He took out his phone.

"I'll go pay the bill. Get the pie to go."

"I don't want pie."

"I bet I know someone who does."

46

I was not expecting to find Mary sitting at the top of my stairs. She wasn't even smoking. "Have you been naughty?" I asked.

"I'm being discreet."

"Oh yes?"

"Your daughter's doing something it would be tacky for me to participate in."

"Too tacky, for you? This I gotta see." I helped her to her feet and we went in.

Miller went through to the bedroom to get his garment bag. Mary led me to a position behind Sam who was at the computer. "What?" I asked.

"I'm chatting with my mother," Sam said.

"Oh."

Miller came back with his bag. I left the grrrls and walked to the door with him. "You all right?"

"I'll tell you in a couple of lifetimes." We did what the pre-hug generation does—shook hands. And he left.

I watched him head down the stairs. I wondered what was in store for him. Him and his Marcella.

Ah well. I returned to the computer. Mary was peering over one of Sam's shoulders. I went to the other. On the screen, lines of oddly written text alternated between the labels of "Lex Gal" and "Me."

Sam said, "Mom's been telling me stories about when she was married to you, Daddy."

"I'm surprised she remembers me."

Mary said, "Your ex-wife seems quite a witty woman."

"She was never stupid," I said, "except on the subject of men. You guys carry on. I'll be next door, eating this piece of cherry pie."

"Cherry pie?" Mary straightened up. "Honey?"

We went to the bedroom and sat on the bed.

"Excuse fingers," Mary said. A piece of pie vanished. "Why did your friend leave?"

"He realized there was someone else he'd rather spend tonight with."

"Oh."

"How you feeling?"

"Adrenalized. Your daughter's good for that."

"Good."

"And she's really *really* pleased to be back in touch with her mother."

"I would ask why the *vache* broke off contact in the first place, but I don't care. I'm glad for Sam."

"She's signing off now. There's something she wants to tell you."

"Oh yes? What?"

Mary shook her head.

"A surprise. Oh goodie. I haven't had enough of those the last few days."

"Be nice, Albert. She's your daughter. You're lucky to have one."

I looked at her.

"There is a lot about me you don't know, Samsdad."

I took one of her hands but instead of letting me say anything she put a cherry in my mouth. "We'll have time to get better acquainted," she said. "Unless you behave like an out-and-out cad after taking my cherry."

"How many of those does a girl have?"

"As many as she needs, of course."

"Tell me one thing now."

After a moment she said, "What?"

"Have you checked the Lotto numbers?"

"The ticket didn't win."

"But if it had, you'd have shared, right?"

"It was my ticket."

"But I gave you the numbers."

" 'Gave' being the operative word." We looked into each other's eyes. I couldn't see a damn thing in hers.

Sam appeared at the door. "Daddy, can I have a word?"

"Sure."

"Go talk to your kid," Mary said. She tore off another piece of the pie.

Sam sat in my Client's Chair, so I sat behind the desk.

"Daddy, there's something I want to say about my future, what I want to do. It's why I decided to contact mother. I wanted her to know."

Samson and Daughter? "And what does your mother think?"

"That I'm crazy, but if it's what I want . . ."

"You are a grown-up type of person."

"I agree."

"Which entitles you to make decisions for yourself."

"So you don't mind?"

"Mind? Why should I mind?" Then, "We are talking about the same thing, aren't we?"

"My future. My career. The letter I got this morning."

"What letter?"

"I had the impression that Grandma was going to tell you. I've been accepted. It's official, Daddy. I'm going to be a cop."

47

Mary was lying on the bed.

"Tired, huh?" I said. I lay down beside her.

"How you doing, Samsdad?"

"You knew."

"About the letter? She told me after you and your pal went out. I thought maybe you knew and I hadn't given you a chance to tell me."

"I didn't knew. I'm always the last to knew."

"No you aren't."

"Mom knew. You knew. My ex-*vache* in Lexington knew. I bet even fucking Norman knew."

"But you come in way ahead of Boris, and Dan Quayle, and Buffy."

"Great."

"I'm trying to help you focus on the bright side here, Samsdad."

"The neon-bright side?" And then I remembered something. "When I suggested 'Samson and Daughter' you told me to ask her first. Did you know then?"

"I knew she'd applied."

"Great."

"She's looking to become a detective. That has to tell you what she thinks of her father."

"Don't tell me. She's proud."

"Of course she's proud. In fact, I think you ought to go ahead and get that 'Samson and Daughter' sign."

"How about 'Samson and Daughter Only Not the Daughter'?"

"If it says, 'Samson and Daughter' potential clients will understand that under one roof they can have access to age and youth, and to male and female points of view. They'll be lining up at your door."

"Apart from my not being able to provide the young, female daughter part."

"She might bust out of the cops. Meanwhile you could adopt. Or better, hire one."

"Hire a daughter?"

"Singing groups do it. You don't think the Everly Brothers are really brothers, do you?"

"They are brothers."

"Well, you know what I mean. Besides, once you get them through the door, you'll be able to charm them into settling for little ol' you." She began to stroke my cheek.

I was about to say something more when she said, "Shhhh."

48

I woke up in the middle of the night. Mary was breathing quietly beside me. That was nice.

Not so nice was waking up with my mind's eye filled with Ronnie Willigar's face. I was seeing him in the picture I'd shown around on first-date night. It was a neutral photo, more a driver's license shot than a mug shot. It didn't do Willigar justice. It made him look like just another guy. Not the monster he was.

I'd sat at a table with Ronnie Willigar. We'd talked. It felt like a nightmare.

Not the nightmare of an innocent man facing execution—I was certain enough of Willigar's guilt.

Nor the nightmare of an evil man going free.

My nightmare was a different one. About my only child choosing a path that could put her eyeball-to-eyeball with the Ronnie Willigars of this world. A path filled with danger, threat, and death.

A father's nightmare for his child.

What was so wrong with a life spent behind the counter of a luncheonette? She could marry Norman. I'd give my blessing.

I eased myself out of bed one inch, one limb at a time. Almost as slowly I made my way into my office. I sat at my desk.

It was not to be "Samson and Daughter" then. Was it just hubris ever to think it might be?

I fished around for notes I knew were there. It was too

dark to read what I had written, but I still wanted to handle them.

One note was from myself about Joe Ellison. I wanted to see the guy, talk to him. I didn't know what I would say, but he had a right to know about the rev. Didn't he?

Then there was a note to call Don Cannon's partner. I would offer to work undercover at Amtrak if he wanted me to. Anything, as long as he wasn't trying to buy a piece of my soul.

The final note was about Brenda. I would work on her behalf re Otis. Whatever her story was . . .

People's stories. That's what I do. What I am. I help work their stories out. I help resolve them. I help. I . . .

"Come back to bed," Mary said from the doorway.

"You're supposed to be asleep."

"And you're supposed to be old enough to know that children go their own ways. Don't worry about her, Samsdad. Concentrate on things you *can* do something about."

Sensible words. Was it time I tried to be sensible? I got up and followed Mary back into the bedroom.

About the Author

MICHAEL Z. LEWIN grew up in Indianapolis although he now lives in Bath, in England. *Eye Opener* is his twenty-first book and the eighth in the Albert Samson series of mysteries. Nominated for Edgars three times, Mike also writes short stories and drama for radio and stage. More details than you'll ever want to know are available at www.MichaelZLewin.com. He has two children and two grandchildren, and a sunny patio where he grows zinnias, popcorn, and arugula.